I0721218

KNOT BENEATH THE MISTLETOE

A WHISPERING GROVE NOVEL

HOLIDAY OMEGAVERSE ROMANCE

HARLEY KNIGHT

Knot Beneath The Mistletoe © Copyright 2024 Harley Knight

All rights reserved.

No part of this book may be reproduced or transmitted in any form or by any means, electronic or mechanical, including photocopying, recording, or by any information storage and retrieval system, without permission in writing of the author, except for use of brief quotations in a book review.

This is a work of fiction. Any resemblance to actual persons, living or dead, or actual events is purely coincidental.

CONTENTS

TW

Knot Beneath the Mistletoe is a sweet omegaverse romance and is not a dark book. However, there may be triggers for some including domestic violence and being trapped in a storm about to freeze.

KNOT BENEATH THE MISTLETOE
A WHISPERING GROVE NOVEL

What's worse than losing everything you own? Having to mate to keep it.

I have twenty-one days until Christmas Eve to find a mate, or my bar goes to my power-hungry cousin. Twenty-one days to deny everything I believe about independence. Twenty-one days until my aunt's will destroys me.

But my best friend has a plan: three blind dates, three weeks, three Alphas who make my Omega instincts scream. A brooding craft brewer with dangerous eyes and skilled hands, an intense outdoor adventurer whose feral smile promises wicked nights, and a dangerous security specialist whose darkness calls to mine.

They say some Omegas need three anchors. I say I don't need anyone.

Too bad my heat isn't listening.

1

I hate the sound of Christmas bells at six in the morning.

They echo through empty streets, bouncing off fresh snow, sneaking through the crack under Flour & Fable Bakery's back door, where I'm currently baking my fourth batch of snickerdoodles. My hands shake as I measure cinnamon—the good kind, Ceylon, because Aunt Eve taught me never to skimp on the important things. The sugar-coating sparkles under harsh fluorescent lights, but all I can think about is how I have exactly twenty-one days left to save everything I have.

Twenty-one days to find a mate.

Twenty-one days until Christmas Eve.

Twenty-one days until I lose my bar to my cousin.

My chest tightens whenever I think about it, which is all the time.

The mixing bowl clatters against the metal counter

harder than necessary as I beat the mixture. Lily's going to kill me if I wake up Chonky, her precious sourdough starter. I swear that blob of flour and water judges me every time I enter her bakery for early morning baking therapy. But that's still better than being alone in my apartment above the bar, where every creak sounds like footsteps and every shadow holds memories.

"At least I don't need feeding every day," I mutter toward the sourdough starter, aggressively creaming butter and sugar. The familiar motion helps calm my trembling fingers. "And I don't live in a jar."

Great. Now I'm talking to bacteria. Next, I'll be singing carols and believing in Santa.

The town speakers crackle to life outside, right on schedule at six in the morning. Whispering Grove's tourism board thinks visitors need twenty-four-seven Christmas spirit. *Silent Night* drifts in, and I reach for the vanilla extract, pretending the moisture in my eyes is from the cold. My nose catches another Omega's scent, something like peppermint, before I hear the creaking door.

I instantly know it's Lily, the owner and baker at Flour & Fable Bakery and one of my best friends.

"If you're going to stress-bake, you could at least text me," Lily says.

I twist around to where she's standing in the kitchen doorway, having most likely just come down the stairs from her apartment on the floor above. She's wearing candy cane pajamas and a puffy winter coat, her dark curls stuffed under a beanie. She sniffs the air, wrinkling her nose.

"Your scent's all over the place. Distressed Omega at six a.m. isn't exactly subtle."

"Sorry." I'm not. "Didn't want to wake you."

"Please." She smirks at me. "Like I sleep when you're broadcasting anxiety across the street." She shuffles to the counter against the wall, returning with a chocolate-cherry scone. She hops onto the counter, swinging fuzzy-socked feet. "So, want to talk about why you're stress-baking instead of decorating your bar for the holidays like a normal business owner?"

I concentrate on my cookie dough while she takes a bite of her scone.

"The bar's fine as it is."

"Ruby, you haven't put up a single Christmas decoration. Even the gas station has a tree."

"The gas station isn't run by—" I stop, but Lily finishes for me.

"A useless Omega? Is that what Marcus said again?"

The wooden spoon cracks in my grip.

Lily's brow furrows.

"You should report him," she says softly. "The Omega Rights Council—"

"Would do nothing. He's an asshole Alpha with connections. I'm just..." I gesture at myself, flour-covered and clearly failing at proper Omega behavior. "This."

"You are amazing. And *this* is pretty great, if you ask me." Lily takes another bite of her scone. "What did you put in them?"

"Dark chocolate, dried cherries, and..." Just like Aunt Eve used to do. The memory hits unexpectedly, and the tightness in my chest deepens. Eve in her kitchen, silver hair escaping its bun, showing me how to fold the dough. *Always add cardamom, Ruby. Gives it depth, like a good story.*

I haven't made these scones since Eve died, but for some reason, I found myself making them today. I also haven't decorated for Christmas since I was fifteen. Haven't let anyone close enough to—

A crash from somewhere outside the bakery makes us both jump. Lily's scone goes flying.

"Just raccoons," she says nervously, but I'm already heading for the door. "Ruby, wait—"

The December air hits like a slap, and my skin ripples with the cold. Snow crunches under my boots as I edge around the dumpster, phone flashlight illuminating scattered garbage. Normally, I don't run toward danger, but I've seen raccoons in this alley before, and last time, there was a baby one I wanted to capture to help, except he got away from me. They come down from the nearby mountains searching for easy food.

A metallic rattle draws my attention to a toppled trash can.

That's when I see it—a young raccoon thrashing against a red ribbon tangled around its neck, caught on the can's handle. My heart stops.

Suddenly, my mind flashes to a memory...

"Just hold still, Ruby-girl. The ribbon has to be perfect for the Christmas photos."

Fingers pulling too tight. Can't breathe. Mom's drinking again, and the ribbon's cutting into my neck, and Dad's getting angry about the waiting photographer's fee, and their scents are all wrong—Alpha rage and Omega fear mixing until I'm choking on it...

The raccoon's panicked chittering snaps me back. I hate the acid in my gut whenever I'm reminded of my past. Refocusing on the furry animal, now thrashing harder, the ribbon tightening with each movement, I move closer.

"Hey," I whisper, crouching slowly. "Hey there, sweet thing. I know exactly how you feel."

It freezes, beady eyes reflecting my flashlight. Up close, I can see it's young and could be the one I saw before. It's probably its first winter alone, like I was that Christmas Eve when everything shattered.

"Being trapped sucks, doesn't it?" I inch closer, keeping my voice soft. "Especially by something pretty. Something that's supposed to be festive."

The raccoon watches me, still breathing fast but no longer struggling.

"I'm going to help, okay? But you have to trust me. Just for a minute."

I reach for the ribbon with trembling fingers. The raccoon snaps, catching my hand between its front paws. I cringe, but it doesn't bite or scratch me, and I don't pull back. I know too well how fear makes anyone bite.

"Yeah, I get that, too. Trusting hurts sometimes. But being trapped hurts more."

Quickly, I work the ribbon loose. It's synthetic satin, cheap and cruel, like the ones Mom used to buy in bulk for *perfect* Christmas photos. One final tug and the raccoon bolts, leaving me holding the torn red strip. My throat feels tight at the memory of my past with my mom.

"Ruby?" Lily's voice floats from the doorway, cutting through my thoughts. "You okay?"

"Fine." I stuff the ribbon into the trash. "Just fine."

When I turn around, she's not alone. Hannah, her sister, stands at the end of the alley, too, already dressed in black pants and a white button-up shirt with a fitted black vest—the bakery's uniform. She's hugging herself in the dim morning light.

"We need to talk," she says seriously in my direction.

"I'm baking." I stroll back toward the bakery.

"You're hiding." Hannah steps into my path.

"No, I'm not." I stuff my hands into my pocket.

"So, the Christmas boxes in your office are nothing? And Marcus' offer is nothing?"

Ice floods my veins at the name of my cousin. I don't want to deal with this so early in the morning.

Suddenly, headlights sweep the alley, painting long shadows across the brick walls. A black Mercedes crawls past, my cousin's silhouette visible through tinted windows.

Speak of the devil, and he shall appear!

My insides squeeze as I watch him prowl down this stretch of Whispering Grove, so far from his mansion in the gated hills on the other side of town. There's no innocence in this drive-by. Every pass of his car is calculated, a silent reminder of the power he holds over the fate of my bar. He knows exactly what he's doing, cruising past my bar like he's already measuring for new signs, picking out fixtures for when the will from my aunty finally forces my hand.

Marcus turns his head just slightly, and even through the tinted glass, I sense his grin.

Mine soon, that smile says. *All mine.*

The car disappears around the corner, but the cold remains. I'm grinding my teeth.

Asshole!

"Come inside," Lily says quickly. "Both of you. I'll make tea."

The bakery's warmth wraps around me as Lily puts on the kettle. Hannah perches on a stool while I move to the sink and wash my hands vigorously with disinfectant soap and hot water. Then, I dry them and return to my abandoned cookies, methodically rolling the dough into balls and coating them with cinnamon sugar. The motions are automatic and soothing. Aunt Eve taught me this recipe the day she found out my parents kicked me out.

"Ruby." Hannah's voice is gentle. "Talk to us. Did Marcus pay you another visit? What did he say this time?"

I lift my gaze, staring at the sisters who always have my back. "Nothing new. He just reminded me that very soon, none of this will matter. The bar will be his."

"There has to be a way—" Lily starts.

"There isn't." I move by the counter covered in flour. "I've checked every legal angle. Eve's will is clear. I have to be mated and married to an Alpha by Christmas Eve, or everything goes to Marcus. The bar. The building. Her apartment. All of it."

"It's barbaric," Lily murmurs, her lips downturning. "Making mating a condition of inheritance."

Hannah sighs heavily, her shoulder rigid. "I hate him so much. And your aunt shouldn't have put you in this situation."

"She thought she was helping." The tears finally spill over. "She worried about me being alone. Wanted to make sure whoever I chose would be committed enough to share the business, so I can't even marry anyone, then divorce them later because they automatically get half of the bar and apartment, as in my aunt's will. But she didn't know Marcus would..."

Would what? Transform from the cousin who once shared my crayons into an Alpha determined to put me in my *proper place*? Use his connections to drive away any potential mates? Make it clear that no *real* Alpha would want a defective Omega in her mid-twenties who hasn't experienced her heat, who ran a bar instead of a home, who couldn't even handle Christmas without breaking down.

The kettle whistles. Lily pours three mugs of Eve's special chai blend. The spices fill the air, mixing with cookie scent.

"We did something," Hannah says finally, glancing over at Lily, who's nodding. "It's what we wanted to talk to you about. It's something you might hate us for, but I hope you don't."

"Please don't hate us," Lily pleads.

That tone never means anything good. I narrow my eyes, slightly scared.

"What kind of something?"

Lily takes a small sip, holding my gaze, and the longer she drags it out, the worse I know it's going to be. "We arranged some Alphas for you to meet. Three of them until the deadline."

The mug slips from my hands, shattering on the floor. Tea splashes my legs, but I barely feel it. My chest tightens as a phantom ribbon constricts my throat.

"No." The word comes out choked. "No dates. No Alphas. No—"

"Ruby, breathe." Lily's at my side instantly, helping calm my racing heart. "Deep breaths."

"You don't understand." I grip the counter, knuckles white. "I tried dating, remember? Six disasters in two months. One Alpha actually lectured me about how Omegas shouldn't own businesses. Another just wanted to *help* by buying the bar himself. And the last one..." I shudder. "Let's just say Marcus made sure he understood what happens to Alphas who touch his property."

"These are different," Hannah insists. "We vetted them personally. They're not under Marcus's influence."

"You're both bakers, not matchmakers!" I retort, maybe harsher than I intended, but I'm freaking out internally. I've only had bad experiences with Alphas, not to mention I keep remembering how my father brutally treated my Omega mom and how she never fought back. I don't want to end up that way...

"We're your friends, and I'm watching you lose yourself in fear," Lily says.

"I'm not afraid!" The words echo off steel appliances. Chonky's jar almost rattles on its shelf. "I'm practical. The bar is all I have. Eve's memories are all I have. I can't risk—"

"Risk what? Being happy? Having a real mate instead of just surviving?" Hanna interrupts.

My hands shake as I try to clean up the broken mug. A sharp edge catches my already injured hand, and I wince.

"Ruby." Hannah crouches beside me, also gathering ceramic shards. "Let us help you."

I close my eyes, seeing Marcus' smirk as he leaned across my bar yesterday afternoon. His Alpha scent had filled the space, making other customers unconsciously submit. Making me fight every Omega instinct to bare my neck and submit. To admit I was submissive and that he could make decisions for me. Just the thought has me breathing faster, my heart racing.

"He said he'd make it easy." My voice sounds distant. "Sign over the bar now, and he'll let me manage it. Under his supervision, of course. Because clearly, an unmated Omega can't handle business decisions." A bitter laugh escapes. "Said he'd even let me keep my apartment upstairs. If I learn my place."

Lily growls, a surprising sound from an Omega. "He can't—"

"He can. In twenty-one days, he will." I stand abruptly, needing to move. "Unless I mate someone. Anyone. Let them own half my business, half my life, half my soul, just to keep Marcus from taking all of it."

"Just try meeting these Alphas," Hannah pleads. "If it's terrible, then you've lost nothing. But what if one of these guys is the one?"

Outside, *Jingle Bells* plays. Inside, my cookies are definitely burning, and I go to remove them from the oven. Then I stare across the street to the Winterscape Bar, my bar's windows glowing warm against the darkness.

Not long before I lose everything.

"I can't." The words catch in my throat. "Hannah, Lily, I... I'm not ready. I can't do this again."

"Ruby—"

"No." My nerves spike with distress. "I'd rather lose the bar than lose myself to an Alpha and end up like my mom." Even as I say it, I know it's a lie; it's my fear. Even as Hannah's face falls and Lily hugs me and the town speakers switch to *Let It Snow,* I know I'm lying.

Because in twenty-one days, I'll lose both, anyway.

The Mercedes engine rumbles past again. Waiting. Watching. Knowing.

I stand frozen, each breath coming shorter than the last, like a noose slowly tightening—and I'm running out of ways to fight it.

I think of what I told that raccoon earlier in the alley.

Trusting hurts sometimes. But being trapped hurts more. Funny how advice has a way of coming back around.

2

RUBY

Whoever decided Christmas lights should have minds of their own deserves coal in their stocking—for eternity.

My hands tremble as I wrestle with a tangled string of white lights, which somehow managed to knot itself between my car and my booth along Main Street at the Whispering Grove Winter Craft Beer Festival. The trembling isn't just from the cold or from half the night's sleepless baking session. It's the kind that starts in your bones when you know you're running out of time.

"I swear these things breed just to mock me," I mumble to myself, trying to keep my voice steady. Twenty days. The deadline looms like a guillotine blade.

I take a deep breath, trying to push the worry to the back of my mind.

The festival bustles around me, vendors setting up booths under grey morning skies threatening more snow. My booth—technically just an extension of my bar's regular spot at local events—sits sadly undecorated compared to the winter wonderlands popping up around me. Even the sign looks tired, the gold lettering that Aunt Eve had hand-painted beginning to fade: *Winterscape Bar & Brewery - Established 1962.*

"You know," Erica calls from her cupcake booth next door. "Normal people decorate before the day of an event."

"Normal people sleep at night instead of baking." The words come out sharper than intended. I see the flash of hurt in her eyes and immediately regret it. It's not her fault I spent last night alternating between stress-baking and having panic attacks about Marcus's latest *offer* to take the bar.

"Speaking of which," I add, softer now, trying to smooth things over. "I hear you've got beer-flavored cupcakes this year." Whispering Grove may have more bakeries per capita than anywhere else in America, but Erica's creations are unique and delicious.

She brightens, arranging perfectly frosted cupcakes. "You have no idea how good they turned out. We can do an exchange later... beer for a cupcake?"

"You got yourself a deal." The lights fight back as I climb on a chair, my fingers numb from the cold and exhaustion. The metal wobbles beneath me—of course, it does because everything in my life feels like it's about to collapse.

"Need help with that?"

The deep voice startles me. My chair tips, lights tangling around my arms as I flail. Strong hands catch my waist, steadying me. The scent hits me hard—pine needles and hops, yes, but underneath that, there's the familiar darker and richer smell, like coffee beans roasted with vanilla. I love how it feels so right as I breathe it in, my insides starting to soothe, and I might be gushing. What has he done to me? It makes my chest ache with want, and a fire ignites between my thighs, which immediately sets off warning bells in my head.

"Those lights are a fire hazard," the stranger says, his hands still gentle on my waist, and I'm struggling to think about anything but his burning touch. How my body is buzzing all over. When I finally look up, I nearly lose my balance again.

He's tall—most Alphas are—but it's not just his height that commands attention. Dark hair swept back from a face that belongs on a men's sports magazine, though the silver at his temples softens what might otherwise be intimidating perfection. His eyes remind me of forest green with hints of blue, crinkled at the corners with concern. A full-sleeve tattoo of the brewing process winds down one arm, visible beneath a rolled-up Henley, and cargo pants do nothing to hide all those muscles. I'm smitten.

Breathe, Ruby. Breathe.

"So is my cousin, but the health department hasn't shut him down yet." The words slip out before my brain's filter kicks in, and I immediately tense, waiting for the reaction. Alphas don't like Omegas who talk back. I learned that lesson young, usually with a hand around my throat.

He laughs, deep and genuine, setting me carefully back on solid ground.

"Fair point. Though I'd take questionable wiring over questionable relatives any day." He steps back, hands raised in mock surrender. "Want a hand? I'm kind of an expert at untangling disasters."

Warning bells shriek louder. He seems... safe. Which makes him more dangerous than any openly aggressive Alpha. Trust is a luxury I can't afford, not with Marcus breathing down my neck.

"I've got it," I say quickly, putting the chair between us. "But thanks..."

"Garrett." He gestures to the booth across from mine. The sign reads *Mountain Gate Brewing Co.* in hand-painted letters. No fancy banner, no corporate logo. Just passion and—my heart skips—a coffee stout on his draft list.

Focus, Ruby.

I've seen the brand around town and even tried some of their offerings, which are always exceptional, but I never knew who owned the brewery... until now.

"You're Eve's niece," he says suddenly. "The one who inherited Winterscape Bar."

My shoulders tense. Every muscle in my body prepares for the usual lecture about how Omegas can't possibly run a business alone, how we need Alpha guidance, how we should focus on finding mates instead of trying to compete in a world that wasn't built for us. Lily faces the same issues, but because she runs her bakery with her sister, it seems more acceptable somehow.

"Ruby," I answer shortly. "And yes, I run the bar. Successfully. Without help."

"I know." His grin catches me off guard. "Your German Imperial Stout won best in show last spring. And your version of Eve's Winter Ale? Adding cardamom was genius. Gives it depth."

I blink. "You know my Aunt Eve's original recipe?"

"Used to help bottle it during my summers in high school. Eve let me study her techniques when everyone else said Alphas didn't have the patience for craft brewing and should be left to Betas." His smile turns wry. "She had strong opinions about people's *proper places* in society."

I laugh. "That's her."

Something in his voice resonates with old pain, but before I can respond, a shadow falls over me, and the temperature seems to drop ten degrees. A familiar cologne cuts through the festival buzz, expensive and calculated, designed to mask an Alpha's natural scent. Only one person in town would bother.

My blood curdles.

"Well." Marcus appears like a nightmare in a tailored wool coat that probably costs more than my monthly rent. Everything about him screams old money, old power—from his perfectly styled dark hair to his Italian leather shoes. He's handsome in that cold, cruel way that makes prey animals freeze in their tracks. "Networking already, little Ruby? How... progressive."

My hands clench on the lights, the plastic digging into my palms. Garrett's gaze narrows sharply on my cousin, but I step forward before he can speak. The last Alpha who tried to defend me ended up in the hospital with a broken jaw. Marcus made sure everyone knew it was a *skiing accident.*

"Shouldn't you be at your country club?" I keep my voice neutral, careful. Show no fear. Show no weakness.

Marcus moves closer, using his height to loom over me. "Twenty days, little one." His voice drops to a whisper that scrapes down my spine like ice. "Though we could speed that up if you keep... disappointing the family. What would your father say, seeing his only daughter spreading her legs for any Alpha with a brewery?"

The crude words hit like a slap. I taste blood where I've bitten my cheek, trying not to show how much he's rattled me. But my hands shake as I attempt to untangle another section of lights, and I know he sees it. He always sees the cracks in my armor.

He knows that bringing up my father unravels me. My mom always took his side against me, despite the way he treated her, and since she passed, he's never once reached out.

"I hear the health inspector's making rounds today," Marcus continues, still too soft for others to hear. "Be a shame if something was... amiss. These old buildings, so many potential violations. One bad report and the bank might reconsider that loan extension."

"Is there a problem here?" Garrett's voice could freeze hell.

Marcus straightens, still not as tall as Garrett, but his public mask slides back into place as he squares his shoulders.

"Just a family discussion. Though I'm surprised you'd waste time on this one." He grins mockingly at my expense, his chin pointing in my direction. "Ruby has quite the reputation for... instability. But perhaps that appeals to your sort."

"My sort?" Garrett's question carries a growl.

"Second-rate brewers playing at success." Marcus adjusts his already-perfect collar. "Though I suppose beggars can't be choosers. Twenty days, Ruby. Tick tock."

He leaves, but his presence lingers like a bruise. My legs want to buckle. My hands won't stop shaking. At the booth next to me, I catch Sophie and her Alpha watching with naked pity in their gazes, and something in me crumples. I hate this—hate being the spectacle, the joke, the Omega who dared to think she could stand on her own.

"Ruby?" Garrett's voice is gentle. Too gentle. "Are you—"

"I'm fine." The words come out brittle. "You should go. Marcus has ways of making problems for people who help me."

"Good thing I like problems." There's steel under his easy smile now, rage carefully banked. "Want to trade samples later? I've got a bourbon barrel-aged porter that needs an honest opinion."

Part of me wants to say yes. A larger part remembers the last Alpha who offered to *trade samples*—remembers waking up three days later in the hospital, the doctors saying I was lucky they caught the bonding hormones in time.

"I don't think that's a good idea." I focus on hanging lights, pretending my hands aren't trembling. "But thanks."

I feel his eyes on me throughout the morning, between pouring samples and explaining Eve's recipes to customers. He's not obvious about it, but I'm too used to being watched to miss the weight of his gaze. It should make me nervous. Instead, it feels like standing in a patch of sunlight—warm and dangerous in its comfort.

The health inspector arrives just before noon. I see Marcus smirking behind him, and my stomach drops. Not today, Satan. Please, not today. I need this festival revenue to make next month's loan payment.

They move across the busy street of people to Garrett's booth.

I freeze on the spot.

I don't hear their conversation, but my blood runs cold. This is my fault. Marcus is targeting him because he talked to me, because he dared to be kind to the wrong Omega. Words bubble up in my throat—defiance, anger, retribution—but fear closes my windpipe. One wrong move and Marcus could accelerate the loan deadline. Could make sure I never work in this industry again.

I watch helplessly as the inspector writes citations. Nearby, Sophie's pity has turned to resignation. She knows how this goes. We all do.

The festival continues, but something in me feels cracked. I pour samples on autopilot, smile mechanically, and pretend I don't notice how conversations stop when I walk by. Pretend I don't see Garrett watching me with something like understanding in those sea-glass eyes.

Twenty days until I lose everything. Twenty days until Marcus wins.

I should have known better than to hope for anything different. Though I think about Hannah's and Lily's offering of three dates and if there's a possibility there. I also contemplate the notion of maybe marrying an Alpha to ensure Marcus doesn't get the bar... but each time I do, my stomach knots as flashes of my father beating my mother flood my thoughts. And how she never stood up to him, never left him. Instead, she kicked me out of the house, saying it was for my own good.

I breathe heavily and push the past and the drowning thoughts aside.

As the afternoon light fades, I discover a coffee stout sample on my counter. A note underneath reads, *Some disasters are worth untangling.*

I pour it down the drain. I have to.

Hope is a luxury I can't afford right now.

3

GARRETT

ours after the festival wound down and the sun descended, Ruby's scent lingers in my nose like honey and cardamom. The delicate scent that marks her as an unmated Omega should repel me. I've spent years avoiding unmated Omegas, keeping my distance and staying professional because I thought I never wanted to settle down. In truth, I have never been drawn to one so powerfully as I am to Ruby.

She's different. Everything about her is different.

From inside the bar, the winter festival's lights flicker outside through the windows as we clean up, casting dancing shadows across the worn wooden floor. Christmas lights strung across Main Street pulse gentle colors through the frosted glass, making Ruby's skin glow as she moves between tables. She keeps insisting she's fine handling the clean-up and carrying her merchandise from the booth outside into her bar alone.

I can't walk away. I've been watching her all day, keeping an eye on her, close to murdering that fucking ass harassing her. Then, thinking that by bringing an inspector to my booth, I'd be scared off. He has no idea who he's dealing with.

I contacted my two closest friends, Knox and Dominic, to update them on the incident with Marcus and the steps we need to take to handle him. They'll be meeting Ruby in the next week or two as potential mates. Ideally, we want an Omega to share, but in my mind, she's already mine. Whether she fits with them or not won't change how I feel—or my claim on her.

My priority is Ruby and her safety. Don't ask me what the fuck's gotten into my head so fast, but seeing she's the first Omega to ever affect me this way, I'm inclined to follow my instincts. Even if it means just ensuring she's safe.

So now, I'm helping her clean up in the closed bar.

She's changed from her festive red dress into black jeans and an oversized sweater that falls off one shoulder, revealing freckles I want to trace with my fingertips. Her boots make soft sounds against the floor as she works. She belongs here, among the gleaming bottles and brass fixtures, as much a part of the bar's soul as the ancient hardwood beneath our feet.

I grin, knowing that feeling. It's how I am in my bar.

"You really don't have to help," Ruby says for the third time, dropping another crate by the recycling bin. Her reddish-blonde hair has mostly escaped its messy bun, forming a wild halo around her face. There's a smudge of dirt on her cheek that my fingers itch to brush away. "I'm sure you have better things to do than clean up someone else's mess."

"Your cousin was out of line," I say abruptly, making her pause. "Bringing the health inspector to the festival, then to visit me? That wasn't about me. That was about getting to you." My hands clench around the rag I'm holding, remembering Marcus's smug smile. "He's a fucking coward, using bureaucracy to fight his battles."

Ruby's laugh is sharp and bitter. "Welcome to the Marcus Winters' playbook. He's been trying to get this place condemned since Aunt Eve died twelve months ago." She starts aggressively sorting bottles, the glass clinking like angry wind chimes. "Says a bar's no place for an Omega, but it was okay for my aunt, who was a Beta. Says I'm disgracing the family name." A bottle slips from her fingers, but I'm right at her side and catch it before it can shatter. The movement brings us close enough that I can see the tiny scar near her left eyebrow and smell the lingering festival spices in her hair.

"Careful," I murmur, setting the bottle safely aside. My hand brushes her arm, and electricity crackles between us. "These are getting heavy."

"I've been doing this alone for two years," she says, but there's less bite in her tone now. More exhaustion. "Ever since my aunt Eve..." She trails off, rubbing her temples. "Sometimes, I think Marcus is right. Not about Omegas running bars—that's bullshit—but about me not being strong enough to keep this place going."

My grip tightens on the rag until my knuckles go white. The thought of Marcus's smug face makes violence curl in my gut. I've seen his type before— wealthy Alphas who think their status gives them the right to control others.

"I should pay him a visit," I say quietly, watching her reaction. "Explain the concept of professional cour- tesy." Images flash through my mind—Marcus's shocked face as I corner him in his precious country club, my hands around his throat, teaching him what happens when you threaten someone else...

Ruby whirls to face me, eyes flashing. "Don't. Please. He's not worth risking your business over."

"He's already risking my business." I move closer, drawn by the way her pulse jumps at her throat. A strand of hair has fallen across her face, and before I can stop myself, I brush it back. Her skin is warm beneath my fingers. "More importantly, he's threat- ening yours."

"Why do you care?" She backs away, but there's nowhere to go—the bar's behind her, bottles gleam- ing. "You barely know me."

The question hits harder than it should. Why do I care? Why does watching her fight that bastard make my chest ache? Why do I want to destroy anyone who puts that haunted look in her amber eyes?

"I travel a lot," I say instead of answering directly. I lean against the bar beside her, close enough to feel the heat of her body but not quite touching. "Built my brewery's reputation across three continents. Told myself relationships were too complicated. Saw too many Alpha friends lose everything in messy bond-marks and broken claims. So, I accepted that it wasn't for me, but I watched my two younger sisters and how they struggled with fitting in, with how many treated them for being Omegas. I helped them as much as I could... well, in truth, it's as much as they allowed me." I chuckle, remembering their stubbornness, half reminding me of Ruby.

She watches me from the corner of her eye, fingers playing with the label on an empty bottle as she stands by the bar. "Smart policy."

"That's what I thought." I stare into those fiery eyes, trapping her between my arms as I grip the bar on either side of her. Not touching, but close enough to share breath. Every inch of me is attentive to how close she is, how quickly her chest rises and falls. "Then you almost fall off a chair this morning, and suddenly, I can't think about anything else. Can't stop wondering what you look like when you smile. What makes you laugh. Whether you sing along to the radio when you're alone in the bar."

Color floods her cheeks. "Don't say that stuff. That's the pheromones talking. It happens sometimes—"

"It's more than that." I cut her off, needing her to understand. "I've met plenty of compatible Omegas. None of them made me want to commit assault over a health inspection. None of them made my skin feel too tight just by existing in the same space."

That startles a laugh out of her—a real one this time, soft and surprised. Fuck me, but my balls are tight, pulling up at the beautiful sound. What is she doing to me?

"My knight in shining brewery gear." She eyes my Henley top, with my logo embroidered on my sleeve, my deep cargo pants, and down to my waterproof boots.

"I'm serious, Ruby." I catch her wrist when she tries to move past me, my thumb finding her racing pulse. Her skin is silk and fire against mine, and I have to fight the urge to pull her closer. "What Marcus did today? That's just the beginning. He's going to keep coming after you, keep trying to wear you down."

"I know." Her voice cracks on the words. "Trust me, I know. But I can handle it."

"You shouldn't have to." The words come out rougher than intended. My hand slides from her wrist to her waist, and she shivers. "Let me help."

"Why?" She looks up at me, defiance warring with something darker in her eyes. In this light, they're more gold than amber, flecked with shadows that make me want to chase away every bad memory she's carrying. "Because I'm some damsel in distress? Some Omega who needs an Alpha's protection?"

"Because you're extraordinary." The truth of it burns in my chest. My other hand rises to cup her face, thumb brushing across that smudge of dirt I've been wanting to erase all night. "Because watching you work today, seeing how your customers light up when you talk to them, hearing you explain the brewing process to that kid who wanted to start a home brewery... you're not just surviving, Ruby. You're thriving.

"Marcus wants to take that away because he can't stand an Omega being more successful than him. And because I know how damn hard it is to start against all odds. I started with fucking nothing, borrowed money, and was in debt to my eyeballs, but I worked damn hard to get my business off the ground. So, to see that shithead try to squish your dream, it hits something personal in me."

Her breath catches. We're too close now, the heat of her body calling to mine. She smells like honey and vanilla and determination, like everything I never knew I was missing. My head fogs, thoughts floating away.

"I can't..." She swallows hard. "The bar, Marcus, everything... I can't afford distractions right now."

"Is that what I am? A distraction?" I have no idea how I'm already feeling so obsessed with her. Yet I know the answer... Sure, it's pheromones, but it's so fucking much more, and I have no intention of walking away.

"You're a forest fire." Her laugh is shaky. "And I'm already burning."

I can't stop my free hand from sliding into her hair, cradling the back of her head, tilting her head back. Her eyes flutter closed at the touch, and something primal in me roars to life.

"Ruby..."

This time, when she shivers, it's not from fear. Her scent deepens, flooding me with desperate desires, with a hunger so strong, it makes my head spin. I lean closer, giving her time to pull away.

She doesn't.

The first brush of my lips against hers is gentle. The second is pure possession. She tastes like winter spices and sex, her mouth opening on a gasp that I swallow hungrily. My fingers tighten in her hair, tilting her head to deepen the kiss, our mouths mashing together, my body pressing against her, feeling the softness of her breasts, the trembling of her body. Her hands clutch my shirt, nails scraping my chest through the fabric.

I kiss her like a starved man finding air. Every soft moan she makes vibrates through my bones, setting off primal instincts I'd thought long buried.

Protect.

Claim.

Keep.

Mine.

Her back arches, pressing harder against mine, her nipples hard, and I growl into her mouth. My free hand slides down her side to her hip, drawing her closer, eager to feel every inch of her. She makes a desperate sound that nearly undoes me, her fingers moving to tangle in my hair.

I need more—I need all of her.

When I finally pull back, my hands on her hips to lift her up on the bar, we're both breathing hard, but she instantly places a palm on my chest, pausing me. Her lips are swollen, her pupils blown wide, her hair a mess from my hands. I want to kiss her again. Want to fuck her right here on the bar, to make her scream.

Then she shoves me away so hard, I stumble.

"No," she says, voice shaking. "No, no, no. This isn't happening. I'm not ready for an Alpha, not sure I can trust..."

I can still taste her on my lips, can smell how our scents have mixed together into something intoxicating. Fuck, it's an addiction.

"Ruby—"

"Get out." She wraps her arms around herself, looking smaller somehow. "Please, just... I can't do this. I can't."

Everything in me fights against leaving her like

this, my cock so hard in my pants, it aches, but I force myself to step back.

"I'll go if that's what you wish."

"Yes, it is." But she won't meet my eyes, and we both know she's fighting her own temptation.

I make it to the door before turning back. Ruby is still pressed against the bar, looking lost and frowning and fucking beautiful.

"For what it's worth," I say quietly, "I'm not trying to save you. I just want to know you."

Then I walk out into the night before I can do something stupid like kiss her again until we end up fucking. The cool air does nothing to clear my head—I can still smell that delicious sex scent, still taste her honey, still feel the pressure of her lips against mine.

I force myself to keep walking.

Ruby might not believe in fate, might not want anything to do with Alphas or relationships or me, but I know one thing with bone-deep certainty.

She's mine. She just doesn't know it yet.

4

GARRETT

I've become *that* Alpha. The kind who watches an Omega from across the street, on my third cup of coffee in two hours this morning while pretending I'm not completely fixated on her every move. But here's the thing—when your soul recognizes its mate, rationality goes straight to hell.

Mom always said I'd know. *One day, Garrett, you'll scent an Omega, and everything will shift. It'll terrify you, but you grab that chance with both hands and don't let go.*

I didn't expect it to ever happen, let alone so quickly over Christmas lights and craft beer. Yet, that's exactly what happened.

I'm inside Cocoa & Cheer Cafe, which offers the perfect vantage point of Ruby's Winterscape Bar. Snow falls softly outside, coating Main Street in fresh white, but it doesn't stop too many people doing last-minute shopping. Garlands and twinkling lights deck every storefront, and *White Christmas* plays for probably the hundredth time today. Usually, I love this season—the lights, the music, the way the whole town transforms into something magical.

But right now, all I can focus on is Ruby.

Three days since the festival. Three days since that kiss that damn near brought me to my knees. Three days of her scent—honey and cardamom—flooding my dreams.

I've been out of town for the last two days for a meeting with a new supplier, so today, I intend to see my sweet Ruby. But first, I want to ensure she's safe, as I've heard from a couple of friends I had watching her place that her cousin has been hanging around.

My coffee's gone cold, vanilla syrup pooling at the bottom. I should be at my brewery. Should be working on that new winter stout. Instead, I'm here.

Something's way off about Marcus. The way he looked at Ruby at the festival, like she's property to be claimed rather than the fierce, independent woman who nearly knocked me on my ass with one smile. I've been doing my homework on Whispering Grove's golden boy. The things people whisper when they think no one's listening... The fucker is rich, has connections, all inherited from his stepfather's side. Never worked a day in his life.

That's when a black Mercedes coming down the snowy street grabs my attention, and I spot Marcus in the driver's seat. My hand tightens on my cup.

"Time to play," I murmur, pulling out my phone. One quick text to Dominic.

Your boy's making his move.

The response is instant.

Watch the show.

Marcus parks illegally practically in front of the cafe door—of course, he does—and straightens his designer coat. He takes one step toward Ruby's bar.

That's when the tow truck appears from around the corner, grunting toward the Mercedes, and parks in front of it.

My new cup of coffee arrives, and I smirk at the blonde who stares at me too long.

Quickly, I turn my attention back to the show.

Two massive guys jump out of the truck. Before Marcus reaches the sidewalk, they're already hooking up his precious car. I grin as his face turns the color of Christmas lights.

"What do you think you're doing?" His voice carries even through the cafe door slightly ajar. "Do you know who I am?"

The bigger guy—must be close to seven feet—looks supremely bored. "Someone parked in a snow removal zone."

"This is my town!" Marcus pulls out his phone. "I'll have your jobs for this!"

"Your town?" The second guy steps into Marcus' space. "Funny. Paperwork says it belongs to the city council." He taps the sign Marcus definitely saw and ignored. "Can't remove snow with cars in the way. Public safety issue."

A crowd's gathering now. Phone cameras appear. Marcus's perfectly tailored suit doesn't appear so perfect as he gestures wildly, face getting redder by the second. The huge guy doesn't move an inch, just stands there like a mountain in a high-vis safety vest.

"My stepfather will hear about this!"

"Sure." The first guy keeps working, chains clinking. "He can pick up your car at the impound. After paying the fines. And the boot removal fee."

"Boot?" Marcus looks down. Somehow, while he was ranting, they'd slapped a boot on his back tire. "You can't... I'll sue..."

"City ordinance 47-B." The mountain shrugs. "Double parking during snow removal gets a boot once we deliver it to the impound to ensure you really learned your lesson when you receive two fines."

I hide my smirk behind my cup as Marcus's composure cracks. He's on his phone again, pacing, that perfectly bred Alpha control slipping with every step. The crowd's loving it, hanging on their every word. Several people are definitely livestreaming.

The Mercedes rises onto the truck bed as a cab appears, right on cue. Marcus storms toward it, trying to maintain dignity while foaming at the mouth.

"This isn't over!" he shouts at the tow truck.

"Sure is," Mountain-man drawls. "Unless you want a citation for threatening city workers."

The cab door slams. The tow truck pulls away. The crowd slowly disperses, but their phones are still out, still sharing the town's latest entertainment.

"Enjoying the show?" Dominic says from behind me abruptly.

He slides into the chair across from me. Fifteen years of friendship and I still haven't figured out how he moves so silently, I don't hear him approach.

"Your guys do good work."

He grins, all sharp edges and he looks dangerous wrapped in his black expensive suit. "Former special forces tend to. Amazing how many find work in private security."

"Incredible how they always show up right when needed," I say sarcastically.

"I do love a good coincidence." He signals the waitress, who sprints over. Her Beta fruity scent floods as she takes in both of us. "Bourbon caramel latte, extra shot."

"Anything else?" She's batting her lashes so hard, I worry she'll strain something.

"Just the coffee." Dominic's smile is pure sin.

She actually stumbles leaving.

I chuckle. "You're giving her false hope."

"You're one to talk, stalker." He nods toward Ruby's bar. "Three days you've been here. Getting a little obsessive, aren't we?"

"Says the man who has Marcus' entire history, including his kindergarten report cards."

"He bit three kids and blamed a dog. Very telling." Dominic's expression turns serious. "He's dangerous, Gar. Not just spoiled-rich-boy dangerous. There's something wrong there."

I think of Ruby's face when Marcus threatened her at the festival. The fear she tried to hide. "Tell me."

"Three Omegas filed complaints against him in the last year for sexual assault and battery. All withdrawn suddenly. All moved away shortly after."

My growl makes nearby customers jump. Dominic continues like he doesn't notice.

"His father's got half the town council in his pocket. Local cops won't touch him. But..." His grin returns. "Federal agencies don't give a fuck about small-town politics."

"What did you find?"

"Let's just say the IRS is very interested in certain financial discrepancies at Daddy's company. Might take them a few weeks to fully investigate. Right around Christmas, probably."

The waitress returns with his coffee, all smiles.

"Thanks, darling." He winks.

"You're still a shithead," I tell him.

"Please. Like you weren't just marking your territory all over the festival." He sips his coffee. "Speaking of marking territory, Hannah and Lily weren't exactly forthcoming about her little matchmaking scheme, were they? Or why they wanted us on such short notice to try dating Ruby, but they made it clear this isn't a one-night stand. Ruby is looking for a long-term commitment, and that's why we agreed."

In truth, we researched her background before agreeing to anything, our trust issues demanding we dig deep. But the moment we laid eyes on her that busy night when we stopped in for drinks, we knew instantly she might be the Omega we'd been searching for. We've known Hannah and Lily, who we buy all our baked goods from, for years, so I trusted their judgment when they approached me for help with Ruby. They were well aware that Dominic, Knox, and I were bachelors without an Omega. One thing led to another, and here we are... stalking the girl.

"I think fear is stopping her from following her heart. Anyway, my first attempt could have gone better," I admit.

"Could have gone worse." Dominic's eyes fill with interest. "Did anything happen that I should be aware of?"

I can't help the longing rumble in my chest. "I kissed her. Fuck, she had me so switched on even before the kiss."

"And?" He leans forward, suddenly intense.

"And nothing's ever felt more right." I run a hand through my hair, remembering the way she tasted, how her scent had me rock hard in seconds. "It was like... everything clicked, but also like something was missing."

"Missing?" His eyebrow raises.

"Can't explain it. Just know I want more. Need more. And she's holding back." I meet his eyes. "You'll understand when you meet her."

"If she forgives us and her friends for the setup." He grins, but there's hunger in his expression. "Knox gets his shot next to meet her since he insisted."

My hands clench at the thought of my friend near her, but strangely, it doesn't feel like jealousy. More like... anticipation. We've decided against traditional dating, wanting to meet her in more organic situations, for her to see us as we are in our jobs, like I met her at the festival. Dates are always fucking awkward for everyone.

Dominic's gaze gleams. "Think her friends know what she's really set up here?"

"Does it matter? We've all been searching for our Omega, and I think she might be the one for us. I swear I feel my scent matches with hers, but I need more time to be close to her, to be sure."

Dominic whistles, then chuckles loudly, gaining some glances our way. "Guess we'll find out." He checks his phone. "Speaking of Knox, he's asking if Marcus is handled." He types his response, already knowing the answer.

I watch Ruby through the window outside her bar, accepting something from the mailman. She's laughing at something he said, and my chest aches.

"Think she can handle us all?"

Dominic's gaze follows mine. "From what you've

told me... I'm more than ready to find out." His voice drops lower. "When my turn comes, she'll have to be ready."

"She's perfect."

"You've got it bad, my friend."

"Yeah." I don't bother denying it. "But something tells me I'm not the only one who will."

He doesn't deny it, just watches her with that calculating look I know too well. The one that says he's already planning his approach, already imagining his own chance.

"Well," he says finally. "This should be an interesting Christmas."

5

RUBY

The Wednesday night crowd at my bar keeps me busy enough to almost forget about the flowers. Almost. They sit at the end of the bar, winter rose camellias in various shades of pink, making my heart skip every time I catch their sweet, floral scent mixed with the lingering memory of Garrett's kiss.

"Boss, table four needs another round." Ash's voice pulls me back to reality. My bouncer in the bar and bartender moves behind the bar, his sleeve tattoos catching the warm lighting. The nautical scenes wrapping his arms seem to move when he works, waves and ships dancing as he mixes drinks. I told him that once I make more money, I will hire a bouncer, so he focuses on the bar side of things.

I met Ash five years ago when Eve was still alive. He'd wandered in looking for work, fresh out of the

Navy with too many tattoos for most places to hire him. Eve took one look at his gentle Beta nature, hiding behind that tough exterior, and hired him on the spot. Now he's more family than employee.

"You're staring at them again," he says, nodding toward the flowers while pouring drinks.

"Am not." I busy myself wiping down the already clean bar top, my skirt swishing around my knees with my fast movements. "Just making sure they're not dying."

"Uh-huh." He grins, showing the small gap between his front teeth that somehow makes him look more charming. "Nothing to do with the Alpha who sent them?"

"Just a guy I met at the festival." I throw my rag at him. "When you abandoned me for your grandmother's birthday."

"Hey!" He catches the rag with the reflexes that make him such a good bouncer. "Nana's only turning 100 once. Besides, sounds like you managed just fine without me." His eyes twinkle. "Unless there's something you're not telling me about this festival guy?"

I'm saved from answering by a customer ordering my newest brew, Midnight Porter. To me it smells and even has an aftertaste of roasted grains, chocolate, and toffee, one of the reasons it's so popular.

"We're almost out," I tell Ash as I pour. "Can't believe how fast it's selling."

"Because it's amazing. Eve would be proud—" He

stops mid-sentence, eyes widening as he looks toward the door.

My heart knows who it is before I turn around.

Garrett walks in like he owns the place, all confident Alpha energy wrapped in a blue-and-black checkered shirt that stretches perfectly across his shoulders as he shoulders off his jacket. Three days' worth of stubble darkens his jaw, and his short, dark hair is slightly messed up from the snow outside. He hangs his jacket by the door, and I definitely don't watch the way his muscles move under his shirt.

"Oh," Ash whispers behind me. "That's festival guy? Damn, boss."

"Shut up," I hiss, but my whole body's already humming with awareness. My Omega instincts purr at his presence, remembering how his lips felt against mine, how his masculine scent whirls around me like protection and promise and—

"You're drooling." Ash nudges me as Garrett chooses a quiet spot at the side of the bar, glancing my way.

I pretend I don't see him. Is it suddenly really hot here?

"Go get him, tiger, but play it cool. Alphas love the chase."

"I hate you," I whisper.

"Love you too, boss." He grins. "Now go *serve* your man before I do."

I take a deep breath, trying to ignore how my skin

prickles with electricity as I approach, a grin dying to spread across my lips. Up close, his eyes are even greener than I remember, his lips turning upward at the corners when he sees me.

"Couldn't stay away?" I manage to sound casual despite my racing heart. "Here to check out the competition?"

His laugh does things to my insides that should be illegal. "Maybe I just missed your cardamom ale."

"Sure it wasn't my sparkling personality?"

"That, too." He leans forward slightly, and his masculine scent makes me want to bare my neck. "How've you been, Ruby?"

The way he says my name melts me. "Oh, you know. Just running my bar, avoiding Christmas spirit, the usual."

"And how's that working out?" He gestures to the subtle holiday decorations I finally put up.

"Temporary insanity. What can I get you?"

"Surprise me."

The way he says it, deep and trusting, sends shivers down my spine. I turn to hide my reaction, pulling out my special reserve glass. The porter pours dark as night with a perfect cream head, and I catch myself making it extra perfect, taking more time than usual. Since when do I try to impress Alphas?

"You always take such care with every pour?" His voice carries genuine interest, not mockery.

"Only for customers who appreciate the art." I slide

the glass over, hyper-focused on how his fingers brush mine. "Though some just want whatever's cheapest and fastest."

"Their loss." He takes a slow sip, and the way his throat moves should not be this fascinating. "Perfect temperature. You know most places serve craft beer too cold?"

"Kills the flavor profile." I lean against the bar, falling into the comfortable rhythm of beer talk. "Eve used to say if you're going to do something—"

"Do it right or not at all," he finishes. Our eyes meet, and something electric passes between us.

"You really did know her well."

"Yep. She'd let me study her recipes after hours, taught me about proper temperature control, fermentation times..." His hands move as he talks, and I notice a small scar across his right knuckle. "Eve knew everything." His smile turns softer. "Including how to spot someone who needed a chance."

The weight of memory settles in my chest, reminding me of how badly her loss still sits inside me. Time might help me accept the loss of a loved one, but I find time also deepens the ache. Noticing a new customer, I excuse myself and get busy making another customer's whiskey sour, too aware of Garrett's gaze following my movements.

"You're different here," he says when I return. "More... yourself."

"This is my territory." I gesture to the bar, the

warm wooden walls, the Christmas lights I finally let Ash put up.

"It suits you." The intensity of his gaze makes my skin tingle. He inhales deeply, eyes darkening as if inhaling my scent, admiring it.

Heat floods my cheeks. An Alpha making such a move should feel invasive to me.

He takes another drink, throat working, and I definitely don't imagine how it would feel to run my tongue along his pulse point.

"Excellent beer."

I snort a laugh. "Flattery will get you everywhere."

"That a promise?"

Before I can formulate a response that isn't embarrassingly needy, he pulls out a small notebook. It's worn leather, pages crowded with notes.

"What are you doing?"

"Occupational hazard." He jots something down, and I lean over to peek. His handwriting is surprisingly elegant, describing flavor notes and possible brewing techniques. "Been keeping journals like this since I was eighteen."

"A good brewer learns from every pint," we say together.

His grin is devastating up close. This near, his scent overwhelms me and makes my Omega hindbrain whisper *mate*. I straighten quickly, heart pounding.

"Another?" I gesture to his nearly empty glass, proud my voice remains steady.

"Actually..." His eyes intensify with a challenge. "I've heard interesting things about your Midnight Pine. Word is it's the best porter in three counties."

My stomach drops. "Ah."

"Something wrong?"

"We might be temporarily out." I glance at the tap that was running low earlier. "Unless..."

"Unless?"

"There might be some in the basement. We keep extra supplies down there, but..." I bite my lip, remembering Ash mentioning a delivery.

"But?"

"But I'd have to check. Give me two secs." I round the bar and head over to his side of the bar as he's sitting right next to the door into the basement.

He stands, and suddenly, he's so close I can feel his body heat.

All I sense is that damned anticipation again. Like every cell in my body is pulling toward him. I reach for the door, wrestling to yank the stubborn thing open.

"That door sticks," I murmur.

He reaches past me, arm brushing mine, and the contact sends electricity shooting through my veins.

"Allow me."

The door opens easily under his strength. The stairs descend into warm darkness, and as I take the first step, his scent curls around me like a promise.

Or a warning.

The basement's warm darkness embraces me when I look back and notice he's joining me.

Warning bells should be ringing. An Alpha, alone in my basement? Instead, my body buzzes with wild abandonment.

Garrett's hand brushes the small of my back, steadying me on the narrow stairs, and that simple touch sends sparks through my entire body. The scent of aged wood and stored beer mingles with his increasingly intoxicating Alpha presence.

"Watch your step," he murmurs.

"Are you going to catch me again?" I tease. "Though I am fully capable of looking after myself."

"I know you are," he answers.

I flick on the dim lights, revealing rows of kegs and stored supplies. I busy myself checking keg labels, checking them all, trying to ignore how his presence fills the space.

"Most Alphas don't like that about me." I peek at him from behind a shelf. "The whole 'not knowing my place' thing."

"Most Alphas are idiots." He moves closer, helping me shift some boxes. The muscles in his arms flex beneath his shirt, and my mouth goes dry. "My sisters would love you, you know. They're both fighters, too, always getting into trouble, standing their ground."

I pause, studying him in the dim light. The way his eyes shine when he mentions family, the gentle pride in his voice. There's something so careful about his strength, so controlled.

"So, you see me as a sister?" I aim for banter, but my voice comes out husky. "Interesting."

The change is instant. His scent darkens and fills with want. He moves closer, backing me against the shelf, and suddenly, the basement feels too small, too hot.

"Trust me, Ruby," his voice drops lower, sending shivers down my spine. "What I feel for you..." His hands cage me in, and my breath catches as he leans close. "What I want to do to you... it's nothing like what I feel for my sisters."

My heart pounds so hard, I'm sure he can hear it. "And what exactly do you feel?"

"Been keeping me up at night." His fingers trace my cheek, feather-light. "Thinking about your laugh. Your fire. The way you light up talking about brewing. How you taste..."

His closeness makes me feel drunk on desire and need. Every Omega instinct screams to submit, to let this Alpha claim me. That thought should terrify me. Instead, it has heat pooling low in my belly, drenching my underwear.

"I'm not going to rush you," he continues, thumb brushing my lower lip. "But I need you to know... I like you. More than I should. More than makes sense after just a few days."

"Garrett..." His name comes out like a prayer.

"Tell me to stop." His forehead rests against mine. "Tell me this isn't affecting you too."

I should. Everything I've built, everything I've fought for, screams at me to push him away. To run. To hide.

"Kiss me," I whisper. "Please, I'll die if you don't—"

His mouth claims mine, and this kiss obliterates our first. It's heat and hunger and desperation. I soften into him as he presses me against the shelves, one hand tangling in my hair while the other grips my hip. A sound escapes me, something between a whimper and a purr that should embarrass me but only makes him growl.

"God, your scent," he groans against my lips. "It's driving me crazy."

"I feel so hot." My skin's on fire wherever he touches, my body moving against him. "Is this normal? To feel like I'm burning up?"

"Let me take care of you." His kisses trail down my neck, and I tilt my head instinctively, baring my throat. "Let me show you how good it can be."

I've never felt like this—like my body's not my own, like I'll combust if he stops touching me. My hands clutch his shoulders as he leaves open-mouthed kisses along my throat, each one sending sparks of electricity straight to between my thighs.

"You taste like heaven," he whispers against my skin. "Like everything I've ever craved."

His thigh slides between mine, and I gasp at the

pressure. My hips rock without my permission, seeking more. Heat builds between us, desperate and wild.

"Garrett, I—" I can't finish the thought. Can't think at all with his hands roaming my sides, his scent filling my lungs.

He's kneeling in front of me suddenly, one hand pushing my skirt up to my stomach, the other hand curling around the elastic of my panties.

He glances up at me, and I hold my breath.

"Do you want this?"

I nod, unable to find my words, more sure of this than anything else in my life. In seconds, he tucks my dress into my belt and pushes my underwear down my legs. I step out of them, still unable to believe I'm doing this.

My inhales are coming too fast, and he's smirking, lowering his gaze to my offering, studying me unapologetically.

"So beautiful and shaved for me, too."

There was primal darkness in his voice.

My nipples tighten against my shirt as he gently nudges my thighs apart, leaning in, and his fingers pry me open, the others pinching my clit.

My breath catches in my throat, my body tensing up. I've played with men before, but it was never serious. Yet, I've never felt like I was about to self-combust before.

Then his mouth is pressing against me, pushing his tongue between my folds.

A moan bursts past my lips, and I lean against the shelves, gripping them like I might fall over. Two hungry fingers slip into me as his tongue flicks my clit. My hips rock to the rhythm of his fingers working in and out of me.

I squirm while he makes sexy slurpy sounds, lips clasping my pussy, fingers pushing into me. More moans roll over my throat.

Somehow, a slice of sanity still remains to remind me that I shouldn't draw attention from anyone upstairs, seeing I've left the door to the basement open.

Fuck!

It's the same moment his fingers curl inside me to a spot so specific, so electrifyingly perfect, I cry out as a shuddering climax tears through me. It comes so fast, I'm seeing stars while Garrett removes his fingers and licks my hole like he can't get enough of my juices. I'm soaking wet, trembling, all those endorphins rippling through me. I'm in damn love with the way he laps at me, taking quick jerks and devouring me.

He grunts, keeping me spread, not releasing me. The sound turns me on as flutter after flutter rolls across my pussy.

Squirming against me, I'm floating, holding onto the shelves, struggling for breath.

Coming down from my high, I can't stop smiling.

"That was incredible."

He breaks away and gets to his feet, towering over me, his mouth and chin glistening. His body is pressed up against me, his fat cock nestled against my stomach. Now that's all I can think about—him pushing inside, spreading me, making me cry out.

"You're so wet, so sweet, so fucking ready," he whispers, and it should scare me, but I'm still smiling, desperate for everything he offers. His eyes darken to forest green, wide with hunger, but there's something else crossing his expression.

Should I be concerned?

"My sweet Ruby," he whispers, voice rough, my heady scent all over his mouth. "Did you know you're starting to come into your heat?"

Ice floods my veins even as my body burns hotter. "What?"

"BOSS LADY!" Ash's voice suddenly booms from upstairs, making me jump. "Need a hand up here!"

"No." I push against Garrett's chest, panic rising. "You're wrong. That doesn't happen. I don't get heats. I haven't had one—"

"It happens when you meet your scent match." His voice is gentle, but his eyes burn with possession. I know he's right, but I'm struggling to admit it to myself. "When you find your Alpha."

Terror and desire war in my chest. This can't be right. I'm not ready to succumb to an Alpha, to have them control me, everything I've fought for. My head's swimming with too much confusion to make sense of everything he's saying.

"I have to go." My voice shakes as I duck under his

arm, lowering my dress, my legs like jelly. "Customers... I need to..."

"Ruby, wait!" He reaches for me, and the raw need in his voice almost breaks my resolve.

"No!" It comes out sharper than intended. "No, you're wrong. This isn't. I'm not..."

I flee up the stairs, leaving him in the darkness with the taste of him still on my lips, panic clawing at my throat, and drenched. That's when I realize I left my underwear behind, but I can't bring myself to go back. My body screams to return to him, to let him claim me, to submit to what every instinct says is right.

But it also terrifies me to lose control so easily.

Heat. Alpha. Mate.

The words echo in my head along with something else...

What if he's the one... the answer to my Marcus problem? Am I ready to take on a mate so quickly for the sake of the bar? I feel torn on the inside, hating the fear that comes over me when it comes to my feelings toward Marcus.

6

RUBY

I shouldn't be here in the mountains.

The thought pounds through my head with each step up the snow-covered trail, as persistent as the memories of Garrett's second kiss the other night—from my panties missing when I went back down to the basement to collect them to him sending me more flowers but not returning to visit me himself. I contemplated going to his brewery, but I worried it made me seem desperate. So, here I am, about to scale a local mountain often used for treks.

My body still tingles when I think about him bringing me to orgasm, which is another reason why I'm here—to stop thinking about him and clear my thoughts. Yet, in my mind, I keep seeing him smiling at me and heading out of the bar the other night, and I haven't been able to get him out of my head since.

Then, there was his scent, which made me practically purr.

When do I purr?

So, I took a day off from the bar, unable to face anyone there, let alone Marcus if he returned. Not to mention Ash, with his smug teasing, well aware of what was happening in the basement.

The problem is, I want Garrett to come back.

Of course, I've thought about him being the one to help me with my Marcus problems, yet something inside of me stiffens when I remind myself of the commitment to mate and marry someone I barely know. What if he turns out to be exactly like my dad? An abusive Alpha?

Us Omegas, we're made to be at the mercy of Alphas, and that terrifies me.

I feel torn, broken, confused.

Nope, I need a break, and it helps that this morning, I found a flyer for Pine Peak Adventures stuffed under my bar's door. It seemed like divine intervention.

First Trip Free - Discover Your Mountain Spirit!

The walk to their office earlier today, across town, wasn't grueling. Now, here I am in the fresh mountain air, surrounded by snow and a small group of attendees in the group, along with our teacher, Knox Anderson. I've heard of him running ski tours from the town, but I've never had the time to explore the mountain area.

The air is crisp and clean, cutting through the fog of confusion that's never left my thoughts since I fell hard for Garrett in the basement. Later that night, I googled *Omega suppressants* on my phone out of curiosity, so I had a clear head when making decisions, rather than my hormones controlling me. The ads had promised freedom, control, and a way to silence these traitorous instincts that make me weak. To avoid being like my mother.

"Everyone keeping up okay?" Knox Anderson's deep voice carries easily over the group in a lazy drawl that somehow manages to be both commanding and comforting, seeing it drew me from my thoughts. Our tour guide looks like he just stepped off the Australian beach—all sun-bleached hair sticking out from under his hat, tanned, and ice-blue eyes so bright, I can't stop staring.

Of course, it doesn't help that the man is drop-dead gorgeous.

I adjust the straps of my borrowed backpack, glancing around at the rest of the group trudging through snow. Knox is leading us up an open, worn trail in the low snow, Mrs. Peterson keeps offering her homemade trail mix from a Ziploc bag, and Sarah and James can't keep their hands off each other. It would be cute if it didn't remind me of everything I'm worried about.

Then there's Mia and Kym, Omegas I've never seen

in town, but that doesn't mean they don't live there. Whispering Grove is enormous.

I've been watching them hover around Knox all morning, giggling at his every word, finding excuses to need his help. He handles it professionally, but I catch their predatory glances, the way they position themselves to accidentally brush against him.

"And then last summer," Kym gushes. "I tried rock climbing for the first time. Maybe you could give me some private lessons?"

Knox's polite smile seems forced. "The guide office offers group courses—"

"But you're the best instructor," Mia interrupts, batting her lashes. "Everyone says so."

I roll my eyes hard. Their desperation reeks stronger than their perfume, which is saying something. Who wears perfume on a mountain trek?

I glance over at Knox.

There is something about him that makes blending in impossible. Maybe it's the way he moves—silent and graceful despite his height. Maybe it's how his gaze finds mine, staring a bit too long, lowering his gaze to my lips. I'm confused about what's going on and why I can't look away. Or maybe it's his scent...

God, his scent. It's nothing like Garrett's, but equally intoxicating—chocolate and crisp snow and something wild that reminds me of thunderstorms. My Omega side perks up every time the wind shifts, bringing his scent to me in teasing waves. It makes my skin tingle, my body too warm despite the mountain chill.

Knox pauses at a switchback, pointing out a distant peak. The midday sun catches his profile, high-lighting the sharp line of his jaw, the slight scruff that would feel rough against my skin if I—

You're no better than other Omegas, my father's voice sneers in my memory. *Another Omega slut, always begging for it.*

The memory comes at me fast—my mother cowering in the kitchen, my father's alcohol-soaked rage filling the house with bitter pheromones. I was twelve, watching through the crack in my bedroom door as he grabbed her arm, leaving bruises.

"It's not his fault," she'd told me later, covering the marks with makeup. "Alphas can't help their instincts, baby. And we Omegas, we provoke them. It's our nature."

I dig my nails into my gloved palms. I'm nothing like her. I'm in control. And if that control is slipping lately... well, that's what the suppressants are for. The website had promised delivery within twenty-four hours, no questions asked. The price made me wince, but maybe it would be worth it to silence these urges, to stop my body from betraying me. Though I'm still not sure yet if I will order any.

"Watch your step here," Knox calls out, extending a hand to help Mrs. Peterson over a rocky section of trail. His thorn tattoo flexes on the side of his neck, and I imagine what it would be like to run my fingers over it.

I catch myself, sighing. What is wrong with me? Was Garrett right that my heat is coming? And now look at me, falling for all the Alphas. I'm no better than Mia and Kym, drooling all over Knox. Heats can come on anytime from eighteen to twenty-five, and I'm at the tail-end of that.

A perky laugh nearby pulls me from that dangerous train of thought. Sarah, the Omega from the young couple, is practically glowing as James helps her over the same rocky patch. She leans into his touch like she can't help herself, like his presence is gravity, and she's happily in orbit. He stares at her like she's the only person on the mountain, his hand protective at the small of her back. They move in perfect sync, lost in their own little world.

Something in my chest aches at the sight. For just a moment, I let myself imagine what it would be like to have that—to trust someone enough to let them in, to feel safe instead of trapped. To not flinch when an Alpha raises his voice, to not constantly fight my own biology...

"Beautiful view, isn't it?"

I startle at Knox's voice right beside me. When did he get so close? I can see the golden flecks in his blue eyes and the tiny scar above his left eyebrow. He's younger than I initially thought, maybe mid to late twenties.

"I suppose," I manage, stepping away to put some distance between us. My heart is racing, and I'm sure he can hear it. Can probably smell the confusion and want rolling off me in waves. "If you like that sort of thing."

His laugh is low and warm, stirring something primal in my chest. "Not a nature enthusiast?"

"More of an indoor cat." I gesture at my obviously new hiking boots, purchased in a panic at the sporting goods store this morning. "This is... an experiment."

"Trying to shake things up?" His nostrils flare slightly, and I watch his pupils dilate. "Or running from something?"

The question hits too close to home. I open my mouth to deflect, but a shout from ahead breaks the moment. We both turn to see James sprawled on the trail, clutching his ankle. His face is white with pain.

Knox moves instantly. I follow without thinking, my first-aid training from the bar kicking in.

"Everyone stay back. Give him some space," Knox orders, already kneeling beside James. The rest of the group hovers anxiously as Knox checks James' vitals. "Can you tell me what happened?"

"Slipped on some loose gravel." James voice is tight with pain. "Tried to catch myself, but..."

I drop to my knees on James' other side, hands already reaching for his ankle. "May I? I have some medical training."

Knox's eyebrows lift slightly, but he nods. Our

hands brush as we both support James' leg, and the contact sends electricity shooting up my arm. His gaze locks with mine for a heartbeat, and the intensity in them makes me shiver.

Focus. The ankle is already swelling, but when I carefully manipulate it, James winces, suggesting a sprain rather than a break. The skin is hot to the touch, but there's no obvious deformity.

"A sprain, I think," I murmur to Knox, fighting to keep my voice steady despite his proximity. "He needs elevation, compression, and ice, but it could have been worse."

"There's a first aid kit about a mile back," Knox states, then frowns at the murky sky. "The weather is coming in faster than anticipated. It shouldn't have reached our town until later tonight."

I follow his gaze to see dark clouds gathering ominously over the peaks. The temperature has dropped noticeably in the last few minutes, and the wind carries the sharp scent of approaching snow. We've got weather coming in.

The wind also brings Knox's scent, and this close, I catch something else in it—something familiar that tugs at my memory. Something that reminds me of old paper and faded ink, of freshly baked apples, and his masculine scent, which leaves me swooning.

"I know this group was supposed to go another three miles," Knox addresses everyone, switching seamlessly into serious mode. His voice carries that

Alpha timbre, and I'm catching my breath at how much I enjoy hearing it. "But with James' injury and the weather, we need to evacuate. There's a cabin about a quarter mile ahead—we'll shelter there until the storm passes."

He pulls out his satellite phone, and immediately, Mia edges closer. "Will we be safe there, Knox?" She touches his arm, voice sugary sweet.

"The cabin's fully stocked for emergencies," he says, already making his call. "Let me notify base about our change in plans."

"I can help you with anything you need," Kym offers.

After his phone call, Knox sends Sarah ahead with Mrs. Peterson to prep the cabin while the Henderson couple takes charge of distributing emergency supplies from his pack.

"I'll help with James," Mia volunteers instantly, but Knox shakes his head.

"Ruby has medical training. Ruby, take his left side. I've got his right."

I move into position, catching the daggers Mia and Kym shoot my way. The group clusters together as the temperature plummets, and snow starts to fall more heavily now.

"I can carry the first aid kit," Kym announces, pressing close to Knox's free side. "It looks heavy."

"Actually," Knox says. "Could you and Mia help Mrs. Peterson? The trail gets tricky here."

They retreat, whispering furiously, while James groans between Knox and me. The weather's deteriorating rapidly, the wind whipping snow into our faces.

"Nearly there," Knox murmurs, but all I can see around us are trees. "You're doing great, Ruby."

Behind us, I hear Kym's stage whisper to Mia. "Could she be any more desperate?"

I shake my head and ignore them.

With the storm closing in, I have bigger problems than two jealous Omegas.

My phone buzzes in my pocket, but I have no hands to check it, so it'll have to wait. Finally, we reach the huge wooden cabin which is larger than I anticipated. It's nestled in a clearing of trees covered in snow.

Inside, the main room has couches positioned in front of a fireplace. There's a basic kitchenette and what looks like sleeping quarters and a bathroom through a side door. And another hallway to more rooms. While Knox and I get James settled, I notice Mia and Kym whispering, shooting me venomous looks. I ignore them and recheck James' ankles while Knox grabs the first aid kit and compresses the area with a bandage, while I grab several cushions to elevate his foot.

"Everyone, I'm going to update the base on our arrival," Knox announces. "They will know we're waiting out the storm here. No need to risk rescue teams in this weather for a minor sprain."

James is nodding like he agrees, while Sarah is kneeling at his side, grasping his hand.

I use that moment to check my phone to find three missed calls from my bestie, Lily, and a text that makes my blood run cold.

> Marcus was just here asking about you. Said something about making sure you're taken care of. Ruby, what's going on?

The words blur as my vision swims. What the hell does he want now? I quickly message her back that I'm fine and will speak with her later.

Stuffing the phone into my pocket, I glance around to find James lying across one of the couches facing the fireplace, his leg propped up. Knox is throwing more logs into the growing flames, trying to get it to build up.

Being up here in the mountains was my getaway from Marcus, yet seeing Lily's message leaves me feeling cold all over.

"Hey, you okay?" Knox's tone carries genuine concern as he steps closer. "You look a little pale."

While I attempt to focus, everything feels too intense—the cabin's warmth, feeling trapped, and, most of all, Knox's presence getting stronger with each step he takes toward me.

"I'm fine, just..." I sway slightly, and his hand

catches my elbow. Even through my jacket, his touch is a tempting fire.

"Come on." His voice drops lower, meant just for me. "Let me make you some hot chocolate. James is resting, and we can't do anything but wait out this storm."

I follow him to the small kitchenette at the rear of the room, watching as he shrugs off his winter gear. Without his bulky jacket and hat, I stare at this hunk. Where Garrett is all broad shoulders and powerful, Knox is athletic and captivating. His dirty blonde hair falls in his eyes as he rummages through cupboards, and the long-sleeved thick t-shirt he's wearing shows off strong arms. A thin leather cord around his neck disappears beneath his collar, and I find myself wondering what hangs on it.

"You're watching me closely," he says without turning around, amusement filling his voice.

"Just trying to picture how you got so tanned in a town like Whispering Grove, where it's snowing more often than not."

"I just got back recently from a surfing competition in Hawaii."

"Seems a long way from mountain guide. How was it?"

He chuckles, and I stare at the dimple in his chin.

"We were up on the north shore of Oahu at Banzai Pipeline. Man, the waves were just beasts... perfect overhead barrels, glassy conditions until the wind picked up." He runs a hand through his salt-bleached hair. "Then these hammerheads decided to crash the party... came in way too close to the lineup. Had to call everyone in."

The way he talks about surfing transforms him—there's this wild freedom in his voice that makes something in me ache—as though he's most alive when he's challenging nature itself.

"Sounds terrifying," I admit.

"Nah, that's the rush of it. Same as climbing, really, just you against the elements."

"And sharks weren't impressed with your skills?"

He grins, and my insides soften at the most beautiful smile I've ever seen.

"I came in fourth." He shrugs, but I catch the disappointment in his voice. "The competition was intense this year."

"Fourth place is incredible. So, you travel often, then?" I watch him measure cocoa into a mug.

"Here and there." Steam rises as he adds hot water to the cup. "But nothing feels quite like being home in Whispering Grove." Something shadows his expression. "Grew up here. My parents have passed now, but..."

"I'm so sorry." The pain in his voice is hard to ignore.

"Traffic accident." He shrugs, turning to grab marshmallows from the cupboard on the wall. "Ten years ago now." The words are clipped, holding back emotions it feels. I can't blame him. "Marshmallows? I'm a two-minimum kind of guy."

"Two sounds perfect."

The mug warms my cold hands as he guides me to a window seat. The beige cushions look well-loved, clearly a favorite spot. Through the glass, the storm intensifies, snow swirling in angry patterns while tree branches shake violently.

He guides me to the window seat, and I catch Mia whispering something to Kym that makes them both glance in my direction. I ignore them.

"Knox?" Kym interrupts us, standing a few feet away. "Can you please help? I think I have a splinter..."

"You're still wearing gloves," he points out without looking away from me, but I notice her scowl as she slips away.

"I don't mind if you help her. She's your girlfriend, right?" Part of me is playing dumb, but I need to hear it from his lips.

"Fuck no!" he answers abruptly, his brow furrowing as if it hurts him just thinking about such a notion. "I don't have a girlfriend right now. Anyway, you should come trekking more often," he says to me, settling down near.

Not too close, but close enough that his scent wraps around me, leaving me buzzing all over. Especially with hearing he's a free man.

"Amazing how you can find yourself in the wilderness," he continues.

I laugh, but it comes out shakier than intended. "I would love that more than you can imagine."

"Tell me about you. What makes you buzz?" His tone is so casual.

"My brewery is my life." I go on to explain my creations in detail and end up speaking more than expected, then pause to take a sip of my drink. He's watching me closely, with more interest than just being polite. "But more recently, life has been a bit of a bitch."

His laugh is unexpected and rich. "You sound like me. When I lost my parents, I went dark. Really dark. Hated fucking everything." He runs a hand through his hair again, and the gesture is so endearing, it makes my chest ache. "That's actually how I found out about trekking in the mountains. Needed something to pull me out of the darkness."

"Did it work?"

"Not at first." He glances outside, then back at me. "First few trips, I just walked until I couldn't anymore. Then I collapsed wherever I ended up. Probably lucky I didn't freeze to death."

"What changed?"

"Met this old guide. Complete asshole, but he saw something in me. Made me learn proper survival skills, navigation, and first aid. Said if I was going to be stupid enough to walk into the wilderness, I should at least be smart enough to walk back out."

I find myself smiling. "Sounds like Eve." He gives

me a questioning look. "My aunt. She had this way of helping people by pretending she wasn't helping at all."

"The best ones do." His smiles, his piercing eyes never leaving me, and something in my stomach flips. "Anyway, he got me into proper training. Then, I discovered surfing on a trip to California. Something about catching waves... it's like time stops. Nothing exists except you and the water."

I know very little about surfing except that those who do it are super brave to ride those huge waves.

"Is that why you compete?"

"Partly." He shifts, and his arm brushes mine. Tingles zip through me at the contact, and there's something so comforting just chatting with him. "Mostly it gives me purpose. Something to work toward, you know?"

The question hits deeper than he probably intended. What is *my* purpose? The bar, obviously. Eve's legacy. But is that enough? Is that why I'm fighting so hard to keep it?

"Sorry." His voice brings me back. "Got philosophical there. Want to hear a really bad joke instead?"

"Hit me." I recline, adoring the way he smiles at me.

"What did the buffalo say to his kid when he dropped him off at school?"

I frown. "I'm afraid to ask."

"Bison!" His grin is ridiculous and perfect.

I groan but can't help laughing. "That's terrible."

"I've got worse. What do you call a bear with no teeth?"

"Please, no."

"A gummy bear!"

"Stop!" I'm giggling now, and the way he looks at me makes my heart stutter.

This is dangerous. I shouldn't feel this pull toward him, not when Garrett's kiss still burns on my lips. Not when my body responds to both of them in ways I've never experienced with other Alphas.

"Knox?" Mia appears beside us suddenly, frowning. "Could you check the weather updates? I'm worried about my family back in town with this storm..."

He sighs. "Sure. Ruby, stay put. I've got more terrible jokes when I get back."

The moment he leaves and heads to the back of the room with Mia, Kym materializes at my side. "Having fun?"

"Loads." I sip my cocoa. "Your splinter feeling better?"

"Listen carefully," she hisses. "We've been working on Knox for weeks. He's ours. Back off, or you'll regret it."

I laugh, which clearly isn't the response she expected. "He's not a project to *work on*. He's a person."

"You have no idea who you're dealing with." Her sweet smile is crooked. "We've seen how he looks at you. It stops now."

"Everything okay here?" Sarah asks, joining us.

"Just explaining to Ruby how things work," Kym says brightly. "About respect and territory."

"And I was just leaving." I stand, but Mia blocks my path.

"You know what happens to homewreckers in these mountains?" she asks. "Such dangerous terrain. Accidents happen all the time."

Her threat sits heavily on me.

Before I can respond, Knox returns. "Storm's getting worse. Looks like we're here for the night. Settle in and get cozy."

Through the window, the storm intensifies. Snow whips past in white sheets, and the wind sounds almost alive. Something about it raises the hair on my neck.

Or maybe that's just the knowledge that I'm trapped in a cabin with two Omegas who stare at me like I'm their arch-enemy.

This should be fun.

7

RUBY

Mac and cheese never tasted so much like tension.

The powdered sauce and boiled noodles mix with beef jerky chunks—Knox's suggestion to add protein—while canned green beans and stale crackers round out our five-star mountain cuisine dinner. Still, after the day's hike and drama, even this basic meal feels like heaven. And hot chocolates for dessert.

Outside, it's pitch black with the storm howling while we gather around the fireplace, its warmth the only real comfort in this situation. Mrs. Peterson has claimed one of the couches, stretching her legs across it, while Sarah sits on my couch and James on another one, with his ankle propped up. Mia and Kym arrange themselves artfully opposite me. Knox is currently at the rear of the room, checking in with the base on the radio.

"I just think it's sad," Mia says loudly to no one in particular. "When people don't respect boundaries."

Kym nods sagely. "Or established relationships."

I shove another forkful of mac and cheese in my mouth to keep from responding. The cheap pasta tastes like cardboard and spite.

"Some people just don't understand their place," Sarah chimes in, surprising me. When did she join Team Bitch Girls?

The fork freezes halfway to my mouth. "I'm sorry, what exactly are you implying?"

"Oh, she speaks!" Mia's fake surprise would win her a high school drama award. "We thought you only talked to Alphas."

"Only specific Alphas," Kym adds with a sneer.

James shifts uncomfortably. "Hey, maybe we should—"

"It's fine," Sarah cuts him off, and I get up to set my plate on the table before I'm tempted to throw it. It's also when I notice Knox is still on the phone, not paying attention to our conversation, though I wish he would.

Back on the couch, they're all watching me, clearly waiting for my response.

"I'm used to people making assumptions about me. Though usually, they're better at it."

"Was that a threat?" Mia sits up straighter.

"An observation." I force my voice to stay casual. "Like how I've observed you two throwing yourselves at Knox all day with zero success. Must be frustrating."

Kym's face turns an interesting shade of purple. "You little—"

"Everything okay out here?" Knox's voice cuts through the tension. "Radio says the storm's settling in for the night."

"Perfect!" Mia's transformation from fury to sugar would give me whiplash if I wasn't so nauseated by it. "We saved you a spot."

Knox drops into the space they make for him between them, and they immediately press closer like bookends. The sight shouldn't bother me, but it irritates me to no end.

"I found some games in the back," he continues, seemingly oblivious to the way Kym's practically in his lap. "And books, if anyone's interested. We should also figure out sleeping arrangements - there are five single beds in the back room. James has one, obviously. And Sarah next to him, perhaps?"

She nods eagerly.

"One for me," Mrs. Peterson quickly pipes up.

"I'll take a couch," I offer. Anything to avoid being trapped in a room with my new fan club.

Knox stares at the two girls. "You both take the last beds?"

"Where will you be staying," Mia coos, batting her eyelashes at him.

"The couch since I want to keep watch on the weather."

"Then we'll stay, too!" Kym announces. "In case you need help. Plus, it's so much warmer here."

Great. Just great.

While part of me contemplates going into the bedroom, I feel safer near Knox. Especially seeing Sarah turned against me, too.

Knox shrugs. "Sure. Your choice. Okay, that's settled. Now, anyone want to hear a story?" Knox asks, and something in his voice makes me lean forward despite myself. "There's an old legend about these mountains in winter."

"Is it scary?" Mia clutches his arm.

"Sounds great," I add, and others nod.

"Only if you believe in the Yuki-onna." His eyes lock with mine as he begins, and suddenly, it's like everyone else fades away. "The Snow Woman. They say she walks these peaks during the worst storms, beautiful and deadly. And if you're found alone in the mountains at night, she will come and kidnap you." A log shifts in the fireplace, sending sparks flying. Someone gasps.

"They say she appears like a ghost," Knox continues, his voice dropping lower. "A woman in white, with skin pale as moonlight and lips blue as frostbite. Her feet never touch the snow... she glides above it, leaving no tracks."

"Stop it," Mia whispers sarcastically, but she's leaning in, too.

"Ten years ago, a hiker went missing up here. They found his camera two months later when the snow melted." Knox pauses, letting the silence build. "Want to know what was on it?"

We all nod, the fire crackling ominously.

"The last photo showed a white figure in the distance, barely visible through the snowstorm. But when they zoomed in..." He leans forward. "They saw she was looking directly at the camera. And smiling."

The wind howls outside, rattling the windows. Half the group jumps. Goosebumps race up my arms.

"They say that's how she hunts. She creates devastating snowstorms, waiting for someone to get lost. Then she appears, pretending to help..." He glances around the circle. "And if you follow her..."

Another log shifts, sending up a shower of sparks. This time, most of us yelp, except for James.

"What happens then?" Sarah whispers.

Knox's tone drops to just above a whisper. "They find you in spring when the snow melts. Frozen solid. With a peaceful smile on your face... and your hair turned pure white from terror."

The fire pops loudly, and Mia screams, burying her face in Knox's shoulder. Kym's laughing nervously at her.

"But that's just an old legend," Knox says, his normal voice returning. But when his eyes meet mine again, there's something else there. "Although... they never did find that hiker's body."

The wind picks up outside, whistling through the trees, and suddenly, the warmth of the fire doesn't feel quite enough.

Knox is staring right at me, grinning, softening the fear he's caused.

That's when I notice Mia's and Kym's glares toward me, while Knox's lips curve in a small smile as he starts a new story.

Eventually, he's told us three tales, and I'm curled up with my pillow into a ball. Mrs. Peterson is on her feet, clearly had enough, starting to distribute blankets and pillows before she goes to bed. Knox helps Sarah take James to the bedroom.

Then he's back, setting up the couch somewhere behind mine

"Sleep well," he murmurs. Mia and Kym take the remaining couches, aggressively fluffing their pillows and in my line of sight.

The fire crackles, casting shadows on the walls. Outside, the storm rages, but here, it's almost peaceful... if I ignore the death glares from across the room. And I pretend I'm not hyper-aware of Knox in the room with me.

Thinking of him makes my skin tingle and my heart race.

How am I supposed to sleep when he looks at me like that?

Or when Mia and Kym might murder me in my sleep?

And why, despite everything, do I keep thinking about Garrett's kiss while drowning in Knox's scent?

Pain explodes through my shoulder as I hit something hard and cold. For a moment, I can't process what's happening—why am I not on the couch, why is everything so dark, and why can't I breathe? Then snow fills my mouth as I gasp, and the metallic click of a lock sliding home brings reality crashing into focus.

I scramble to my feet to find myself standing outside the cabin and in the snow, the door shut. I blink the sleep out of my eyes, and I know I'm a deep sleeper, often not hearing my own alarms in the morning, so it hurts to know I slept through being carried.

Not to mention, those psychotic bitches must have thrown me outside!

Fuck!

Wind whips around me like invisible claws, and the absolute darkness seems to close in around me as I rush to the door. I'm wearing only what I fell asleep in —jeans, long-sleeved thermal shirt, and socks. No jacket. No shoes. No chance if I don't get back inside.

"Hey!" I slam my fists against the main door, my voice scraped raw by the wind. "Let me in! Open the door!"

Nothing. Of course, nothing. Through the window, I can spot the mud room door is closed—no one will hear me over the storm. I think back on the couch where I'd been sleeping. They must have waited until I was deep under. Two of them to carry me? Oh, I bet they had help from Sarah. Dread coils through me, colder than the wind.

Another gust nearly knocks me off my feet. I hug myself, trying to preserve what little warmth remains, but my clothes are already soaked from the snow. How long before hypothermia sets in? Twenty minutes in these conditions? Less? Knox's story about the Yuki-onna echoes in my head—beautiful and deadly, claiming lost travelers in storms just like this one.

I glance behind me to complete darkness, and I feel exposed and so alone.

"Not like this," I whisper through chattering teeth. "I'm not dying because two Omegas can't handle rejection."

I force my already-numbing feet to move, fighting through knee-deep snow around the cabin's perimeter. Pine branches whip against me, dumping more snow down my back. Each breath feels like swallowing ice.

"Please," I whisper, though I'm not sure who I'm begging—God, the universe, or the snow woman herself. "Please don't let me die like this."

My breath comes in ragged clouds as I stare into the darkness, Knox's story clawing at my mind. The wind whips through the skeletal branches overhead. Something howls from the mountains, or is that a woman's keening cry? Terror slides down my spine as I bolt along the side of the house. My heart pounds against my ribs, and every shadow seems to reach for me.

The first window I find belongs to the back bedroom. Through a gap in the curtains, I can make out the shapes of beds in the darkness. I pound on the glass harder than before.

"Help! Someone wake up!" But my voice and banging on the glass are stolen by the howling storm that rattles the windows.

They don't hear me. They're dead to the world.

My fingers have lost all feeling by the time I find the back door. More pounding, more screaming, more silence. The wind cuts through my wet clothes like knives, and my thoughts are starting to get fuzzy around the edges. Bad sign. Very bad sign.

One more window a few steps away. I just have to try one more window.

I'm so cold I can barely lift my arms to bang on the glass. My legs give out, dropping me into the snow. Ironic, really. I survived my parents, survived Marcus so far, survived everything life threw at me, just to die because of two stupid Omegas.

A hoarse scream rips past my throat, but it's drowned out by the storm.

Through the darkening edges of my vision, light suddenly spills across the snow. A door opens. Warmth. Please be warmth.

"Ruby?" Knox's voice carries pure horror. "Oh God, Ruby!"

Strong arms scoop me up, cradling me against a chest that feels like fire against my frozen skin. I try to speak but my jaw won't work right.

"I've got you," he murmurs, already moving. "When I saw your couch empty, I searched for you through the cabin until I saw movement outside through the back window and came to find you. But I have you now. Just hold on."

We pass through the door into blessed warmth, but I'm shaking so hard, I can barely process where we're going. Upstairs? I didn't know the cabin had stairs.

"C-Cold," I manage.

"I know, sweetheart. I know." His voice carries barely contained fury as he shoulders open another door. He sets me on the edge of a bed piled with blankets.

"We need to get these wet clothes off you. Now." His tone brings no argument from me as I sit there, shaking, struggling to move. "You're in the early stages of hypothermia. We have to get your core temperature up."

I try to grip my shirt, but my fingers won't cooperate. Knox's hands replace mine, stripping each wet layer. There's nothing sexual about it, though in other circumstances, having an Alpha undress me might send my reaction into overdrive. Right now, I can't think past the bone-deep cold.

"Arms up," he instructs, peeling off my soaked shirt. The rest follows quickly—jeans, socks, everything—then he's wrapping me in layers of thick blankets. "Lie down."

I collapse onto the bed, shivers wracking my entire body. Knox slides in next to me, pulling me against him so we're face to face. He's adding another blanket over us both. His body heat seeps into me slowly, painfully, as feeling returns to my extremities.

"F-Found me," I manage after what feels like hours.

"Heard the front door close." His arms tighten around me, his voice rough. "When I saw your couch empty... Fuck, Ruby. Did they hurt you? Besides..."

"J-Just threw me out." Speaking is easier now, though I'm still shaking. "Didn't expect the psycho level of j-jealousy."

"I'm so sorry." He presses his face into my hair. "I knew they were intense, but this... this is attempted murder."

"O-Over you."

"I'm so sorry." He pushes strands of hair off my face. "I'll take care of them for doing this. I give you my word."

There's silence between us, and I can't stop staring at this handsome man and how I ended up in his arms in this situation.

He blinks, those hypnotic blue eyes catching the faint light overhead, and I find myself sinking into them, trying not to notice how his arms feel like shelter around me.

My thoughts are a storm—the biting cold, the terror, the way he found me... and oh God, he'd seen me completely naked before he wrapped me in these blankets. Heat crawls up my neck despite the persistent chill in my bones.

"Oh look, there's color coming to your face. Good." He rubs his knuckles across my skin, his touch impossibly gentle. "You had me worried."

"Only a minute?" The words slip out before I can stop them.

His expression darkens. "If I'd been even a minute later—"

"But you weren't," I murmur, trying to stop shivering. "You found me."

"I would never forgive myself for setting all this in motion," The words come out like a growl, possessive and protective all at once. His hand cups my cheek, and I lean into its warmth without thinking. "Rest now. You're safe."

"W-What does that mean?" My eyes are getting heavy, but I fight it.

"Mm? Just rest now."

"Thank you for... for coming after me."

He pulls me closer, tucking my head under his chin. "Sleep," he commands softly. "I'm not going anywhere."

I want to stay awake, to memorize how this feels, but exhaustion pulls at me. The last thing I register is his heartbeat against my ear, steady as a drum, and his whispered words that sound almost like a threat.

"No one will ever hurt you again."

8

KNOX

The sunrise paints Ruby's skin gold.

I can't stop staring at her—the way the early morning light streams through the cabin's window, catching the copper highlights in her messy hair, softening the worried line between her brows. Ruby's curled up in my bed like she belongs there, her breathing soft and even, one hand tucked under her cheek. Last night feels like something from a fever dream—finding her locked outside in the storm, her skin ice-cold, those bastards Kym and Mia thinking it was some kind of joke.

Fuck. My hands clench, remembering her violent shivers, the way she'd practically collapsed against me when I found her. Pure luck that I'd woken up and found her gone from the couch, and I started checking the cabin. If I hadn't...

My insides tighten at the thought, a possessive

rage burning through my veins. When Garrett told me about her, said I needed to meet her, I thought he was exaggerating. But that first day she walked into my office, clutching the free trek voucher I'd carefully planted under her door... Christ. Her scent hit me like an avalanche—honey and vanilla and something wild underneath that called to every protective instinct I possess.

Even now, with her sleeping peacefully after the being-locked-outside ordeal, that scent wraps around me like a physical touch. It's subtle, delicate... nothing like the overwhelming pheromones most unmated Omegas put out. There's something about it that makes me want to desperately get closer, to taste...

I push away from the bed before I do something stupid like bury my face in her neck. The wooden floor creaks under my boot as I head for the door, and I twist my head around, but she doesn't wake. Good. She needs the rest after what those idiots put her through.

The cabin's main room is quiet when I reach the kitchen. Mia and Kym are sprawled on the couches where they still sleep, and my lip curls at the sight. The urge to drag them outside, leave them to freeze the way they did to Ruby, burns hot in my chest. It would be so easy. So satisfying to let them experience what they put her through...

But I can already see the headlines: *Guide Throws Clients Out In Blizzard.*

My fingers dig into the kitchen counter as I fight

down the urge. There are other ways to handle this. Better ways. Ways that won't end with my business in ruins.

You two have no idea who you're messing with, I think darkly, watching them sleep. They'll learn soon enough. I tolerated them long enough for the business, even their insistent flirting, but they crossed the line when they messed with Ruby.

The kitchen's pretty bare—we don't keep much here besides emergency supplies—but I know where the good stuff is hidden. The instructors' private stash is behind a false panel in the pantry—premium hot chocolate, fancy granola, dried fruit, the kind of comfort food that makes long shifts bearable. Ruby deserves something better than trail mix after last night.

As I heat milk for hot chocolate on my single burner, my mind drifts to the empty house waiting for me back in Whispering Grove. Memories of parents long gone and the endless wanderlust that's driven me since losing them. The mountains filled that void for a while—the constant movement, the solitude, the simple purpose of keeping others safe while they explored the wilderness.

But lately... fuck, lately, it's not enough. I want more than empty rooms and silent mornings. Want someone to share stories with, to build something permanent with.

My thoughts travel to Ruby and how quickly she

captivated me. Her beauty, how easily we click, how I want to steal her away from the world and get to know everything about her. The thought follows me up the stairs as I balance the hot chocolate and a plate of granola, dried berries, and the last shortbread cookies from my secret stash.

The door creaks when I nudge it open with my shoulder. Ruby stirs at the sound, and I'm caught again by how right she looks in the bed.

"Rise and shine, sleeping beauty," I say. "You know what the difference is between a good morning and a bad morning?"

She peeks out from under the blanket. "What?"

"About 100 degrees." I grin as she groans and pulls the blanket over her head.

"Too early for jokes," she mumbles, but I can hear the smile in her voice.

When she emerges again, reality crashes back in. Awareness floods her gaze—where she is, what happened last night—realizing most likely that she's naked. I kept it all professional last night, though who am I fucking kidding? Hard to be completely detached when faced with cream-colored skin, curves that have my cock throbbing, full breasts calling to me...

Fuck!

"You're safe," I tell her, setting down the breakfast offerings on the bedside table.

She sighs heavily, pulling the blanket tighter to her neck. "I can't believe they did that to me."

"Don't worry." My tone drops lower, a growl threading through it. "I'll be taking care of them."

"You don't need to protect me," she protests, then tugs at the blanket. A blush spreads across her cheeks as she tries to cover herself more.

And fuck if my brain isn't helpfully supplying every detail from last night. The smoothness of her hips as I peeled off her wet jeans. The strip of blonde hair at the apex of her thighs. The small snowflake tattoo just above her right breast that I definitely shouldn't have noticed. But the images are inked on my brain, and I can't forget them.

I clear my throat. "I brought you breakfast. And your clothes are dry; I put them by the heater." I nod toward the pile of neatly folded clothes. "There's a bathroom through there." My chin lifts across the room at the white door.

She's looking at me with a mix of gratitude and confusion that makes my chest tight. A small smile plays at the corners of her mouth. Those lips are tempting, torture...

"I'll let you get dressed," I say, backing toward the door before I tell her how gorgeous she looks and climb under the blanket with her.

"I mean, you already saw me naked." She smirks, and her attempt at humor is adorable, especially with that blush staining her cheeks.

"And it was beautiful." The words slip out before I can stop them, low and rough with honesty. I shut the door quickly, leaning back against it while my heart pounds.

Smooth. Real fucking smooth.

I can hear her moving around inside - soft footsteps, the rustle of clothing, a quiet humming that makes me want to curl up and purr. Last night shouldn't have happened the way it did, but having her here, in my space, feels right in a way I can't explain.

"You can come back in," she calls, and I'm through the door embarrassingly fast.

She's perched on the edge of the bed now, fully dressed but still looking deliciously rumpled. Her sock-covered feet are tucked under her as she cradles the hot chocolate, and something inside me actually aches at how fucking adorable she is. Her hair's been somewhat tamed, but there's still a stubborn piece curling around her ear that my fingers itch to touch.

"Is this like a secret bedroom?" she asks, glancing around the area that's definitely nicer than the main cabin downstairs.

I sink down onto the bed beside her. "It's for instructors to get away from the chaos sometimes. Everyone needs an escape."

"Especially when you have stalkers in your group."

The reminder of what Kym and Mia did makes my hands clench.

Ruby takes another sip of her drink, and a tiny smile curves her lips as she savors it.

"This is amazing, by the way," she says, then peers at the plate. "Where did you get all these goodies in the middle of nowhere?"

"I have my sources." I watch her take a cookie, fighting back a grin at her expression of pure bliss.

"Mm-hmm." She eyes me over the rim of her mug. "So, what other secrets are you hiding up here in your mountain fortress?"

"I can't give away all my secrets." I lean back on my hands as she curls to stare at me, her hand collecting a second cookie.

"You're not what I expected."

"No? What did you expect?"

"I don't know. Some macho Alpha guide who'd try to mansplain hiking to me. Or treat me like I'm made of glass because I'm an Omega." She shrugs. "Not... you."

"Sorry to disappoint."

Her gaze lifts instantly. "I didn't say it was disappointing." Her eyes meet mine, and fuck, there's heat there that has nothing to do with the morning sun streaming through the window.

I force myself to stay still as she studies me, her head tilted slightly.

"So what am I like then?" I ask.

"You're..." She pauses, worrying her bottom lip in a way that's fucking distracting. "Approachable, but not soft. Strong without being domineering. And you tell terrible jokes."

"My jokes are amazing."

Ruby shifts closer, maybe without realizing it. Her knee brushes mine, and the contact sends a buzz right to my balls.

"Thank you," she says quietly. "For last night. For not... taking advantage."

A growl builds in my chest at the implication she thought I might. "I would never—"

"I know." She cuts me off, laying her small hand over mine. "That's what I mean. You didn't have to be so careful with me. But you were."

Her touch is like a brand on my skin. I turn my hand over slowly, letting our palms press together. Her fingers are tiny compared to mine, but they fit perfectly between the spaces.

"You deserve *careful*," I tell her, meaning it more than I've meant anything in a long time.

Something vulnerable flashes across her face. "Even after I proved how helpless I am? Getting locked out, needing rescue..."

"Hey." I catch her chin with my free hand, tilting her face up to mine. "You're not helpless. You survived hypothermia-inducing conditions until I found you. You kept your head, kept moving, kept fighting. That's not weakness, Ruby. That's strength."

She blinks rapidly, but I keep hold of her chin, thumb brushing along her jaw.

She's smiling, too, not pulling her hand from mine.

The morning sun catches her hair again, turning it

into a living fire. That stubborn curl taunts me, and before I can think better of it, I reach up to tuck it behind her ear. Her breath catches at the touch, pupils dilating slightly.

"Knox..." My name is barely a whisper on her lips.

A door slams somewhere downstairs, breaking the moment. Ruby freezes, quickly getting off the bed and putting her cup down. I have to bite back a growl of frustration. *Right.* The rest of the world exists. Including two soon-to-be ex-clients I need to deal with.

"I should go handle that," I say reluctantly, standing. "You can stay up here as long as you want. No one else comes to this part of the cabin."

She nods, already drawing back into herself slightly, but then she catches my hand as I turn to leave. "Knox?"

"Yeah?"

"Thank you. For... everything."

There's so much I want to say. Want to tell her about Garrett, about her friends asking for us to date her, about how I've been looking for her my whole life without knowing it. Want to pull her into my arms and never let go. Want to track down everyone who ever hurt her and make them pay.

Instead, I squeeze her hand gently. "Anytime, angel."

I force myself to leave before I lean in and kiss her.

Ruby is something special. Something rare and

precious and worth taking time with. Worth doing right.

Fuck Garrett for being right.

I am completely and utterly screwed—I had no idea what I was getting myself into.

9

My hands shake slightly as I type the message to my bartender, Ash.

> Got caught in the storm up at Pine Peak. Long story, but I'm safe. Can you open the bar today? Will explain everything when I get back.

I pause, my thumb hovering over the send button. Should I mention Knox? Ash will want details if I mention a guy. The way Knox saved me last night, carrying me from the freezing darkness into warmth and safety? The way his scent wrapped around me, making me feel protected for the first time in years?

No. Just thinking about it makes me sound over-dramatic, and Ash will never let me forget it. So, I add something else.

> Some crazy stuff happened with the tour group. Tell you later.

The message sends, and I take a deep breath, letting my head rest against the bathroom wall as I stand there. The mirror shows me what a mess I am—hair barely contained in its messy ponytail, my extra sweater I brought with me in my backpack hanging off one shoulder, and my amber eyes too bright with left-over adrenaline and lingering fear from last night.

From downstairs, Knox's voice reaches me—deep and authoritative—yet I can't make out his words. Just the sound of him has my stomach bursting with butterflies, which is... inconvenient. A ridiculous reaction. The last thing I need is another Alpha complication in my life. Though the notion that perhaps he might be somehow able to help me with Marcus comes to mind... as does Garrett and our kiss, and I'm suddenly pacing from the door to the shower. How can I be drawn to two guys? Talk about making my life even more complicated. Or is this some kind of side effect from starting to experience initial signs of my heat?

I push those aside because, first, I have some bitches to deal with.

I straighten my shoulders, channeling Aunt Eve's steel-spine energy. *In life, you need to stand up for your-self,* she always said. *No matter how uncomfortable, how terrifying it makes you. Because if you can't face your demons, honey, they'll eat you alive.*

Downstairs, the main room falls quiet when I arrive. James is testing his ankle, grimacing but mobile, while Sarah and Mrs. Peterson hover nearby, ready to catch him. My attention locks onto Kym and Mia, huddled by the fireplace like they're trying to make themselves small.

Good. They should be afraid.

"The rescue team should be here in twenty," Knox announces, heading for the front door with James, Sarah, and Mrs. Peterson, who is waving at us. I assume she's decided to take a quick flight off the mountain. "I'll show them the best landing spot. The rest of you wait for my return."

"Well, look who survived the night." As soon as he's gone, Kym's fake-sweet voice cuts through the silence.

The mockery in her tone has my blood boiling, but I keep my voice steady.

"Funny you should ask about last night."

"Is it?" Mia examines her nails.

I step closer, arms tight at my side. "You don't remember locking me outside in a blizzard? Ignoring me while I pounded on the door?"

"Sounds like a bad dream." Kym's smile infuriates me.

"I know it was you two!"

"Do you have proof?"

"You mean besides Knox finding me half-frozen?" I watch their smug expressions falter slightly.

"Have you considered seeing a doctor? It sounds like you sleepwalk," Mia mutters, chin high.

"You could have killed me." My laugh sounds bitter even to my own ears. "But I guess that was the point, wasn't it? Can't have some Omega catching Knox's attention."

Kym's face twists with ugly jealousy. "What lies did you tell him about us?"

"Nothing he didn't figure out himself." I smile, sweet as poison. "You're not as clever as you think you are."

"Listen, bitch—" Kym starts forward, but Mia grabs her arm.

"Don't," she hisses. "Not here."

The door opens before Kym can respond, and Knox's presence fills the space. His gaze narrows on us as he strides toward us, something dangerous flickering in their depths.

"Everything okay here?" he asks, but his gaze is fixed on me.

"Perfect," I say, not breaking eye contact with Kym.

His jaw tightens. "Get your gear," he orders them. "We're heading down."

I move to gather my backpack, but he's suddenly there, close enough that I'm inhaling his scent, and my head spins.

"You good?" he asks quietly.

"Yeah, thanks." I nod, hyperaware of Kym and Mia's glares burning into my back.

His hand is on my lower back, and my body buzzes with adrenaline, with an excitement that startles me. When I glance up, we stare into each other's eyes, and he feels the connection, too.

I'm trembling slightly, more to do with what he's doing to me, with how heat burns between my legs so quickly, it scares me.

My mother's words come to mind, a memory from that night she came home with bruises across her neck, tears tracking through her makeup.

"Don't ever let them fool you, Ruby. An Alpha's magnetism is nature's cruelest trick. Your body betrays you first—the heat, the need, the way your mind goes fuzzy around the edges. By the time you realize what's happening, it's too late. They take everything—your choice, your dignity, your soul—and they make you think you wanted it."

The words twist in my gut, bitter as bile. I remember how she'd gripped my shoulders, fingers desperate, eyes wild with a fear I didn't understand then. I was twelve, watching my beautiful, strong mother shatter into pieces.

"Promise me you'll be smarter than I was. Promise me you'll never let an Alpha make you forget yourself."

But here I am, my body singing with want for a man I barely know. My skin burns when he's near me, and part of me wants to lean into that fire, let it consume everything—my fears, my doubts that keep me awake at night. It would be so easy to give in.

And that terrifies me more than Marcus ever could.

Maybe I'm not fighting for the bar at all. Maybe I'm sabotaging myself, pushing away help, choosing failure over the risk of letting someone in. Maybe I'm so broken that I'd rather lose everything than trust an Alpha who looks at me like I'm something precious instead of something to be owned.

Another memory surfaces—Mom coming home after that last terrible fight, her eye swollen shut, lip split. But she still went back to my dad the next day. "*He needs me,*" she'd whispered. "*And when an Alpha needs you, it feels like breathing. Even when it's killing you.*"

"Hey, are you okay?" Knox's voice is gentle as he touches my hand, tenderness lacing his words. "We don't have to leave the cabin right away. We can wait here a bit longer." The softness behind his words lulls me toward him, but Mom's voice keeps echoing, keeps warning.

"I'm here for you, you know that." His thumb traces circles on my palm.

"That's what I'm scared of," I whisper, the truth slipping out before I can catch it.

"You don't have to be," he says softly, but I'm already pulling away.

"We better go." I push all those thoughts down,

locking away the emotions threatening to break free. My spine straightens as Mia and Kym watch from across the room.

"All right, let's do this," Knox announces, taking the attention away from me, thank goodness.

Outside, the morning sun sparkles off fresh snow. I spot sets of footprints leading away from the cabin, James' and Sarah's trail to their rescue pickup. Strange how peaceful it looks now, this place that nearly killed me.

I adjust my backpack straps as Knox locks up the cabin. Mia and Kym are already moving down the slope. Who would have thought a simple day trek could turn into a night of hypothermia and ghost stories or me unable to stop staring at Knox?

Then we're off. Knox positions himself between me and the others like a shield, his broad shoulders blocking their view of me. The gesture shouldn't make me so happy, shouldn't make me want to press closer to his warmth.

"So, Knox," Kym's voice breaks the quiet after about ten minutes. "We missed you last night. When we woke up, everyone was gone."

"Imagine that," he says flatly.

"Is there something going on?" Mia asks, her tone suggestive. "Between you and her?"

I can't help the sharp laugh that escapes me. "Seriously? After what you did?"

"Hey," Knox cuts in suddenly, his voice brightening

with obviously fake enthusiasm. "Will you look at that? There's some mistletoe growing over there."

I follow his gaze to snow-covered bushes, confusion washing through me. I'm unsure what it is, but that's definitely not mistletoe, yet Kym and Mia hurry forward immediately.

"They say it brings luck if you gather it in winter," Knox continues. "The scent is incredible, too—unique to each person who touches it. Want to try?"

The girls practically trip over themselves, heading for the plants. I watch in disbelief as they strip off their gloves, breaking off branches and—oh my God—actually rubbing them on their skin.

"Can you smell it?" Kym asks breathily, pressing the leaves to her neck. Knox's hand finds mine, squeezing gently as I watch the girls being so dramatic, batting their eyes at Knox. He's already strolling forward and past them, me at his side.

We've been walking for at least half an hour, and my calves are burning from the descent, but I wouldn't dream of complaining—not when Knox keeps finding excuses to steady me with those ridiculously sexy and huge hands of his. Who even has hands that big? Every time he touches my elbow or lower back to guide me around a sketchy section of trail, my skin practically sizzles.

Behind us, the bitches are whispering to each other and scratching while still carrying those damn twigs they snapped off the bush. They are so desperate to please Knox, they'll do anything he says. Not that I'm paying them any attention. I learned my lesson. Let them stew in their bitchy juice. I've got better things to focus on, like how Knox somehow makes hiking feel like a walk in the park.

"Careful here," he murmurs, and I swear his voice has dropped an octave since we started down the mountain. The sun's doing this unfair thing where it catches his jaw just right, highlighting a day's worth of light stubble that makes my fingers itch to touch it. He towers over me like some mountain god, all broad shoulders and quiet strength. Yeah, I totally get why Omegas lose their minds around him. I'm not exactly keeping my sanity intact, either.

"See that peak?" He points to a jagged monster of a mountain piercing through the clouds. His sleeve rides up, revealing a forearm that belongs in a rock-climbing calendar. "That's where I had my worst accident. Broke my leg in three places last year."

I almost trip over my own feet. "Three places? Jesus, Knox. Were you trying to wrestle a mountain lion up there or something?"

His laugh rumbles through the air between us, and I swear I feel it in my chest.

"Nothing that exciting. Just got cocky, didn't respect the mountain. Spent six weeks laid up, reading every climbing manual I could find. Nothing like a broken leg to teach you humility."

More furious scratching from behind us, followed

by what sounds suspiciously like cursing. Knox's fingers find mine as we navigate a steep section of rocks and snow, and my heart does this embarrassing flutter-skip thing. His hand practically engulfs mine, and it's way too distracting for someone trying not to faceplant on a mountain trail.

Kym makes this weird, strangled sound behind us, and I glance back to see her clawing at her wrists, which are turning an angry shade of red. She catches me looking and turns away so fast, I'm surprised she doesn't give herself whiplash. Whatever. If she wants to be over the top, that's her business. I've got a gorgeous view ahead of me—and the mountains aren't bad, either.

Knox is moving again, those long legs of his eating up the trail.

"It's so... tingly," Kym murmurs.

"Tingly, huh? That'll be the urushiol oil." Knox is glancing behind him at the girls, itching like mad now.

"The what?" Mia's already clawing at her wrist.

"From the poison oak you're currently covering yourselves in."

The silence that follows is absolutely beautiful.

"Poison... what?" Kym stares at the branches in her hands like they might bite her.

"Oak," Knox says helpfully. "Causes quite a nasty rash. Especially when you rub it directly on your skin like that."

The branches hit the snow as both girls start frantically wiping at their necks and arms. But it's too late—red patches are already blooming across their skin.

"You told us it was mistletoe!" Mia shrieks, scratching frantically.

"Did I?" Knox's voice is all innocent confusion. "Pretty sure I just pointed out some interesting plants. Not my fault you didn't check what you were grabbing and went to the wrong shrubs."

"We need help!" Kym's voice rises hysterically as the rash spreads up her arm as she pulls her sleeve up. "Call the rescue team back!"

"For poison oak?" Knox shrugs. "Not really an emergency. You'll just have to tough it out for the walk down. Actions have consequences, after all."

Understanding dawns on their faces as they look between us. Kym's expression turns murderous despite the red blotches covering her neck.

"You bastard," she hisses. "You did this on purpose."

"Let's get moving," Knox mutters without a hint of sympathy. Hell, I adore him at that moment for making them suffer.

He winks at me, and my knees actually go weak. The gesture shouldn't be so attractive, yet it is. Watching him defend me, orchestrate such perfect karmic justice... I might be swooning! No Alpha has ever stood up for me before.

He takes my hand like we're taking a casual stroll

rather than hiking down a mountain with two itchy, furious Omegas trailing alongside us.

I hold on to him, trying to ignore how right it feels to touch him.

The rest of the descent passes in a blur of Kym's and Mia's complaints and increasingly desperate scratching. Knox keeps up a steady stream of conversation with me about everything and nothing—favorite hiking trails, best local restaurants, the way the mountains look different in every season. It's easy, natural, as if we've known each other for years instead of hours.

And that's the problem.

I'm starting to like Knox way too much. Like the way he smiles, the dimple in his chin, and the protective rumble in his voice when he talks about keeping people safe on the mountain. Like how he can be both ruthlessly clever and unfailingly kind.

It's dangerous. Terrifying. Everything I swore I'd be careful of.

"Hey," Knox says suddenly, breaking through my thoughts. "Why did the mountain climber bring dental floss on his expedition?"

I eye him suspiciously. "I'm afraid to ask."

"In case he got stuck between two peaks." He grins, looking absurdly pleased with himself.

A startled laugh escapes me before I can stop it. "That's terrible. Like, genuinely awful."

"You laughed, though." His dimple makes an appearance again, and my heart does a somersault.

"How can you possibly be joking right now?" Kym snarls from near us, scratching furiously at her arms. "We're literally dying here!"

"Seriously," Mia chimes in as she claws at her neck. "This is hell. Actual hell. And you, our guide, are doing nothing to help us."

"Right now, my priority is getting everyone safely down before that storm system returns," Knox says, his tone light but firm. "Poison oak's uncomfortable, but hypothermia's worse." He flashes them a smile. "All part of the authentic wilderness experience."

They don't say much more for the rest of the trip... well, not to us, anyway. And that brings me all kinds of joy.

Before long, we're all in Knox's store, where I booked my trekking yesterday morning.

I pretend to be fascinated by the rental return form, but my attention is completely focused on Knox pulling Kym and Mia into the corner of the office. Their faces already show fear.

"What you did?" Knox's voice drops to that dangerous tone that makes my skin prickle. "Wasn't just stupid. It was attempted murder." He takes a step closer to them, shoulders lifting, and even from across the long room, I can tell he's barely holding himself back.

"We didn't—" Kym starts, her voice trembling.

"Shut. Up," he commands. "You think this is a joke? You locked someone outside in subzero temperatures during a snowstorm. Do you have any idea what hypothermia does to a person?" His hands clench at his sides. "Their blood literally freezes. Their organs shut down. They suffer before they die."

Mia starts crying, but Knox shows no mercy.

"I'm so fucking pissed at you both that I've decided to press charges myself, and I've called the police, so you're not going anywhere. Though Ruby might do the same, and trust me, I'll support her every step of the way. That shit you pulled showed exactly who you are and I will not accept anyone pulling such stunts under my watch." He leans in closer, and both girls shrink back. "You're also banned from Pine Peak Adventures. Forever. And outside the charges I'm placing on you both, if I see either of you anywhere near this place, near me, or God help you, anywhere near Ruby, I'll show you exactly how it feels to be left in the cold."

I risk a glance. Their faces are ghost white. I quickly look away when Kym's gaze finds mine, and I fight back a satisfied smirk as I hand over my borrowed gear. I'm still blown away by the fact that Knox is getting the police involved. It means so much that he is fighting for me.

"Have an amazing time?" the clerk asks cheerfully, oblivious to the tension.

"Oh, a once-in-a-lifetime experience. Won't forget it. Ever." I can't keep the sarcasm from my voice.

Knox materializes beside me, his presence warm and solid. "I'm walking you back as I have to wait for the police to arrive. And the girls are doing to wait here." The protective gesture shouldn't make my heart flutter, but it does.

"It means a lot that you are doing this. And—"

"They deserve so much worse," he admits. "And you don't need to press charges as long as you are willing to testify. Though let's see what the police say as I suspect they will confess easily."

"Absolutely I will."

His smile chases away any tension I might have experienced. "Okay, let's go."

Outside, Whispering Grove is a Christmas wonderland more than usual. They seem to have added more decorations. Every lamppost now wears a garland crown, and every window sparkles with twinkling lights. The morning sun catches the fresh snow, making the whole street glitter.

"You okay?" Knox asks softly as we walk. "Really okay?"

I consider lying, but something in his voice makes me honest. "I'm getting there. Last night was... intense."

"Those bitches had no right! And now they will pay." His shoulder brushes mine as we dodge a group of tourists. "I still can't believe they—" He stops himself, jaw clenching.

"Hey," I nudge him gently. "I'm alive. Thanks to you."

He shakes his head. "You shouldn't have needed saving in the first place."

"Thank you."

Holiday music drifts from hidden speakers, *Santa Clause is Coming to Town* mixing with the chatter of shoppers.

"This town loves Christmas a bit too much," he chuckles, falling back in step with me. "I've traveled everywhere—Nepal, Switzerland, even Alaska—but nowhere's quite like Whispering Grove."

"Really? I would love to travel the world one day." I try to ignore how his arm keeps brushing mine, how each touch sends little sparks through me.

We pass Mason's Bakery, and the scent of fresh pastries makes us both stop mid-sentence.

"God, their apple turnovers," I groan, inhaling deeply.

"You, too?" His eyes light up with genuine delight. "My favorite."

"Oh my God, same! My homemade snickerdoodles are to die for, though, too." I shake my head dramatically.

"Snickerdoodles, huh? Bold claim."

"I sense doubt?"

"Let's just say I've been disappointed before." His eyes twinkle with challenge. "I'll have to judge for myself sometime."

"Is that an official request for cookies, Mountain Man?"

"That depends. Is that an official offer, Cookie Queen?"

I chuckle just as we pass Flour & Fable Bakery, and I spot my best friend, Lily, inside, serving a customer. Her eyes go saucer-wide at the sight of me and Knox, and she starts immediately making exaggerated kissing faces in my direction. Horror floods through me as Knox begins to turn—I grab his hand and tug him away.

"Oh, I'm just over there!" I point across the street to my bar, probably too quickly to be casual.

He lets me pull him along, but I swear I see a knowing smirk play on his lips. We stop in front of my bar door, which has a new Christmas garland I can only assume was put there by Ash. Knox studies the building, then glances down at me with a captivating smile.

"So, this is your brewery, huh? I'm impressed. How long have you owned it?"

"It was my aunt's," I say softly.

Something in his expression shifts, becomes more intense. "Family legacy. That's rare these days."

"Yeah, well..." I swallow hard. "Want to come in for a drink? On the house? Least I can do after last night."

He sighs, looking genuinely regretful. "I wish I could, but I've got rescue paperwork to file and need to check on James." He takes my hand, his grip gentle but sure, thumb brushing over my knuckles. "But I promise to make it up to you. Deal?"

I soften under his intense stare. There's something almost predatory in the way he looks at me, but it doesn't frighten me. It thrills me. And with it comes my trepidation, my mom's warnings, and all the reasons why I am still unmated at age twenty-five.

"Tonight, then. I'll pick you up and we'll do something fun," he says with a grin, stepping closer, and that turns my insides to jelly.

The warmth of his grin collides with the ice in my veins as memories crash through me. Mom sprawled on our kitchen floor, blood streaming from her nose, mascara tracking down her cheeks. *They're all the same, Ruby. Every Alpha. No matter how sweet they seem at first..."*

"I'm quite busy," I manage to Knox, the words tasting like ash. "Maybe not now."

Knox studies me, and I see the moment he recognizes my retreat for what it is. The concern in his eyes makes it worse somehow. Gentleness has always been more dangerous than anger.

Dad's voice echoes in my head, sharp with contempt. *"Useless Omegas, both of you. Can't even take a simple correction without crying."*

My throat thickens. This is why I'll end up alone. Why I'll probably lose the bar. I can't take a simple risk, can't trust a genuine smile, can't stop seeing Mom's bruises every time an Alpha shows interest. I'm so fucking tired of being broken.

"How about you think about it?" Knox says softly,

taking my hand. The touch is gentle, but my pulse still spikes. He pulls a pen from his pocket and starts writing on my palm. "If you change your mind, message me."

He winks, and God help me, I melt all over again. Yet, I'm exhausted from fighting this constant war between want and fear, trapped in my own cage. The key is right there, but my hands shake too much to use it.

"They'll charm you first." Mom's voice whispers in my memory. *"Make you feel special, wanted. Then they own you."*

"Of course," I finally answer Knox, forcing brightness into my tone. The numbers on my palm seem to burn.

"Well, I better let you go." His smile hasn't dimmed. "I hope to hear from you."

He strolls back down the street, winter sunlight catching on his hair, making him look like something out of a dream. A fucking great dream. The kind I'm not allowing myself to have.

"What is wrong with you?" I whisper once he's out of sight. The answer is right here, walking away, and I'm still frozen in place, still hearing Mom's warnings, still feeling phantom pain from wounds that aren't even mine.

I push through the familiar bar door, and the bell's jingle is loud.

There, perched on a barstool as if he owns it, is

Marcus. His smile spreads slow and cruel when he spots me.

Dread drops through me. All the warmth from my walk with Knox vanishes in an instant.

I recall Knox's story about the Snow Woman, thinking that sometimes, the monsters aren't in the mountains at all.

10

RUBY

Two weeks. Fourteen days until the will's conditions expire, and every time I see Marcus, I'm reminded of the looming deadline.

His shark-like grin greets me from the bar, and something inside me snaps. Maybe it's the whole situation up in the mountains. After years of swallowing my mother's fears, of seeing her broken and bloody on our kitchen floor, of hearing my father's contempt—*useless Omega, just like your mother*—I'm done. Fucking done.

"I don't have time for you," I bark, marching toward the bar, where Ash shoots me a concerned look. The afternoon sun slants through the stained-glass windows, painting Marcus in sickly shades of red and purple. Fitting.

"You okay, boss?" Ash asks, already moving closer.

Marcus leans over the polished wood as I move behind the bar, his expensive cologne stinking up the place and that predatory grace irritating me. His perfectly tailored suit probably costs more than I make in a month.

"Having a tantrum? I can fix all this stress for you, Omega. Just hand over the bar now, stop worrying your pretty little head—"

"Get the fuck out of my bar, you piece of shit!" I yell, my anger flying past my lips.

Marcus's mouth actually drops open.

"You heard me," I snap, heat rising in my chest. "I don't need to be nice to you now or ever, so leave before I have Ash toss you out. And trust me, he'll make it hurt."

Marcus's smile turns wide, reminding me so much of my father, it makes my stomach turn.

"Such language from our little Omega bartender. Though I shouldn't be surprised... you always were uncouth. Just like your mother." He places a hand over his heart, and the gesture is as fake as his concern. "I came to offer you a position when you lose this place. That's what family does."

I'm shaking now, teeth grinding so hard my jaw aches. "Shove your offer up your ass. Ash, show him the door."

He steps forward, but Marcus raises his hands, backing away. The fury in his eyes makes my skin crawl.

"I get it. You want to play big girl business owner a little longer." His voice drops to a silky whisper. "Tick tock, Ruby. Two weeks. Don't come begging when you're homeless."

The door shuts behind him with a final-sounding click. I grab a bottle of bourbon—the good stuff—and pour a double with trembling hands. "Fucking asshole," I mutter, downing it in one smooth gulp.

I glance upward, where Eve's old photo watches over the bar. She's laughing in it, holding up her first brewery award. "Did you really have to put me in this situation?"

Ash wraps me in a bear hug, his Beta woodsy scent comforting. "I am so fucking proud of you for finally telling that creep to fuck off."

A slightly hysterical laugh bubbles up. "So long overdue."

"Well, wherever you've been since yesterday has changed you. I like this version of you. And I have news that's going to make you even happier. We got a call for a party booking in our function room."

Something in his tone makes me pause. "Okay..."

"For tomorrow night."

"Tomorrow?" My voice shoots up. "As in just over twenty-four hours from now? That's insane, Ash. We can't possibly—"

"Party of thirty." He's got that look, the one that says he's saving the best for last. "Corporate Christmas gig. Their original venue flooded or something."

I run a hand through my hair, mind already spinning through logistics. "That's so tight. The prep alone—"

"They'll pay triple our going rate."

My mouth might have fallen open. "Triple? You're sure?"

"Cross my heart." His grin is infectious. "Said they're desperate and money's no object."

The possibilities start racing through my mind. That kind of money could help with the bar's mortgage.

"It's very short notice," I say slowly. "But Lily and Hannah can handle the baked goods – they always have extra holiday stuff this time of year. We've got plenty of decorations already up. Drinks we're well-stocked on after today's delivery."

"And I'll handle everything." Ash straightens to his full height, chest puffed out like a proud rooster. "You work the main bar, I'll run the event. Trust me, Boss – this is what I live for. Give me a crowd and some Christmas music, and I'm in my element."

"You sure you can manage alone?"

He actually looks offended. "Please. I was born for this. Besides, what's our motto?"

Despite everything, I smile. "Never turn down good money when it walks through the door." Another of Aunt Eve's lessons.

"Exactly." He's already heading toward the office.

"I'll call them back and lock it in. This is going to be epic, Ruby. Things are finally looking up!"

I watch him go, his enthusiasm contagious. Maybe he's right. Maybe the universe is finally cutting me a break.

Then I look down at the number scrawled on my palm, Knox's messy handwriting slightly smudged but still readable. The ink's slightly smudged from nervous sweat but still readable. Why should I let Marcus win? Why should I let Mom's trauma become mine?

Yet my mom's voice echoes in my head. *"They'll destroy you, baby. That's what Alphas do. They find your weak spots and exploit them."*

But what if my weakness is being too afraid to accept help? Two weeks isn't long enough to save the bar on my own. And here I am with two incredibly successful Alphas showing interest in me. Is it so wrong to explore those connections? My gut churns at the thought of using either of them that way, but survival instincts are hard to ignore.

I wipe angry tears from my eyes and pull out my phone. I message Knox.

Let's meet at 8pm the day after tomorrow.

His response is immediate as my phone beeps.

I'll swing by and pick you up.

Something in my stomach bursts with excitement at seeing him again.

"I feel like it's been too long since I've seen you," a deep voice makes me nearly choke on my breath.

I shove my phone away, looking up to find Garrett standing at the bar, wearing that smile that makes my insides flutter. His button-up shirt stretches across broad shoulders, the brewery logo crisp above his heart. Everything about him radiates sex god—from his rolled-up sleeves showing muscled forearms to the way he carries himself with quiet confidence.

"I came by yesterday, but they said you weren't in."

My gaze drops to his mouth before I can stop it, remembering our kiss, his head between my thighs in the cellar, and the flowers he'd sent after. I'm swooning over one Alpha right after agreeing to date another. But something feels different today. Like I'm finally pushing back against the cage I built around myself. Like I deserve this.

Ash smirks knowingly as he pours a draft, giving me the side sneaky stare... The bastard is dying to tease me.

"Everything okay?" Garrett reaches across the bar, his thumb gentle as he wipes away a stray tear I missed. The touch sends electricity racing down my spine. "Tell me who made you cry, and I'll make them wish they were never born." His words are dark, and I believe he means every word.

"That's dark," I say, but find myself grinning. "And sort of sexy."

"I live to serve." His smirk is hypnotic, but there's steel underneath the warmth. "Though we only ever seem to catch up in this bar. What do you say about seeing what the outside world looks like? Promise I don't transform into anything in the sun."

I laugh despite myself, eyes trailing over how his shirt pulls across his chest when he leans forward. He's stunning in that rugged way that makes my hands itch to touch; deep green eyes seem to see right through me.

"That sounds excellent," Ash chimes in, nudging me in the side with his elbow. "Bar's dead. I've got this."

"Maybe something to eat for a late lunch?" Garrett suggests, and his voice has dropped lower, more intimate. "I know a place."

I'm suddenly feeling hot, my stomach giddy.

I hesitate, guilt twisting in my gut about Knox, but I nod. "Sure." Am I really doing this? Dating two men while my world crumbles around me? Mom would be horrified. But maybe that's exactly why I should.

"Give me ten minutes to dash upstairs and change clothes, and I'm in."

His grin has me needing to please him further. I dart upstairs, ready to dive into the shower for the world's fastest wash.

Clean and dressed, I find Garrett waiting for me by

the bar door, and once we're outside, I swear I spot Marcus's Mercedes idling down the street.

I freeze, but Garrett steps smoothly into my line of sight, his body angling protectively, facing me.

"Hey, I have a better idea. You know the fair's in town down by the park?"

When I peek around him, the car's gone. Still, Garrett read something in my expression because he adds, "Lots of people, good food, Christmas lights."

A warning flares in my mind—Mom's voice, telling me how they draw you in with sweetness before showing their teeth—but for once, I shove it aside. I can't let the past control me forever. I won't.

Buttoning up my coat, I answer his smile with one of my own and a nod.

Minutes later, we're parked near the park, where the winter fair sprawls toward us. A massive Christmas tree marks the entrance, twinkling lights reflecting off the frozen waterfall behind it. Carnival music plays, and the air is thick with delicious smells—popcorn, fried dough, grilling meat.

"I haven't been to the fair in years," I admit as we walk, our arms brushing.

"No? Then we're definitely doing this right." Garrett steers me toward a red-and-white striped food truck with a sign reading, *Klaus's Krazy Krauts - Award-Winning Artisanal Wursts*. The elderly man behind the counter greets Garrett by name.

"You haven't had one?" he asks me incredulously,

and I shake my head. His hand settles on my lower back, warm and steady, then lifts his head to the food truck. "Klaus, we need to fix this tragedy immediately."

In no time, I'm holding a massive Polish sausage hot dog loaded with sauerkraut, mustard, and fried onions. The first bite makes me moan; the skin snaps, juices flooding my mouth with smoky perfection.

Garrett watches me with heat in his eyes that reminds me of that night in the cellar, his mouth on my skin, his hands...

"Good?"

"This is heaven!" I manage.

He laughs, taking a bite of his own, then grabs the bottle of water he ordered. A drop of mustard catches at the corner of his mouth, and I have to physically stop myself from reaching up to wipe it away or from tasting it off his lips.

We end up on the arched bridge spanning the frozen river, snow-laden trees creating a winter wonderland around us. Fairy lights twine through the branches, and people wander around. It's not that busy; the temperature is dropping quickly.

"I hope you don't mind me asking, but why were you crying earlier?" he asks quietly.

I savor my last bite, letting the flavors ground me before reality crashes back.

"Family really sucks sometimes, and mine's the worst. They don't believe Omegas should have any rights. And I miss my aunt. She was my whole family after I got kicked out of my home at a young age." The words just flow out. I can so easily speak with Garrett.

He presses against my side, solid and warm. "It's okay to cut toxic people out of your life, even if they're family. You don't owe them anything."

"I know." I shrug, watching my breath cloud in the cold air. Part of me wants to tell him everything—about Marcus, the loan, my two weeks of freedom left—but I can't bear the thought of him offering to help, of seeming like I'm angling for rescue. I want to trust him, to let him in, but I need to do it slowly. "Sometimes, you're just tied up in things that aren't that easy."

His hand finds mine, fingers intertwining. The touch is gentle but possessive, sending warmth spiraling through my chest.

"You don't have to tell me everything," he says softly. "But I'm here when you're ready."

I look up at him, at the way the fairy lights catch in his green eyes, at how he's watching me like I'm something precious. For a moment, I let myself imagine a future where I'm not alone in this fight, where I have someone to lean on who won't use it against me.

But Mom's words whisper somewhere in the back of my mind. "*That's how they get you, baby. With kindness. With understanding. Then, one day, you wake up and realize you've given them everything, and they've given you nothing but scars.*"

I squeeze his hand once before letting go. "We should head back. I need to check on Ash."

"Ruby." His voice stops me as I turn away. "Whatever's going on, whatever you're afraid of, you're stronger than you think."

Tears prick at my eyes, but I blink them back. Two weeks. Two Alphas. And one terrified Omega trying to outrun her mother's ghosts.

I have time, I tell myself, but the lie tastes bitter on my tongue. Two weeks isn't any time at all.

The fair lights blur around us as we stroll together, my body humming with an awareness that's becoming harder to ignore. Every brush of Garrett's arm against mine has my skin covering in goosebumps. I'm burning up despite the winter chill, my Omega instincts going haywire every time he glances over at me.

Knox's forthcoming date flits through my mind, but it's getting harder to focus on anything except Garrett's mouth when he talks, the way his throat moves when he swallows, how his hands keep finding reasons to touch me on my elbow, my lower back, my shoulder.

"The haunted house is pretty impressive," he says, nodding toward a looming Victorian structure draped in fake cobwebs. There's a line to go into the fun house. "Want to check it out?"

I laugh, maybe a bit too sharply. "I have enough

horror in my life." The words slip out too quickly, and I feel him tense beside me.

"Come on," I say quickly, grabbing his hand and pulling him toward a roped-off section to the far right of the fair that catches my attention. "Let's check this out instead."

A village spreads before us, a dozen tiny elf houses nestled among snow and twinkling lights. Each structure is like a tree house in size but on a small field of snow, each single home made of wood and painted in reds and greens, others like fairy tale cottages. It's whimsical and completely at odds with the darkness swimming in my head.

Garrett studies my face instead of the display, his expression intense. His thumb traces circles on my palm, and the simple touch makes my knees weak.

"If you're in danger," he says softly, "you would tell me, right? You can call me anytime, day or night. I'll be there."

I blink up at him, questions crowding my throat, but my body has other ideas. The heat that's been building all afternoon crashes over me in a wave. I'm up on my toes, pressing my mouth to his. I know I'm distracting him from peppering me with questions, but I don't stop.

Garrett responds instantly, one arm wrapping around my waist while his other hand tangles in my hair. My hands fist in his shirt, hauling him closer.

Suddenly, he breaks away, eyes wild. "Come here,"

he growls, ducking under the rope barrier and pulling me with him. I should protest—we definitely shouldn't be back here—but then he's leading me toward one of the larger elf houses, and all I can think about is getting my hands on him again.

A quick glance around and there's hardly anyone around this area, let alone anyone spotting us.

The door barely closes behind us before he has me pressed against it, his mouth hot on mine. He has to duck to avoid the ceiling, and the absurdity of this massive Alpha in a tiny elf room should be funny, but there's nothing humorous about the way he's kissing me. It's all lips and tongue and desperate hunger.

Fabric curtains cover the windows, but enough light filters through to illuminate his face when he pulls back to look at me. The small space feels electric.

"We shouldn't be here," I manage, but my hands are already sliding under his shirt, tracing the hard planes of his stomach, the thin line of hair traveling down those ridiculous abs.

"We shouldn't be doing a lot of things." His voice is rough as he nips at my neck. "Tell me to stop."

"I can't." The admission tears from my throat. "God, I'm burning up. What's happening to me?"

"It's your heat, gorgeous." His hands slide down to grip my hips, pulling me against him. The hardness pressing against my stomach makes me whimper.

That's the last thing I want to hear, yet I feel like I

can't pull myself away from him if I tried. Yet part of me wants to try.

"Tell me you don't want this." His thumb traces my bottom lip, his eyes dark with want. "Tell me to walk away."

Instead, I bite his thumb lightly, drawing a growl from deep in his chest.

"I want you to make me forget everything except your name."

He kisses me again, harder this time, more demanding. His tongue is long and smooth as he licks against my lips, then he invades my mouth, his body hard against my body, his hips grinding hard against me. My back hits the wall, and I wrap one leg around his waist, trying to get closer, needing more friction. His hand slides under my thigh, hitching me higher.

We kiss like feral things, so sexual, so wet, a moan in my throat. I claw at him, needing more.

"You're going to destroy me," he growls against my mouth. "Do you have any idea what you fucking do to me? How much I want to ram into you right here?"

His words burn me up, making me rock against him with desperate need. "Please," I whimper, not even sure what I'm begging for as I try to make sense of everything through my sex-starved, fogged brain.

Through the haze of desire, I hear distant voices, fair workers or security making their rounds, but right now, I don't care if we get caught. Don't care about anything except Garrett's hands on my skin and the way he makes every warning voice in my head go blissfully silent.

For the first time in my life, I understand why Mom kept going back to Dad, even after the worst fights. This pull, this need... it's like gravity. Like drowning. Like flying.

Garrett's hand presses into the wall behind me, his other hand sliding over my breast, kneading, pinching my nipple. I moan, and my whole body thrums with desire, desperation, and fire. The growl in his voice sends shivers down my spine, awakening something primal I didn't know lived inside me. I can't stop the whimper that escapes when he pulls back, my fingers twisting desperately in his shirt to keep him close.

"Just kiss me again," I plead, hating the neediness in my voice but past caring. His laugh is rough, almost pained, and the sound shoots straight through me.

"If I kiss you right now, I won't stop." The raw hunger in his words makes me weak. "And sweetheart, when I finally make you mine, it won't be against some elf house where anyone could interrupt." But he's leaning closer even as he says it until we're breathing the same heated air, and my body arches toward him of its own accord, seeking more. My nipples are so taut, they hurt, desperate for his touch.

"I don't ca—" I start to say, but he cuts me off with a sound that's almost feral. The strain in that sound, the savagery, only feeds the flame burning under my skin.

"Right now, I'm hanging onto my control by a thread."

It feels like he's taking all the oxygen with him when he's not kissing me. My body aches with an emptiness I never knew existed before him, and I hate how much I need him to fill it. Hate how much sense it suddenly makes why people risk everything for this feeling. Why they burn their whole worlds down just to feel it again.

Yet, here I am, on my knees in moments in front of him, my breaths coming too fast, and I have no control of myself. I know what I want, and he's standing in front of me.

"Dammit," he grinds out as I pull at his belt, then at the buttons on his jeans. "Seeing you on your knees is going to kill me."

I grin up at him, nibbling on the corner of my lower lip as I tug down on his jeans and boxers, his huge cock bouncing out. A purr strokes my throat at the sight. I wasn't prepared for his size, that thick vein running down his length, or the beads on the tip of his cock. And my sights set on the thick knot at the base of his erection, the one that swells once inside of me, keeping us locked. I've never been with an Alpha before, but my initial thoughts are... how am I supposed to fit that inside my pussy?

"Kiss me on the tip," he asks with almost a command, distracting my thoughts.

"You'll be my first," I admit while reaching out to curl my fingers around his erection.

He hisses, his hand running through my hair.

"Fuck, you're saying I'll be the first dick to ever be in your mouth?"

I nod, and his breath speeds up. There's something wonderful about seeing such a strong man lose control over me.

Not being shy, I lean in and slip my lips over his tip, tasting his saltiness.

"That's it, slide deeper." His hand is on the back of my head now, and I sense his pressure.

Keeping my mouth tight around him, I take more of his cock into my mouth, and I'm not sure if I can fit all of it in.

As if he can sense my concern, he pushes my head closer to him, sliding himself deeper still.

"Slowly work me in. Take your time."

So, with my hand reaching to cup his balls, I work him in and out, my mouth working to take all of him. I have no idea if I'm doing this right, but he's growling, his body tensing, and I know he's enjoying it. That's all that matters.

"Look up at me," he asks.

I lift my gaze, my mouth full, and meet his eyes.

"Fuck, Ruby, I'm about to come so hard, burst into your mouth. And you're going to be a good girl and swallow it all down, aren't you?"

I make an agreeing sound.

He has my hair tighter around his fist, and he's growling, still holding my stare as his hips rock, meeting my sucking. Every inch of me is humming with arousal, and I'm completely drenched. I squeeze my thighs, heightening the sensation as it builds and builds.

Running my tongue along his shaft, I grin at him with my eyes, and he hisses again, his balls so tight. I whimper with the fire lighting me up from the inside.

"It's so fucking sexy to see my fat cock all the way in your mouth," he murmurs, then growls, his hips pushing forward, his knot pushing into my mouth too. The tip of his erection hits the back of my throat, instantly bringing tears to my eyes, but there's excitement, too, and I work to take more of him.

"FUUUUUCK!"

Warmth spills into my mouth suddenly, creamy and sticky, almost sweet, and I swallow it. There's so much of it, and it keeps coming. I work my throat, taking it all in, trying to also breathe.

"My sweet Ruby, you're working so hard, taking all of me. I'm dying to sink my cock into your pussy, to knot you, to fuck you until you pass out!"

His words are hungry, savage, and sinful. Turns out I love them because, in seconds, I'm shuddering, my own orgasm tearing through me. I'm buzzing between my thighs at having such a massive cock in my mouth, picturing him fucking me. There was no way I could have prevented what was coming. I moan against him, riding my own climax that tears through me.

"Never fucked a more beautiful mouth. Next time you are going to come on my dick because I need to see you coming on my face or dick."

Finally licking away the last drop, I pull free and wipe my mouth with the back of my hand. He's grinning wildly as he tucks himself away and helps me to my feet. My face is flushing as he collects me in his arms.

"You were beautiful and so perfect."

I open my mouth to respond, leaning into him despite my face blushing, but a voice outside freezes us both mid-smile. My heart leaps into my throat as Garrett moves swiftly to the window, peering past the curtain's edge. In the panic of the moment, I can't help noticing how his shoulders tense protectively.

"Security doing cabin checks," he whispers, turning back to me with a glint in his eye. "Let's get out of here."

Before I can answer, he takes my hand, leading us to the door of the elf house. The thrill of almost getting caught sends nervous giggles bubbling up in my chest, which I try desperately to suppress. Garrett holds my hand a bit tighter, and we wait there as he peers out the ajar door. The moment the voices fade, he eases the door wider and pulls me into the crisp winter air.

We hunch low and dart around the small cabins in the opposite direction of the voices, finally reaching the rope and frantically scrambling under it. We run like teenagers, ducking behind festival stalls and weaving between carnival rides. The wind whips into me, and I can't remember the last time I smiled this hard. When we finally break free of the fairgrounds, we both burst out laughing.

"Quick, get in." He grins, opening the door to his black SUV. The warmth inside is welcoming, and I sink into the leather seat, still catching my breath.

As he pulls onto the road, where there are cars everywhere, something warm unfurls in my chest—so different from the wariness I usually feel around Alphas. Since that first meeting at the festival, every interaction with Garrett has chipped away at me, showing me something about him I never expected to find—maybe he's not a monster in hiding like my father had been.

"What are you thinking about?" he asks softly, glancing over as we stop at a red light.

I just grin, watching the way the shadows play across his face. That tiny spark of hope in my chest feels dangerous, wonderful, real. And I'm starting to believe that maybe some risks are worth taking.

11

RUBY

I wake up burning up. Not the gentle kind of warmth that lingers after a dream, but the kind that makes your skin feel too tight, your bones too heavy.

The snow falling outside my window seems to mock me—all that cold, and here I am, tangled in sweat-soaked sheets, clutching my middle as another wave of cramping heat flares over me.

"Not now," I groan into my pillow, but my body isn't listening. It's been building for days, if I'm honest with myself. Garrett saw it before I did—the way I kept leaning into his touch at the bar last night, how even Knox's scent and smirk couldn't make me pull away. It's my heat.

Forcing myself up, my bare feet find the plush rug beside my bed. The room spins a little, and I grab the edge of my nightstand to steady myself. My coat from last night is draped over my reading chair, and before I can stop myself, I'm reaching for it. The fabric is still cold from the winter air, but underneath that...

I bring it to my face, inhaling deeply, and my knees nearly buckle. His scent is there—pine needles and hops, yes, but underneath is his richer scent of coffee beans roasted with vanilla. It's faint, but it's enough to make the aching in my core both better and worse. I stumble back to bed, clutching the coat like a lifeline.

Last night feels like a dream now. The way we kissed in the elf house, how I went down on him and greedily swallowed his cum.

Another cramp hits, and I curl tighter around the coat, watching snowflakes dance past my window. The rational part of my brain—the part that isn't currently drowning in hormones and need—knows this is moving too fast. A week ago, I had only bad Alpha dating experiences. Now, here I am, practically nesting with Garrett's scent.

My Aunt Eve's words float back to me from that summer I spent with her. We were sitting on her porch, watching thunderclouds roll in when she told me about meeting her now-passed husband, James.

"The smart ones," she'd said, tapping her temple with a knowing smile. "They choose their mate before their heat even makes a showing. That way, you know it's your heart picking, not just your biology."

She'd met Uncle Jim, her Beta partner, at a farmer's market and argued with him about the price of peaches. Three months later, she said she never even considered another man.

"When you know, you know," she'd tell me, even years after he was gone. She never remarried, saying she'd rather have those perfect years with him than a lifetime of settling for less.

I take another deep breath of Garrett's fading scent, feeling the way it settles something wild and restless inside me. It scares me how fast this is all moving. How natural it feels to think of him as mine. Now, I'm lying here, burning up, craving the presence of an Alpha like I never have before.

The snow is coming down harder now, coating my windowsill in white. Another wave of heat burns through me, and I let out a laugh that's a half-groan.

"Well, Ruby," I mutter to my empty room. "For someone who swore off Alphas, you're doing a bang-up job of turning into a walking Omega cliché."

Even as I say it, I press my face deeper into the coat, chasing that last trace of pine and coffee and something that feels dangerously close to home. I know I should be fighting this harder. Except, the rest of me just wants to surrender to whatever this is becoming.

I reach for my phone, seeing a message from him already waiting.

> Good morning, beautiful. Missing you already.

Despite the fever burning through me, despite

every warning bell in my head, I find myself smiling. Maybe Aunt Eve was right. Maybe sometimes you do just know.

I curl up tighter under my blanket, and I clench my eyes, contemplating a cold, cold shower to see if that helps.

The winter wind chases me into Sugar & Spice, bringing a flurry of snowflakes that melt on the warm wooden floors. The difference between the biting cold outside and the bakery's cozy warmth makes me pause in the doorway, letting my frozen cheeks thaw. Classical music drifts from hidden speakers—definitely Hannah's choice, not Lily's—and the scent of vanilla, butter, and something citrusy has my stomach growling for food.

After the cold shower, my heat seemed to subside, so I took that as my sign to start my day and hope the heat doesn't return.

Now, the mid-morning light streams through snow-frosted windows, catching on the gleaming display cases that line the walls. Each shelf is filled with delicious baked goodies, from macaroons in perfect pastel rows and chocolate eclairs with ganache so glossy, I can see my reflection, to tiny lemon tarts crowned with fresh berries. Then there's what appears to be today's new creation near the cash register—a decadent chocolate tart swirled with caramel and dusted with flakes of sea salt that sparkle like morning frost.

"Well, I was going to send a search party out for you!" Lily's voice rings out from behind the counter. She's wearing a butter-yellow dress that makes her golden-brown eyes pop. Her wild deep brown curls are attempting to escape from a messy bun, and there's a streak of what might be chocolate on her cheek. "I was wondering how long you'd stay away."

"I'm just here for snacks and to tell you that Ash will pop over later to pick up our order for the Christmas party booking we're running tonight." I make my way to the counter, snagging a sample cookie from the plate near the register. "Ash and I have a slow day at the bar with all this snow."

"Mmhmm." Lily props her elbows on the counter, nearly knocking over a display of cake pops. She catches them quickly. "Nothing to do with avoiding certain conversations about a certain gorgeous specimen I might have seen you with?"

The cookie, still warm, almost goes down the wrong way. "I don't know what you're talking about."

"Oh really?" Lily's grin turns wicked. "So, that wasn't you diving past my shop yesterday when you spotted me? And that wasn't a tall drink of water with shoulders like a linebacker walking you home?"

"That was Knox," I say, trying to sound casual while reaching for another sample. "He's just one of the guides from the tourist company. No big deal."

"No big deal?" Lily whistles low, absently twirling one of her escaped curls. "Honey, please point any other *not-big deals* my way. Those arms alone could—"

I shoot her a look that makes her burst out laughing.

"Yeah, that's what I thought. Though..." She leans in conspiratorially.

Before I can respond, Hannah emerges from the kitchen, her hair twisted in its perfect French knot.

"I thought I heard voices," she murmurs, her warm brown eyes taking in my slightly frazzled state. "How are you holding up, Ruby?"

"Oh, she's holding up just fine," Lily interjects before I can speak. "What with her mystery man from yesterday. Though..." She draws out the word like taffy. "Apparently, you were seen hand in hand with another guy yesterday at the fair."

I narrow my eyes, and I'm not sure why I'm surprised, seeing this town loves gossip.

They both stare at me, and I busy myself selecting another sample of treats—this time a *petit four* that dissolves on my tongue in a cloud of raspberry and dark chocolate.

"It wasn't a date," I mumble around the heavenly mouthful. "We just went to the winter fair."

"Perfect!" Lily claps her hands, nearly upending a tray of croissants. Hannah steadies it without looking, used to her sister's enthusiastic gestures. "You're all set then. Which one are you picking to deal with Marcus?"

I actually choke this time.

Hannah hurries to get me water while Lily continues.

"I mean, they both sound delicious. Tourist Guide or Mysterious Fair Prince? Though I have to say, if you're taking applications..."

"It's not that straightforward," I manage after gulping down water. My eyes catch on a fresh batch of cinnamon rolls Hannah's arranging, desperate for distraction. "And hey, what about those *perfect matches* you said you and Hannah were trying to set me up with? Maybe cancel those since I have my hands full?"

"Yes, you do," Lily purrs. "But maybe you've already met them?"

I stare at her, slightly confused. What is she saying?

Hannah's brow furrows as she places a tray of perfect rosette cupcakes onto the glass shelf case.

"Ruby, you know you can't spend too long deciding on an Alpha. Your timing—"

The bell above the door chimes, bringing in a rush of cold air and customers. Lily springs into action, her yellow dress swishing as she greets them. I watch in amazement as she remembers not only their names but asks about one woman's daughter's dance recital and another's recent vacation to Florida.

Hannah moves to help, but not before giving me a pointed look that says this conversation isn't over. I watch them work while munching on another cookie.

When the rush dies down and before more customers enter, Lily quickly pushes a box toward me. "Here. Extra of the sea salt caramel things because I love you. Come over tomorrow night so we can catch up?"

"Can't," I mumble, suddenly fascinated by the geometric pattern on the coffee cup display. "I'm catching up with someone."

"Oho!" Lily's eyes light up like Christmas came early. "Tourist company god or mystery fair man? Wait, don't tell me. Let me guess by your blush..."

"I hate you."

"You love me," Lily teases. "And you're going to tell us everything, eventually."

"And we want details," Hannah adds, waggling her eyebrows. "Lots of juicy details."

I grab my box and head for the door, but not before Lily calls out.

"And Ruby? Whoever you choose... just make sure it's what you want, not what you think you should want!"

The bell chimes behind me as I step back into the snow, Hannah's words about timing mixing with Lily's parting advice in my head. They're both right—I need to figure this out. Tonight, I'll go out with Knox and get to know him better. Then, I can make a clear decision and stop leading anyone on.

My stomach twists at the thought of having to let either of them down. I peek in the box, and true to her word, Lily's loaded it with those sea salt caramel tarts. There's also a perfect chocolate croissant she knows I love. Sometimes, best friends know exactly what you need, even when they're driving you crazy. Even if what they're saying makes too much sense to ignore.

I head back toward the bar, the snow crunching under my boots, trying to ignore the way my heart speeds up when I think about tonight.

12

DOMINIC

The snow falls in thick flakes around Ruby as she hurries across the street, cradling that pink pastry box like it's precious cargo. Her white coat makes her look like she's glowing against the gray day, that fur-trimmed hood framing her face just so. Those black boots of hers kick up little puffs of snow with each step.

Perfect. She's fucking perfect.

My fingers tighten on the steering wheel as I track her movement. Even from where I'm parked down the road, I can see her cheeks are flushed from the cold, see how she bites her lower lip in concentration as she navigates the slippery sidewalk. Every detail about Ruby is seared into my brain—the way she moves, the exact shade of her hair, how her scent lingers in the air even hours after she's gone.

And I haven't even met her yet.

The passenger door to my SUV flies open, letting in a blast of frigid air and snow. Garrett drops into the seat, shaking snowflakes from his hair and carrying takeout bags.

"Got your usual from Mike's. Though why we had to drive across town when there are perfectly decent sandwiches near the brewery—"

"You know why." My eyes haven't left Ruby as she disappears into her bar.

"Yeah, I do." Garrett's voice holds equal parts amusement and concern. "Knox's first attempt didn't exactly go as planned yesterday when the storm hit, yet he's already obsessed with her."

"And you couldn't resist swooping in yesterday afternoon, could you?" I tear my gaze from the bar's entrance to give him a knowing look.

He grins, unrepentant. "Fuck, man, I can't stay away. She's an addiction."

The scent hits me then—her perfume, mixed with her natural Omega sweetness, still clinging to Garrett's jacket. My jaw clenches.

"I can smell her on you."

"I know." He sobers slightly. "Look, Knox has his date tonight—"

"And I'll wait my turn." The words come out darker than I intended. "I've gotten good at waiting."

Garrett studies me for a long moment before nodding toward the brewery. "Come on. Let's get back before this gets cold."

The drive to Garrett's place takes us through the historic district, past snow-covered brownstones, until we reach the converted warehouse he's transformed into one of the city's most popular craft breweries. The main floor is all exposed brick and weathered wood, with gleaming copper tanks visible behind glass walls. The scent of hops and barley hangs rich in the air.

Cindy looks up from the host stand, her mousey blonde hair pulled into a tight ponytail, her almond eyes absolutely stunning, as we stroll into the building. She's fantastic at playing normal, but I catch the way she scans the room before fully relaxing. Old habits.

"Your Saturday bookings are getting out of hand," she tells Garrett, falling into step beside us. "I had to add another seating area in the back room."

"You've got it handled." Garrett's trust in her is evident. "Everything else good?"

"Always is." She glances between us, professional but distant. "Need anything else?"

Garrett gives her a brief nod as she heads off to handle a delivery. I watch her go, concern etching lines around his mouth.

"I've reached out to my contacts," he says quietly as we climb the stairs to his office. "No sign of her mate, but..."

"You're doing the right thing, helping her." I flop down into one of his leather chairs. "If her fucker of a mate shows up—"

"Then I'll do what I have to." Garrett's voice is steel.

I lean forward, the weight of another problem pressing in. "Speaking of complications... what are we going to do about Marcus?"

Garrett's expression darkens as snow continues to fall outside his window, blanketing the world in white.

"Marcus is getting suspicious," Garrett says, taking his chair behind the massive, reclaimed wood desk. "He cornered me at The Crossings last night, asking why I've been hanging around Ruby's bar so much."

I let out a low laugh, but there's no humor in it. "What did you tell him?"

"That I like her bourbon selection." He runs a hand through his snow-damp hair. "But he knows about Knox's date tonight. Word travels fast in this fucking town."

The mention of Knox's date sends another surge of that dark possessiveness through me.

"Marcus needs to back the fuck off," I growl. "Ruby's bar isn't his territory, no matter what he thinks."

"You know it's more than that." Garrett pulls out a bottle of his latest experimental brew from his desk drawer, along with two glasses. "He's been trying to get his hooks into that property since before she took ownership of it so he can tear it down and build a towering apartment."

The beer Garrett pours is dark as coffee, with a head like cream. I take the offered glass but don't drink yet.

"You think he suspects?"

"That we know she's our Omega, and we're going to make her ours? Maybe. That we're planning something? Definitely."

Unease settles through me that he's paid a bit too much attention to us.

A knock at the door interrupts us. Cindy stands in the doorway, tablet in hand, her posture slightly tense. "Sorry to interrupt, but the Anderson group called. They want to move their corporate tasting to next week."

"Whatever works best," Garrett says easily, but I notice how his eyes track her movements, assessing. "You okay? You seem..."

"Fine," she mutters, fiddling with her tablet. Her ocean-blue dress flows over her slender frame. At just twenty-two, she's already endured more than most, thanks to her asshole parents trying to marry her off to a controlling Alpha a year ago. "I thought I saw someone familiar outside earlier. But it was nothing."

The temperature in the room seems to drop ten degrees. Garrett sets his glass down with careful precision.

"What kind of familiar?" I ask.

"Not him." Cindy shakes her head quickly. "Really, it was probably just someone who looked similar. I'm being paranoid."

"You see anything that makes you uneasy, you tell us immediately. No matter how small," Garrett states.

She nods, some of the tension leaving her shoulders. "Thanks. I'll let the Andersons know about next week."

After she leaves, Garrett lets out a long breath.

"Six months she's been here. Longest she's stayed anywhere since she ran. Hopefully, he won't track her down to Whispering Grove. For now, she's safe, and we'll fucking keep it that way. Anyway, speaking of situations... what did your contact find out about Ruby's lease?"

The change of subject pulls me back to our own complicated situation. I draw out my phone, scrolling through recent messages. "The building's mortgage is underwater. Marcus has been pressuring the bank to call in the loan, trying to force a sale. Ruby has to the end of the year to either buy it outright or find new investors."

"Fuck." Garrett drains his glass. "No wonder she's been looking stressed lately. I'll lend her the money. Anything she needs."

"Goes without saying." I finally take a sip of the beer, letting the deep flavors roll over my tongue. "If she'll accept it. I get the impression she's not one to easily take help."

Garrett raises an eyebrow. "Then we have to make her see we're not the bad guys."

I set my glass down, remembering how she looked in the snow, all in white, like some kind of winter spirit. Pure. Untouched.

"I've never felt this way about anyone before I've met them, but the urgency to claim her grows inside me. A need to possess her, protect her, claim her... it's getting worse."

"Your turn's coming," Garrett reminds me. "We stick to the plan and not rush it to scare her."

Silence.

"I can hear you plotting murder from here," Garrett murmurs. "Want to share with the class? You're thinking about her again, aren't you?"

I give him a wolfish grin. "Just about problem-solving strategies."

"Right." I hear the sarcasm in his voice. "Not anything to do with waiting for your turn?"

I chuckle heavily. I already know I'm not nearly as in control as I pretend to be.

13

RUBY

The Christmas lights twinkle mockingly as I adjust the last wreath on the wall of the function room in my bar. Everything's perfect—too perfect, maybe—which means something's bound to go wrong. No, I can't think like that.

"Ruby, stop fussing." Ash's voice carries from where he's stocking the private bar. "The decorations are fine. The room looks amazing."

I step back, gnawing on my bottom lip. The emerald garland frames the windows perfectly, tiny white lights casting a warm glow across the polished wooden tables we've pushed against the walls. They're filled with silver chafing dishes, platters of baked goods, plates, cutlery, and festive red-and-green serviettes. A Christmas tree stands in the far corner because I couldn't not have one. But I have to admit, even I can appreciate how the vintage ornaments catch the light.

They're all from Aunt Eve's collection, the ones she'd spend hours telling me stories about while I helped her decorate the bar every year.

The silver star on top is slightly crooked, just like every year she put it up, refusing to fix it. "Some things are meant to be imperfect, Ruby," she'd say, but now I wonder if she knew even then that everything would fall apart after she was gone.

"Earth to Ruby?" Ash waves a bottle of premium vodka at me. "Where'd you go just now?"

"Just..." I gesture vaguely at the room, my fingers automatically finding my aunt's snowflake pendant. "Making sure everything's perfect. We can't screw this up, Ash."

He sets down the bottle and comes over, squeezing my shoulder with a grin. "When have we ever screwed up an event?"

"There was the Thompson wedding."

"That wasn't our fault. How were we supposed to know the bride was running away with the cake decorator?"

Despite everything, I snort. "Or the Miller retirement party?"

"Okay, that one was definitely not our fault. Who brings a pet raccoon to a bar?"

The first notes of *All I Want for Christmas Is You* drift through the speakers—because apparently, I can't escape Mariah Carey even in my own establishment—and I check my phone. 7:45 p.m. The party guests for the Christmas work party should start arriving any minute.

"Right." I smooth down my dark green vintage-style dress, grateful I remembered to pair it with comfortable boots. It's going to be a long night. "I should get out there."

The main bar is already humming with the usual crowd. Old Joe's in his corner spot, nursing what I know is his second whiskey of the night. The Henderson sisters occupy their usual table, Margaret's silver hair catching the light as she leans in to whisper, most likely the latest gossip, to Anne. Tommy and his crew from the local lodge are huddled around the pool table.

The familiarity of it all helps steady my nerves, but there's still that undercurrent of tension I can't shake. Less than two weeks until I either marry a mate or lose everything. The thought makes my stomach churn.

The door chimes, and the first party guests start arriving. I direct them down the hallway, admiring the parade of cocktail dresses—a stunning red number with a sweetheart neckline, a midnight blue sheath that shines in the light. The women move casually, their heels clicking against the hardwood floors. A group of men and several women arrive next, and I direct them.

Then the door chimes again, and my world stops.

He fills the doorway like he was carved to fit it, all broad shoulders and lethal grace. Every inch of me suddenly sits up and pays attention. The stranger has to be at least six-four. The mauve button-down he's wearing clings to his chest, showing he works out. It's tucked into black pants that look painted on strong thighs.

But it's his face that makes my breath catch. Strong jawline shadowed with just enough stubble to make my fingers itch to touch it. High cheekbones. Ink black hair that falls past his jaw, some strands tucked behind his ear while others sweep across eyes that... oh God. His eyes are dark, impossibly dark, and they're scanning the room with an intensity that makes heat pool in my stomach.

A small geometric tattoo peeks out from under his sleeve as he runs a hand through his hair. The simple gesture is so casual, it leaves me captivated. He moves like someone who knows exactly how dangerous he is and doesn't need to prove it to anyone. Like gravity itself bends around him.

"Need some help picking your jaw up off the floor?" Ash appears beside me, his voice low and amused. "Or are you too busy falling for Mr. Sexy over there?"

"What?" I blink, trying to remember how words work. My insides feel too tight, too hot. "I'm not... I was just..."

"Sure, sure," he smirks. "I need to grab some stuff for the party room. Try not to drool on the counter while I'm gone."

I watch him disappear down the hallway, grateful

for the moment to collect myself. This is ridiculous. I already have enough Alpha complications in my life with Knox and Garrett. I don't need another one, especially not one who makes me want to bare my neck just by existing in my general vicinity. And this man is all Alpha. One look at him says it all. I turn to put some glasses away, needing to keep myself busy and distracted.

"Ruby, isn't it?" The voice. Deep, smooth, and gravely coming from behind me. I turn slowly, and there he is, leaning slightly against my bar like he owns every room he enters. This close, I can see his eyes aren't just dark, they're practically black, with tiny flecks of gold that seem to spark when they meet mine.

"That's me." I manage to sound almost professional, despite the way my heart's trying to escape my chest. The air between us feels charged, dangerous. "At Winterscape Bar." I suddenly feel stupid for saying that last part because clearly that's where he is.

His lips curve into something too wicked to be called a smile.

"Dominic Chase."

It dawns on me that he's the man who made the booking tonight.

He extends his hand, and when I take it, a buzz jolts up my arm so intensely, I almost gasp. His skin is hot against mine, his grip firm but not overwhelming.

"Though something tells me you're the real welcome here."

Heat floods my cheeks. "Smooth talker?"

"Only when it matters." His thumb brushes across my knuckles before he releases my hand, the touch deliberate. "I own Sentinel Security. Thanks for accommodating our Christmas party on such short notice."

"Sentinel..." The name clicks, and something cold slides down my spine. Everyone knows about Sentinel Security—the ones you call when traditional security isn't enough. When things need to... disappear. "Nice to meet you. And you run a very well-known company."

"Oh, yeah?" That wicked almost-smile again. He leans in slightly, and his scent hits me—cedar and smoke and something darker, something that makes me want to crawl across the bar and bury my face in his chest.

"I've heard of your company's great reputation."

"Always good to hear. Though we try to keep a low profile. And speaking of reputation..." His smile turns wider. "I've heard nothing but good things about this place. Thanks again for taking us on such short notice. You have no idea how often people can let you down."

"Oh, I think I might." A laugh escapes me before I can stop it. "Trust me, I wrote the book on disappointment."

"You did?" he asks sarcastically, yet his head tilts slightly, and I notice how his hair falls perfectly to frame his face. It's unfair how effortlessly gorgeous he is.

"It's why I try to surround myself with only those I trust."

His eyes darken with interest. "Doesn't that worry you? That you might miss out on meeting... new, interesting people?"

I shrug, thinking of Knox and Garrett and how they crashed into my carefully ordered life. "Impossible not to meet people in this town, but being super close?" My fingers find my pendant again. "You only need a few good ones."

"And how do you decide?" He leans in closer, and I catch another wave of his intoxicating scent. "Who's worth letting in?"

The way he's looking at me makes my skin tingle. His eyes drop to my lips for a fraction of a second before meeting mine again, holding them with an intensity that makes the rest of the bar fade away. The Christmas music, the chatter, the clink of glasses—it all becomes distant background noise. There's just him, the heat of his gaze, the slight curl of his lips, the way his fingers have stilled on the bar top mere inches from mine.

I realize with a start how easily I'm talking to him, how natural it is, despite every instinct screaming that he's a stranger.

When I don't answer, he says, "Well. I better join the party. Which direction was it again?"

"Let me show you." I gesture for him to follow me, and as we walk, I'm hyperaware of his presence behind me. The hallway suddenly feels too narrow, too inti-mate, and my body is screaming at me to slow down, to let him catch up, to let him...

"Beautiful place," he says, his voice closer than I expected.

"Thanks. I try."

We reach the party room door, music and voices pouring out, and I gesture inside. "Well, here you are. Ash will take care of anything you need. Enjoy the night."

"Thank you, sweetheart." The endearment rolls off his tongue like a caress, and I practically swoon. His eyes lock with mine, and for a moment, the rest of the world fades away.

He strides into the room, and my heart's racing. Three Alphas—all impossibly attractive and dangerous—have suddenly entered my life after years of terrible luck in that department. It reminds me of Lily and Hannah's insistence that they planned to set me up with three Alphas... Surely, these couldn't be the ones they meant?

Mom's warnings echo in my head. *"They'll draw you in with their scent, their strength, and make you feel safe right before they show their teeth."*

As I head back to the main bar, I focus on pushing those memories away, not wanting to be controlled by my past anymore.

Hours blur together in a haze of pouring drinks and making small talk with the regulars. Every time I check on Ash in the party room, he's in his element, effortlessly keeping glasses full while charming the corporate crowd. The platters of appetizers are down to crumbs, so I replace them, but Ash handles the party easily.

And each time—though I try to convince myself I'm just being helpful—my eyes search for Dominic. He's always in the thick of things. Sometimes, he's leaning against the wall, nodding as people cluster around him. Other times, he's seated at one of the tables, saying something that makes the whole group laugh. Not once does he look my way, and I tell myself the tight feeling in my chest is relief, not disappointment.

You're being ridiculous. I wipe down the main bar for the hundredth time. My heat's coming; that's all this is. Any Alpha would have my hormones doing backflips right now.

The main bar has quieted some, just the usual evening crowd nursing their drinks. Bob's telling his fishing stories again, and the Henderson sisters are debating about the best pie recipe. It's almost peaceful.

Then the door bangs open, letting in a blast of cold air and snow.

A man stumbles in, shoulders off his coat, and hangs near the door, revealing a rumpled dress shirt. He's maybe mid-thirties, with the kind of face that probably looks friendly when it's not twisted into a sneer. Right now, though, his eyes are glazed, and his movements are loose in that dangerous way that means he's well past his drinking limit.

He lurches toward the bar, bumping off tables as he goes. I'm already reaching for the landline phone under the counter when he clips the corner of Bob's table hard enough to send his nearly-full beer sloshing over the rim.

"What the fuck?" Bob stands, his cheeks flushing. "Watch where you're going!"

The drunk whirls around, swaying. "Fuck you, old man. Get out of my fucking way."

My heart hammers against my ribs. "Bob, let me get you a fresh one, no charge." I'm already moving, grabbing a cloth to mop up the spill. The glass, thankfully, stayed upright. "No harm done."

But the drunk is already at the bar, slamming his palm down hard enough to make the glasses rattle. "Serve me, Omega bitch!"

Tommy, from the pool table, takes a step forward. "Hey, man, cool it."

"Fuck off!" The drunk's hand shoots out, catching the wooden bowl of complimentary nuts. It goes flying, scattering peanuts and pretzels across the floor like shrapnel. "I said serve me a fucking drink!"

"Sir." I keep my voice steady, professional, even as my pulse races. "I can see you've already had plenty tonight. I can't legally serve you in this condition. I'm happy to call you a cab—"

"Don't tell me what I've had!" He lunges across the

bar, faster than I expected, and his fingers close around my wrist like a vise. His scent is putrid–stale beer and sour anger.

I'm reaching for my phone with my free hand from my back pocket, thinking I can message Ash, when suddenly the drunk's grip vanishes. A familiar scent of cedar and smoke wraps around me, and there's Dominic, all six-foot-four of coiled strength as he shoves the drunk back. The man trips over a chair, going down in a tangle of limbs and wood with a crash that makes everyone jump.

"Ruby." Dominic doesn't look at me, but his voice is warm honey even as his stance screams danger. His sleeves are rolled up, showing those geometric tattoos I noticed earlier, and the muscles in his forearms flex as he advances on the fallen man. "Let me handle this piece of shit. You shouldn't have to deal with trash like him."

My mouth goes dry, watching him move. He's graceful even now, like a predator stalking prey. I step back, partly because I should give him room, partly because the Alpha command in his voice makes me listen.

The drunk scrambles to his feet, red-faced and spitting curses. "Who the fuck do you think—"

Dominic's hand shoots out, fisting in the man's shirt collar. He drags him close, and even though his voice is quiet, it carries.

"I'm the man doing you a favor right now. We can

do this the easy way, where you walk out that door and never come back, or..." His other hand flexes, and I watch the drunk's eyes widen. "We can do this the hard way. Your choice. But if you take a swing at me?" His smile is all teeth. "Trust me, you won't like what happens next."

The drunk's response is to throw a wild punch that catches Dominic's lip. My heart stops, guilt already churning in my stomach—he got hurt helping me!

Dominic just sighs, touching his split lip with his free hand. When it comes away bloody, his eyes go cold. "Wrong choice, dickhead."

The punch happens so fast, I almost miss it. One moment, the drunk is trying to break free; the next, he's sprawled on the floor, blood gushing from his nose as he howls. Dominic hauls him up by the back of his shirt like he weighs nothing, dragging him toward the door.

The bar is dead silent as they disappear outside. A moment later, Dominic returns alone, grabbing the drunk's coat from the hook and tossing it out after him. The door closes with a final-sounding thud.

When he turns back to me, he's smiling like nothing happened. "I've got the asshole in a cab to take him straight home as per his licence." But I'm too busy noticing blood is still welling from his split lip. A few of those in the bar are clapping. I'm in awe! He tries to wipe the mess away with the back of his hand, but it only smears the blood worse.

"I'm so sorry," I blurt out before I can stop myself. "Your lip..."

"Is fine." He's suddenly right in front of me, close enough that I have to tip my head back to meet his eyes. There's a dangerous glitter in them that makes my breath catch.

"At least let me clean it up." The words tumble out before I can stop them. "You got hurt because of me. It's the least I can do."

"Ruby—"

"Please." I don't know why it matters so much, but it does. Maybe because he defended me without hesitation, or maybe because I can't stand seeing his blood, knowing it was spilled over me.

Ash appears beside us, gaze widening at Dominic's split lip. "What the hell happened out here?"

"Some drunk thought he could manhandle Ruby." Dominic's voice carries an edge that makes me shiver. "He won't be making that mistake again."

"Shit." Ash shakes his head. "You okay, Boss?"

"I'm fine, but can you watch the bar for a few minutes? I need to patch Dominic up."

"You got it. The party's winding down, anyway. They're mostly just finishing their drinks."

I lead Dominic down the hallway to the staff bathroom. It's small but clean, with warm yellow lighting. The ancient first aid kit sits in its familiar spot under the sink.

"Really, I'm fine," he protests as I dig out antiseptic and cotton pads. "It's barely a scratch."

"Humor me." I gesture to the wooden stool in the corner. "Please?"

He sits, and suddenly, the small space feels even smaller. His knees spread naturally to accommodate his height, and I have to step between them to reach his face. My hands tremble slightly as I dampen a cotton pad.

"This might sting," I warn, but he doesn't flinch when I start cleaning away the blood. The split is small, just catching the edge of his lower lip, but it's still bleeding sluggishly.

I'm acutely aware of every point of almost-contact between us—the heat radiating from his body, the way his breath ghosts across my wrist as I work, the intoxicating blend of his scent mixed with antiseptic. He watches me with those dark eyes, trying not to smile as I carefully dab at the cut.

"You really are a beautiful person, you know that, Ruby?"

The words catch me off guard. "Not really. You came here for a party and ended up in a fight."

He chuckles, the sound vibrating through me. "That's my job, remember? Security's what I do."

I'm so close now, I can see the gold flecks in his eyes and could count his eyelashes if I wanted to. My body hums with awareness, every nerve ending alive to his presence. He hasn't touched me once, but I feel branded by his gaze alone.

"You should learn some self-defense," he says softly. "I have a studio I go to where I train. I could show you some moves."

"I can handle myself." But the image of him teaching me, his hands positioning my body, has heat pool between my thighs in seconds. "Besides, Ash usually takes care of any trouble."

"Ash isn't always going to be around." His voice drops lower, sending shivers down my spine. "And I could teach you a few moves that would have guys like that jerk in the bar on the ground before they knew what hit them."

I dab at his lip again as a fresh drop of blood wells up. "You make it sound so easy."

"It is when you know what you're doing." His eyes never leave my face as I work. "The human body has so many vulnerable points. Size doesn't matter nearly as much as people think."

"Says the man built like a brick wall."

He chuckles, the sound dark and sexy as fuck. "All the more reason to trust me on this. I've trained people half your size who can take down men bigger than me."

The bleeding's almost stopped now. No point trying to put a Band-Aid on a lip. "Why do I get the feeling you're not going to let this go?"

"Because I'm not." That dangerous smile, again,

has my stomach flipping. "Come to my studio. One lesson. If you hate it, I'll never bring it up again."

"And if I don't hate it?"

His eyes darken. "Then we'll see where it goes."

Something in his tone makes me feel bold. "You must have dozens of women throwing themselves at you for private lessons. Your girlfriend—"

"No girlfriend." His eyes lock with mine. "No wife. No one who's caught my eye." The unspoken 'until now' hangs between us, and I tell myself I'm imagining the way his scent deepens, his gaze turns hungry.

"Well, you're all done." I step back, suddenly needing space to breathe. "You'll survive to fight another day."

His hand catches mine, and suddenly, I'm in his arms, pressed against the solid wall of his chest. His heat surrounds me, and I can't help the small sound that escapes my throat.

"I'm trying so hard to keep my distance." His voice is rough, desperate. "But your scent... it calls to me. It's so rare to find someone who captivates me like this." His free hand hovers near my face, not quite touching. "I don't mean to come on so fast, but I need to know if it's just me feeling this."

I can barely breathe. Every inch of my skin prickles with awareness, my insides screaming to press closer, to let this powerful Alpha do what he wants with me. His chest rises and falls against mine, his heartbeat as wild as my own. We're sharing the same air, and I'm drowning in cedar and smoke and burning fire.

Three Alphas in my life, and this one—this dangerous, beautiful man—makes me want to throw away every warning, every defense I've built. The energy between us crackles like lightning, and I know with bone-deep certainty that if he kisses me now, I'll be lost.

Maybe I already am.

"Ruby." He breathes my name like a prayer, his lips so close to mine, I can feel the warmth of his breath. "Talk to me. Tell me what you want?"

I should. *God*, I should. But the words stick in my throat as his scent wraps around me, making my world tilt. His hand slides up my arm, leaving a trail of goosebumps in its wake until his fingers brush my neck. Just that slight touch sends tingles racing down my spine.

"I…" My voice comes out hoarse. "I can't think when you're this close."

"Good." That dangerous smile again, but there's something vulnerable in his eyes. "Because I've been thinking too much since the moment I walked in and saw you. Trying to be professional, trying to keep my distance…"

His thumb traces my jaw, and my knees nearly buckle.

"Why?" The question slips past my lips.

"Because…." His other hand settles on my hip, steady and warm. "I don't want to rush this, don't want to scare you away, but..." He inhales sharply. "Your sweet scent is driving me crazy."

I'm trembling now, caught between wanting to run and wanting to climb him like a tree. His fingers thread through my hair, and I'm lost in the sensation, in his scent, in the magnetic pull between us. He leans in, and I can feel the inferno of his lips just a breath away from mine.

My heart pounds so hard I'm sure he can hear it. This is it. This is—

"Ruby!" Ash's voice echoes down the hallway. "Got a situation out here!"

I jerk back like I've been shocked, nearly stumbling in my haste.

"I-I better go." My voice comes out breathless.

Dominic hasn't moved, one hand still raised where it had been in my hair. His eyes are dark, savage, fixed on me like I'm the only thing in his world. He doesn't look frustrated or worried—if anything, he looks like a predator who knows his prey can't escape for long.

"I, um..." I smooth down my dress with trembling hands, trying to find my usual snark. "Duty calls. Places to be, fires to put out. You know how it is." I'm babbling, but I can't seem to stop. "Running a bar. Always something catching fire. Not literally. Usually."

"Go." His lips curve into that brutally sexy smile. "But Ruby?"

I pause at the door, my hand on the knob, glancing back. "Yes?"

"Come to the studio sometime this week. Let me teach you how to defend yourself."

It's not just about self-defense. We both know that. I find myself nodding.

The promise in his voice follows me all the way back to the bar, along with the lingering sensation of his almost-kiss.

I wonder if this is how Mom felt at first—this intoxicating blend of desire and danger—but something feels different about Dominic. Something feels... right.

And that's exactly what scares me the most.

14

The last glass is finally polished and every surface is gleaming. At 2:17 a.m., I drag myself up the back stairs to my apartment, my feet aching from hours in heels. The Christmas party tonight was a success, another event perfectly executed, but God, I'm exhausted.

My apartment is dark and cold. I crank up the heater and strip off my clothes, leaving them in a trail to the bathroom. The hot water hits my shoulders, and I groan in relief, letting it soak into my tired muscles.

That's when his face floods my mind again.

Dominic.

Sitting in that seat, legs spread wide, watching me with those dark eyes that seem to see straight through me. The way he drew me closer, barely touching, until I was standing between his thighs, my heart hammering hard.

"Stop it," I whisper to myself, but my hands are already moving over my skin, imagining they're his. Down my breasts, pausing, then rolling my fingers over my erect nipples. A moan spills past my throat. Those huge hands could probably span my entire waist.

I drop my arms because I shouldn't tease myself.

So, I reach up and pump body wash into my palm, the steamy air filling with vanilla and honey, yet all I can smell is him—that intoxicating scent of cedar and masculine sex.

His voice plays in my head, a low rumble that vibrates straight down between my thighs.

"I'm trying so hard to keep my distance."

He didn't even have to use Alpha command to put me under his spell. I would have done anything he wanted at that moment.

My soapy hand slides over my breasts again, and I can't stop imagining it's him. Under the shower, every drop is like a stroke as the suds rush down my body. My fingers trail lower, and I bite my lip. This is wrong. I already have Knox and Garrett circling me—I don't need a third Alpha complicating things. Especially not one like Dominic, who leaves me breathless.

But God, the way he looked at me tonight. Like he wanted to devour me whole. Like he knew exactly what I'd look like spread out beneath him, begging for his touch.

A soft moan escapes my throat as I let myself imagine it. Those powerful hands exploring every inch of me, spreading me, fingering me. That wicked mouth and tongue marking my skin, tasting me. The weight of him pressing me down, his cock...

"Fuck," I gasp, my legs trembling as an orgasm slams into me so quickly, it takes me by surprise. I lean back against the cool tiled wall, enjoying the way my body hums and how I'm flying through heaven for these few moments. The water's starting to cool, but I'm burning up, lost in the fantasy of him. Dark eyes watching me fall apart. Strong arms holding me together.

The water runs colder, and reality crashes back in. I grab a towel, trying to shake off the lingering heat of my climax. What am I doing? I'm supposed to be figuring out which Alpha might be willing to save my bar, not inviting my heat to make a stronger appearance.

My bedroom is finally warm when I curl up under the covers, hair still damp against my pillow. The digital clock mocks me at 2:43 a.m. I need sleep. Tomorrow—today—is another full day.

But my mind won't quiet. Knox is sweet, strong, protective, everything an Omega could want. Garrett makes me laugh, brings out the flirt in me, and makes me feel safe. Either one of them might be willing to help me, maybe consider a marriage of convenience to save my bar. Perhaps they will even consider not taking half my bar as part of the will agreement... Something legally I'm unsure is even possible.

Then there's Dominic. Who I absolutely should not be thinking about. Who probably would save me but then not be interested in playing the white knight. And that should worry me, yet I'm so desperately drawn to him, I don't know myself anymore.

Tick-tock, Ruby. Time's running out.

Then Marcus's words echo in my head, and I fucking hate him.

I pull the covers tighter around me, trying to ward off the chill those words bring. The thought of asking any of them makes me cringe. "Hey, want to enter into a loveless marriage to save my bar?" God. How pathetic can I get?

But what choice do I have?

My mind drifts back to Dominic again, remembering how he looked in my bar. Like he belonged there. Like he could make a home among the worn wood and whiskey bottles.

Stop, I chide myself. *Get some sleep.*

As sleep finally pulls me under, I feel the touch of his hands on my skin and hear that deep voice in my ears.

And in my dreams, I let myself be taken by him.

"Dominic…" His name falls from my mouth in a desperate moan as an orgasm crashes through me, my fingers already working between the drenched lips of my pussy before consciousness fully takes hold. The dream clings like honey to my skin—dark eyes watching me play with myself, falling apart, strong hands pinning me down, that voice rumbling promises in my ear. My body shudders with one last wave before the morning starts seeping in.

"Oh God." I bolt upright, heart hammering against my ribs, blankets tangled around my legs. Sunlight streams through the gaps in my curtains, painting stripes across my rumpled bed. "Get it together, Ruby," I mutter, running a shaky hand through my tangled hair. The clock on my nightstand glows at 9:17 a.m. *Shit.*

My skin still tingles as I swing my legs out of bed. How is it possible to want someone this bad when I've barely even touched him?

I'm halfway to the bathroom when my phone chimes. Knox's name on the screen has me pausing.

Can't stop thinking about tonight, pretty girl. Been dreaming about how gorgeous you'll look by candlelight.

Heat blooms on my cheeks as I read it again. Before I can even process that flutter of excitement, another message pops up from Garrett.

Missing your smile this morning, your
scent, your taste. When do I get you all
to myself again? The fair wasn't
enough… need more…

A ridiculous grin spreads across my face as I read it once more. My fingers hover over the keyboard before typing back to Garrett.

Morning. And if you must know, I
might be obsessed with the way you
taste, too…

I hit send quickly as doubt already spreads through me at my flirting, but I clearly can't control myself.

To Knox, I reply with…

Better make it worth my while, then…
Promise I'll wear something that'll
make you forget how to breathe.

Standing there in just my oversized sleep shirt, I try to rationalize with myself. I'm not technically dating any of them, right? We're all just… exploring possibilities. Very attractive, increasingly complicated possibilities. So, this isn't wrong. It's just…

I don't even know who I am anymore.

The phone pings again, and I stare down at an unfamiliar number.

Hey, pretty girl. It's Dominic. Got your number from the business booking. Realized I never gave you the studio address last night. Haven't been able to think about anything else but you. The way you smiled, the way you smelled... Hope you'll let me show you some self-defense moves.

My legs soften, and I have to lean against the wall, my pulse racing in my throat. The memory of standing so close to him has my body radiating with fire, the intensity of his gaze, how small I felt despite him being the one seated.

Three Alphas, all wanting my attention.

This is new for me.

God help me, I want to give it to them all. How do people handle multiple partners, anyway? The thought alone makes me worry I won't be good enough.

Before I know it, I'm sending Dominic back a devil emoji followed by a winking kiss.

Careful what you wish for...

Subtle, Ruby. Real subtle.

Heading downstairs, each step feels heavy with indecision. The bar's quiet this early, everything still and peaceful. Morning light catches the bottles behind the bar, sending prisms dancing across the floor. Eve used to say this was her favorite time of day here—the calm before the storm when anything felt possible.

A slow smile tugs at my lips at my upcoming date tonight.

15

RUBY

The purr of Knox's Range Rover fades as we pull into the parking lot. I can't help but think this place looks like something out of those Hallmark movies I refuse to watch. Three stories of rustic wooden grandeur stretch before us, all perfect logs and gleaming windows, practically dripping with old money. What am *I* doing here?

"An Alpha will only hurt you, Ruby. They're all the same in the end." My mother's words echo in my head, the same warning she'd whisper every time she covered another bruise with makeup. I push the thought away, focusing instead on how the snow catches the light from the wrought-iron lanterns lining the circular drive.

When Knox kills the engine, I watch, mesmerized, as he climbs out from the driver's seat. The black suit transforms him from rugged mountain man to something far more dangerous—a predator in civilized clothing. The fabric stretches across his shoulders as he moves, and I catch myself wondering how someone can look even more untamed in formal wear than they did in climbing gear.

He didn't bother with a tie, and the open collar of his white shirt reveals just enough skin to be distracting. A primal part of me wants to trace the strong column of his throat with my tongue.

Jesus, Ruby, get it together.

The cold mountain air hits my face as Knox opens my door, and I'm grateful for the shock of it against my heated skin. He offers his hand with an exaggerated flourish that should look ridiculous but somehow doesn't.

"I never pictured you like this," I say, trying to keep my voice steady as I step out. "All polished and going to fancy places. What happened to the guy who could start a fire with two sticks and his sheer stubbornness?"

His laugh is low and rich, sending shivers down my spine that have nothing to do with the temperature. "Oh, I haven't even shown you my fire skills, but he's still here. I just clean up well when properly motivated."

The way his gaze rakes over me makes it clear exactly what that motivation is, and my inner self preens despite my best efforts to stay cool and detached.

"*Don't fall for it,*" my mother's voice warns. "*Once they know they affect you, it's over.*"

"My lady," he continues sarcastically, and there's also that growl underneath his playful tone that makes me weak. "I grew up in places like this with my parents. Couldn't wait to escape them then, but they have their uses now." His hand finds the small of my back, warm and steady. "I hope it's okay? I wanted somewhere special."

"It's perfect."

Around us, the mountain lodge is a winter wonderland dream. Massive pine trees drip with thousands of white lights, their branches heavy with fresh snow. Wooden sculptures flank the front steps, wolves mid-hunt, bears rearing up, eagles in flight. A long line of luxury cars are parked nearby, all spotless despite the snow-covered roads.

"I have no idea where we're going," I admit. "But I already love it..." The words catch in my throat as Knox's hand slides lower on my back, pulling me against him with casual possession. Heat radiates from him, and his scent—chocolate, fresh snow, and thunderstorms—wraps around me like a physical touch.

"The only beautiful thing I see is you," he says.

I want to roll my eyes at the line, but the raw honesty in his voice stops me. His fingers trace idle patterns on my back through the thin fabric of my dress, each touch sending sparks through my nervous system.

"You weren't lying in your text about wearing something that will make me lose my breath."

I fight the urge to fidget with my aunt's necklace at his compliment. The red dress felt like a statement when I put it on or maybe a challenge. Long-sleeved but with a neckline that plunges deeper than anything I'd normally wear, the fabric clings to my body before falling to my ankles with a daring slit up one side. Lily had insisted I buy it months ago, declaring it *made for a hot date,* but it had hung untouched in my closet until tonight. Something about Knox made me want to be brave. Or reckless. Probably both.

"A dress like that," Knox says, voice dropping to a rumble that I feel in my bones. "Makes a man think dangerous thoughts." His fingers catch a loose curl of my hair, twirling it slowly. "You have no idea what you do to me, do you?"

"Maybe I do." I try for sass, hoping he can't hear my heart thundering.

His grin is sharp enough to cut. "Careful, pretty girl. I might take that as a challenge."

"Run," my mother's voice whispers, but for the first time in my life, I don't want to.

Knox guides me toward the entrance, past a group of guests who look like they ordered their entire ski wardrobes from a magazine spread. One woman is tottering in stiletto heels that would be a death sentence outside, her white ski suit pristine and obviously never worn outdoors in the snow.

"What do you call a snowman with a six-pack?" Knox whispers in my ear, his breath warm against my skin.

I bite back a smile. "What?"

"An abdominal snowman."

The laugh bursts out of me too quickly, gaining a few stares.

"That's terrible! I can't believe I'm actually laughing at that."

"You love it," he says with absolute certainty. "And I'm here to make you laugh."

Instead of heading toward the main restaurant where most guests are gathering, Knox leads me past it, his hand never leaving my back. We move through hallways, where staff members nod at him and point us forward. I want to ask how often he comes here, what other women he's brought to this clearly exclusive spot, but I bite my tongue.

We emerge onto a massive open balcony, and my breath catches at the sight before us—an enclosed cable car waiting just for us, its transparent walls promising an incredible view. It's larger than I expected, more luxury transport than a typical ski lift, with comfortable benches facing each other and soft lighting.

"After you," Knox says, steadying me as I step in, and it's instantly warm inside. I'm grateful for the low heels I chose, especially when the cabin sways slightly. He follows and settles beside me, close enough that his thigh presses against mine, and the cabin begins its smooth ascent up the mountain.

The world opens up beneath us, a landscape of snow and lights. Ski slopes curve down the mountainside, their paths marked by twinkling lights. The main lodge grows smaller, and in the distance lies the explosion of lights from Whispering Grove. Above us, the sky is impossibly clear, stars beginning to peek through the deep blue.

"I used to hate Christmas lights," I admit, pressing my hand against the glass. "Thought they were tacky. But from up here..." I trail off, watching my breath fog the transparent wall.

I'm acutely aware of how he's shifted closer on the seat, one arm stretched along the back of the bench behind me.

"From up here, they're kind of magical." I wrinkle my nose. "God, that was cheesy. Please don't tell anyone I said that. I have a reputation to maintain."

His laugh rumbles through me. "Your secret's safe with me." His free hand finds my knee, his thumb tracing small circles that send heat spiraling through me. "I haven't been able to stop thinking about you since the mountain hike."

I try to keep my breathing steady. "Because I could have died?" I joke, though it's not really funny.

"Yes, and the way you got fought back up, how you

never let it mess with your head." His hand slides a fraction higher, and I bite my lip. "How I held you all night, keeping you warm. Sexy as hell."

"I think the altitude's affecting your judgment."

"I think you don't see yourself clearly." Knox's voice has dropped lower, edged with something that has me paying closer attention. "Do you know what I thought the first time I saw you?"

I twist in my seat to look at him and nearly drown in the intensity of his gaze. "What?"

"There she is. The one I've been waiting for." His free hand comes up to cup my face, thumb brushing over my bottom lip.

"Knox..." My voice comes out embarrassingly breathy. "Just let me look at you for a minute." There's nothing gentle about the way he's looking at me. "You're so fucking beautiful it hurts."

The cabin continues its slow ascent, and I'm caught between taking in the view and watching Knox staring at me. His gaze tracks every movement, every breath, as if he's memorizing me. When I shift in my seat, his hand tightens on my knee.

"Tell me what you're thinking," he says... no, commands.

"I'm thinking this is insane," I admit. "I'm thinking my mother would be horrified, but I hate that I just mentioned her. I'm thinking..." I take a shaky breath. "I'm thinking I don't care about her judgment anymore."

Something dangerous flashes in his eyes. "Good girl."

Those two words shouldn't affect me the way they do or have a tingle down in the pit of my stomach slide to between my thighs. I want to blame it on my impending heat—it has to be close, given how I'm reacting—but I worry it's more than that.

The sky lift carries us higher, and I'm caught between the breathtaking view and the equally breathtaking man beside me. Below, the world has transformed into a glittering wonderland of lights and shadows, but Knox's eyes never leave my face.

"Not having second thoughts about coming out with me tonight?" he asks, voice teasing but with that underlying current of heat that leaves my skin tingling.

I snort, channeling snark to hide how affected I am. "Please. You saved me. If you wanted to hurt me, you had your chance."

His answering grin is pure predator. Then his fingers trail up my arm, feather-light but leaving fire in their wake.

"Why is your pulse racing, pretty girl?"

"Altitude," I manage to say, but we both know it's a lie. The way his nostrils flare tells me he can smell exactly what he's doing to me, and that shouldn't be as hot as it is.

"They'll use your own body against you," my mother's voice whispers. *"That's how they trap you."*

When Knox's hand slides into my hair, gently

tugging my head back to expose my neck, *trapped* is the last thing I feel. Instead, I feel… powerful. Wanted. His eyes are dark, flooded with need, but he's waiting, letting me make the choice.

"The view up here really is spectacular," I say.

"Mm." His thumb traces my jawline. "I couldn't tell you. Haven't taken my eyes off you long enough to notice."

I laugh, but it catches in my throat as his grip tightens slightly. "That was terrible. Do you practice these lines in the mirror?"

He chuckles, and I love the sound of his laugh. He's closer now, so close I can see the hues of blue in his eyes.

The growl that rumbles through his chest is pure Alpha, then he leans closer, and I meet him halfway. His mouth is on mine. The kiss starts slow, but there's nothing careful about the way his hand fists in my hair to hold me in place or how his other arm bands around my waist, dragging me closer.

He tastes like winter air and something spicier. His tongue swirls with mine, and I moan at the effect he has on me. Knox responds with another growl, deepening the kiss until I'm practically climbing into his lap, my hands fisted in his jacket.

"Fucking perfect," he mutters against my lips before trailing kisses down my neck. When he finds my pulse point, he nips lightly, and my whole body jerks.

"Been wanting to taste you since the moment I saw you."

"Knox…" I'm burning up, everything too much and not enough.

"I know, pretty girl." His voice is rough, wrecked. "I know exactly what you need."

The sky lift begins to slow, and Knox pulls back just enough to rest his forehead against mine. We're both breathing hard, and I must look thoroughly kissed—lips swollen, hair mussed, cheeks flushed.

"You're gorgeous like this," he says, tucking a strand of hair behind my ear. "All hot and bothered because of me."

"You're very sure of yourself," I manage to say, trying to gather my scattered wits.

His laugh is dark honey. "I can smell how wet you are. No point trying to pretend."

Heat floods my face, but before I can respond, the cabin doors slide open at the upper platform. Knox helps me to my feet, steadying me when my knees prove less than reliable. Another lodge awaits us, smaller than the first but no less impressive, its windows glowing with warm light.

Inside, a staff member appears to take my coat, and Knox guides me up a curved staircase to a restaurant that steals my breath. The entire space is encased in glass walls, offering a panoramic view of the mountains. Lights twinkle below us like fallen stars, and above… I gasp as the first ribbons of green and pink dance across the clear sky.

"Aurora," I whisper, enchanted.

Knox's hand is possessive at my waist. "I'd hoped we'd catch them tonight. But honestly?" He leans down, his breath hot against my ear. "Watching you is a better show."

My toes are curling in my closed heels at the things he says.

Our table is by the window, intimate without being stuffy. A linear fireplace runs through the center of the room, flames dancing in a straight line. The whole place manages to be upscale while keeping that cozy lodge feeling, all warm woods and soft lighting, with only a handful of other diners scattered around.

"I got us a set menu," Knox says as we settle in. "If that's okay?"

I nod, still a bit dazed from the kiss and the view and everything. "Whatever you think is best. I don't exactly have a lot of experience with fancy mountain restaurants."

His foot finds mine under the table, and the simple contact shouldn't make my breath catch, but it does.

"Trust me?"

The question feels weighted with meaning.

"I'm starting to."

"Good." His smile is slow and satisfied. "I have plans for you, Ruby."

The way he says my name makes it sound like a promise—or maybe a threat.

"Now, let's begin," he says. "What do you call a mountain climber who's really bad at knock-knock jokes?" Knox asks suddenly, eyes twinkling with mischief. He's loosened up even more since we sat down, jacket open, radiating casual authority like it's his natural state. Which, let's be honest, it probably is.

I play along. "What?"

"A cliffhanger."

"Oh my God." I laugh despite myself, shaking my head. "That was worse than the last one. How do you even know these?"

"My dad was the king of dad jokes," he says, something softening in his expression. "But I notice you're still laughing."

"Maybe I'm just being polite."

"Pretty girl, you're a terrible liar." His foot slides higher up my calf under the table, and my breath catches.

Soon enough, the waiter arrives at our table, and Knox orders our drinks, and the food starts arriving soon after. Evidently, it's an eight-course meal, which is new.

The first course arrives—something delicate involving scallops and foam. Knox watches me taste it, his eyes darkening when I can't hold back a small moan of pleasure.

"Good?" he asks, voice rougher than before.

"Amazing." I take another one, trying to ignore how his intense focus makes my skin tingle. "Though I have to say, this is a far cry from the mac and cheese you made us up on the mountain."

"What can I say?" He chuckles. Leaning back in his seat, he reaches for his whiskey in a glass. "I contain multitudes. But speaking of the mountain... you never did tell me why you signed up for that hike."

I focus on my wine glass, watching the light play through the red liquid.

"Would you believe me if I said it was for exercise?"

"Not a chance."

"Fine." I sigh, setting down my fork. "I had a shit few days, then I got this flyer for a free day in the mountains. I seriously needed to escape the town, get away from it all, so it was too good to resist. Though my best friend saw us strolling in town and grilled me recently for falling for a cute mountain guy."

"And did you?" He leans forward against the table.

"Maybe." I meet his gaze, surprised by my own boldness.

The next few courses arrive—something with venison and wild mushrooms that smells incredible, vegetables, and polenta cubes with truffle. His gaze never leaves me as we eat, and I find him comfortable to be with, loving the attention he pays me.

"Tell me more about your bar," he asks, cutting into his meat.

I welcome the distraction, telling him about inheriting it from my aunt, about learning to brew beer in the tiny back room, about the regular customers who've become family. He listens intently, asking questions that show he's actually interested, not just being polite.

"You light up when you talk about it," he observes, voice soft. "It's beautiful."

"Now, who's being cheesy?"

"Just honest. I like seeing you passionate."

"What about you?" I ask, trying to ignore how that simple touch makes my skin buzz. "Always going to be a mountain guide when you're in Whispering Grove?"

Something dark flashes across his face.

"Thinking about it. It gets me into the outdoors, and it's a great way to meet new people. Besides, after my parents passed away..." He pauses, jaw tight. "It gave me some perspective on what really matters."

I reach across the table without thinking, covering his hand with mine. He turns his palm up, interlacing our fingers. I remember him telling me about them back in the mountains, but it doesn't make it just as sorrowful hearing it a second time.

The waiter arrives with our next course—perfectly seared duck breast with cherry reduction—and I welcome the distraction. As I eat, I'm increasingly aware of every little thing. The way Knox's legs brush mine or his fingers graze against my hand when he reaches for his whiskey glass, how his gaze follows my movements. And the heat building under my skin that has nothing to do with the fireplace or the wine.

"Tell me about the bar's regulars," Knox says, cutting into his duck. "I bet you have some characters."

I launch into stories about Old Joe, who claims he once wrestled a bear, and Martha, who knits beer cozies for everyone at Christmas. Every time he leans forward, his scent covers me, and I'm buzzing with the excitement of being out to dinner with him.

By the time dessert arrives—some elaborate chocolate creation with gold leaf—I'm having trouble focusing on anything but him. How his hands dwarf the delicate dessert fork. The slight stubble darkening his jaw that I desperately want to feel against my skin.

"You've gone quiet," he observes, his voice low and intimate. His foot finds mine under the table again, and the simple contact sends sparks up my leg.

"Just... thinking." I take another sip of my wine, trying to cool down, but it's not helping. My dress feels too tight, the room too warm, every nerve ending hypersensitive.

"About?" His thumb strokes over my knuckles, and I realize he's been holding my hand across the table. When did that happen?

"About how this doesn't feel real." The words tumble out. "About how you look at me like... like..."

"Like you're mine?" The possessiveness in his voice makes me shiver. "Like I've been waiting for you without even knowing it?" He brings my hand to his mouth and kisses my pulse point. "Like I'm falling for you while still getting to know you?"

The words wrap around me, and a smile tugs at my lips at hearing his confession. At the acknowledgment that I'm not too far from feeling the same way.

Combined with his touch, his scent, and the way he's looking at me like he wants to devour me whole—it's too much. My skin feels like it's on fire, every breath carrying his scent deeper into my lungs until I'm dizzy with it.

"I need air," I gasp, pushing back from the table. "Please, I just... I need to get outside."

The concern in Knox's eyes is immediate. He's on his feet in seconds, throwing down what has to be an obscene amount of money, his hand steady at my back as he guides me toward the door. Outside, the cold air covers like a blessing. I kick off my shoes without thinking, letting my feet sink into the snow.

"Anything I can do to help?" he asks, but his tone says he knows exactly what's wrong.

"You have no idea," I gasp, my cheeks burning. My heat has to be close. There's no other explanation for how intensely I'm reacting to him.

"Oh, I think I know exactly what you need, pretty girl." He takes my hand, along with picking up my shoes, and walks me to our sky lift as it arrives. The moment we're inside and moving, he pulls me against him. "Let me help you."

His mouth finds mine, and this time, there's

nothing gentle about it. It's all possession and need, his hands roaming my body like he owns it. Maybe he does. Maybe he always has.

"*Once an Alpha claims you, you're lost,*" my mother's voice whispers.

For the first time in my life, I think... fucking good.

His mouth claims mine with barely any control, his body pressed against mine. One hand cradles my face while the other spans my lower back, pulling me closer. The sky lift sways gently as it descends, but all I can focus on is Knox's touch, the way his thumb traces my jawline, how his fingers flex against my spine.

"Do you want to slow down?" he whispers against my lips, but his actions betray his words as he pulls me even closer.

"Don't," I murmur, surprising myself. "Please don't stop."

A growl rumbles through his chest, and his kisses grow deeper, more demanding. His hand slides into my hair, tugging gently to angle my head just how he wants it as his mouth finds the tenderness of skin beneath my ear.

Those lips. That tongue. I moan, losing my mind.

"You don't know what you're asking for," he says, voice rough.

"I think I do." The words come out breathy, desperate. "I want this. I want you."

His response is a kiss that makes my toes curl, passionate yet still somehow tender. He kisses me like

I'm precious, as if I'm his, as though he's been waiting his whole life to find me.

"*You'll regret this*," my mother's voice whispers in my head.

As Knox's arms tighten around me and his mouth moves to that sensitive spot across my collarbone, I know with absolute certainty that she's wrong. For the first time in my life, something feels completely, perfectly right.

16

KNOX

There isn't a man alive on this planet who could resist a temptation like Ruby.

I have her pinned against the glass wall, the light dim in the gondola, concealing me and my beautiful Omega from anyone down on the field. She's trembling in my arms and actually fucking purring, a sound that shoots straight to my balls. I'm so hard, I'm in agony. Her scent is everywhere, sweet and wild with the edge of her approaching heat, mixing with the lingering traces of clementine perfume. It's taking every shred of control I possess not to completely lose my mind.

"Your heart's racing," she murmurs against my throat as I hold her in place, one hand against the wall over her shoulder.

I trace my tongue down to the valley of her breasts where her dress dips low, revealing that gorgeous cleavage, and I'm rewarded by the way she shivers.

"Do you have any idea what you do to me, Ruby? Any fucking clue?"

"Show me," she challenges.

Fuck, this woman is going to be the death of me.

"Careful what you wish for, pretty girl." My voice comes out like gravel. "I might not be as nice as you think I am."

She tugs my hair, forcing me to look at her, and those amber eyes are dark with need. "Maybe I don't want nice."

Something snaps inside me. I capture her mouth in a kiss that's all possession and hunger, swallowing her gasp of surprise. My hand tangles in her hair, angling her head just how I want it, and the little whimper she makes nearly breaks my control completely.

My other hand slides to her hip and lower to the high slit in her dress. Dipping under the fabric, my fingers trace a line to her thin underwear to where she's drenched between her thighs. Exactly where I crave to be.

"How about I finger that needy little pussy, pretty girl? I've been dying to touch you."

"I want…" she pants, her body trembling. "I need…"

"Don't worry, leave it to me." I slip a finger under the elastic of her panties, and with a sudden tug, I rip them right off her.

She cries out, startled with enlarged eyes, but she

doesn't fight me. I tuck her panties into my back pocket, quickly moving my hand back under her skirt.

She's nibbling on her lower lip, staring at me deviously, her eyes fogged with sex. Her heat is moving so fast, I'm surprised she doesn't have an Alpha mate already, helping her prepare. Except that's my job now, and I'm the luckiest fucking man alive.

I run the tips of my fingers across shaved pussy, so soft, so wet.

"Spread your legs for me, pretty girl."

Her breaths are coming fast, her chest moving rapidly, and she follows my order immediately, widening her stance. I love seeing her lost to her heat and her face flushing.

Staring into her eyes, wanting to study her reaction, I slide two fingers between her folds to where she's burning hot, sticky, and ready for me.

Exhaling loudly, she arches her head back, her chest pushing toward me, and I can't resist. With my free hand, I curl my fingers around the V of her neckline and tug it aside, along with her bra, revealing the most beautiful breast. I repeat on the other side, needing them both out. She's very curvy, overflowing in my hand, and I fucking love them. My cock's throbbing in my pants, and it takes every inch of me not to rip him out and fuck her right now. But for our first time, it won't be here, especially if I'm going to knot... and fuck me, I need to knot her.

Her puckered tits—with sexy large areolas so pink,

they're almost pale—are bouncing slightly with every movement of the cable car.

"Knox," she purrs like she can't form words.

"Yes, my sweet," I answer, leaning in and licking a nipple before taking it into my mouth. She tastes like candy. My fingers press deeper along her pussy, finding her entrance, and I don't wait. I push two fingers into her, her walls clamping around them quickly.

"God!" She shudders as I suck hard on her nipple, taking more into my mouth, never wanting to release her.

Her scent strengthens, and the hunger to taste her pussy has me close to bursting. She's running her hands through my hair, moaning, her hips rocking against my hand. I finger her, going fast now, my thumb on her little cherry clit. She's completely mine.

I ignore my own discomfort and remind myself this is about her and not me.

Releasing one breast, I glance up at my Omega, who's panting. My hand is soaked, and I know she's close.

"The way you're doing that," she groans, her eyes fluttering as though they might close. "Please never stop."

"You're made for me. Your pussy is so tight, gripping my fingers. It's all I can think about. It's become my new obsession."

Moving to her other breast, I bite down gently on

her nipple, which has her crying out for me. She's breathing fast now. So close.

Deciding to help her along, I slip a third finger into her already tight cunt. She flinches but doesn't stop me. I fuck her with them deep. There's a sheen of perspiration on her brow, and her breath is racing. Her clit is swollen, and she's so sensitive to my touch.

She's ready to be fucked, and I wish we were somewhere else.

"Knox… ohhhh fuck!" Suddenly, she shudders under me and screams. Her pussy is constricting my fingers as a gush of her juices rush over my fingers.

So fucking sexy.

"Come all over my hand… that's it, pretty girl."

"It feels incredible," she murmurs between breaths, shaking like a leaf.

What I'd give to have my face buried between her legs right now, to hold her down as she bucks, so I can lick her dry.

My cock's in agony. I adjust my balls quickly for slight relief.

Fuck! I'm ready to blow, except we're closing in on the next stop point. I won't let anyone see her like this but me.

"I'm dying to lay you down and spread those legs wide so I can fuck you blind, but not here."

She nods, glancing out to the approaching building. I draw my fingers out, much to her purring protest, which guts me.

"Don't worry, it won't be for long."

"I completely forgot where I was," she says, red spreading over her cheeks as she quickly tucks away those beautiful breasts. I take the moment to lick the honey from my fingers, my balls pulling up tighter at how deliciously crisp and sweet she tastes.

She's watching me, making these addictive little sounds that I want to spend forever pulling from her throat.

I then take out a handkerchief from my pocket, cleaning my fingers dry before removing my jacket and holding it folded over an arm in front of me. Need to conceal the anaconda in my pants somehow.

She's staring at me, grinning mischievously as she straightens her dress with trembling hands.

"You're absolutely stunning," I tell her, my voice rough.

Her blush deepens beautifully. "I'm starting to learn."

"How are you feeling?" I ask, keeping her steady as the gondola rocks slightly on its approach.

"I can't say I've ever done anything like that over the snow before." Her laugh is breathless, and fuck, the sound does things to me.

I hold on to the handle near the door as it gets rougher, one arm tight around her middle, keeping her pressed to my side where she belongs. The doors open to an empty landing platform—thank fuck for small mercies—and I guide her out.

"Ready to leave?" I ask, stealing another quick kiss because I can't help myself.

"Yes," she whispers. "I don't feel as hot anymore, but it's still there, lingering…"

We move through the building quickly. Her scent is stronger, and already I notice a few Alphas turning our way from around the main foyer, where someone's playing a piano, while others are sitting around on lounges, enjoying a drink. My grip on her tightens instinctively. They can look all they want, but if any of them make a move, I'll tear them apart. Not that I want Ruby to see that side of me. Not yet.

The cold air hits us as we step outside, and I'm hurrying her toward my car when I spot someone approaching. Male. Alpha. My body moves on instinct, stepping between them, blocking his path to Ruby.

"Keep moving if you know what's good for you," I growl.

"Marcus?" Ruby's voice is sharp with disbelief. "What the fuck? Are you following me?"

Marcus. The piece of shit cousin Garrett and Dominic warned me about. The one trying to steal her bar.

"Well, well," he sneers, his gaze flicking between us. "You're not wasting any time sleeping with *all* the Alphas, are you? I can smell your desperation. Revolting." His lip curls. "Just like your mother."

"Leave now, and we won't have any trouble." My voice is calm, but there's a lethal edge to it. Marcus stands slightly shorter than me, but the guy carries himself like he's fucking royalty, all designer clothes and entitled sneer.

"Ruby," Marcus says, ignoring me completely. "Didn't expect to find you here. Bit above your... pay grade, isn't it?" His eyes rake over her dress with disdain.

"Just leave us alone, okay?" Ruby's voice is steady, but I can smell the anxiety rolling off her.

"You're brave now, aren't you?" Marcus laughs, the sound sharp and ugly. "Found yourself a guard dog to hide behind?" He steps closer, and my muscles coil tight. "Tell me, does he know what a waste of space you are? How you're running that bar into the ground?"

"Back off," I growl. "Final warning."

"Enjoy it while you can, Ruby. Won't be long before you have nothing left." His lip curls in disgust. "Though I suppose whores like you always find a way to survive."

My fist connects with his face before he can finish the sentence. He goes down hard, and I'm on him in an instant, fisting his shirt.

"You piece of shit. I see you near her ever again, I'll rip your spine out and shove it up your ass. Understand?"

He laughs, blood trickling from his nose, and I've never wanted to kill someone more.

"Knox, please." Ruby's tugging at my arm. "Let's go. Don't waste your time on him."

Marcus spits something vile as we leave, and it takes everything in me not to turn back and finish what I started.

"Don't," Ruby says softly. "He only creates havoc for any Alpha I'm with. He'll try to make your life hell."

I pull her close, glancing back to see Marcus stumbling inside, clutching his bleeding face. My only regret is not hitting him harder.

Ruby suddenly draws away, looking around carefully. "No cameras out here, by the looks of it."

"Never been any, as far as I know." I scan the area, curious. "Why?"

She holds out her hand. "Car keys?"

I hand them over without hesitation, watching as she heads straight for a gleaming Mercedes parked nearby. She drags my key along the entire length of the car, then back again with deep gouges. Both sides.

"I approve," I state when she returns, and we rush to my car.

"Good, because you're now my accomplice."

"Delighted to be." I get her settled in the passenger seat and climb in myself, cranking up the heat. "I won't let that piece of trash ever harm you again."

Her shoulders slump, and she stares out the window. My chest aches at the sight.

"Talk to me," I urge softly. "What's going on?"

"Marcus is a monster. I hate that I'm related to him in any way."

"He comes near you again, I'll do worse than bloody his nose." The words come out as a growl. "No one talks to you like that. No one hurts what's mine."

She turns to me with wide eyes at that last word, but I don't take it back. Can't take it back.

As we start the long drive back to town, she gradually relaxes, leaning toward me.

"I love how you punched him. Protected me." A small smile plays on her lips. "You know girls love that heroic thing."

I laugh. "Wasn't trying to be heroic. Pure instinct when it comes to you."

She stares at me again, that heated haze returning to her eyes as she nibbles her lower lip. Her scent strengthens in the enclosed space, sweet and intoxicating.

"You okay?" I ask, though I know damn well she isn't.

"The fire inside me is coming back," she whispers. "It's so intense."

I grin, reaching for her hand. "Let me help with that. Lift your skirt and spread your legs so I can see your sweet little pussy."

Her mouth falls open, and I chuckle.

"You want my help?"

"What do you have in mind? Flash everyone?"

"Considering there's hardly anyone on the freeway, you're safe."

Lips pinch to the side, and she looks adorable. But to my surprise, she's doing it, shifting her dress so the split is on the front. She lifts a bent leg, revealing her milky white inner thighs, but my attention is on the pink lips glistening with her arousal.

"Now, come closer to me, as much as you can, resting your bent leg on the middle console."

My cock is as hard as a rock. She might actually kill me tonight with how turned-on I am.

"Now, lay back and relax."

As she lifts a knee and spreads, her gaze still on me, I reach over, my hand tracing her inner leg, skimming all the way to her pussy.

"You're such a good girl," I instruct, and I see her tits heaving with each of her fast breaths. How I'd love her completely naked, but beggars can't be choosers. And I remind myself this isn't about me but her.

Watching the road, I keep glancing back to where she's spread for me. I want a better view, but my fingers are already running the length of her seam, and I push her lips open.

She moans as I stroke her the full length. She's wet and so silky, so sticky. Fuck, I might pull over just to ram my cock into her, complete with my balls. I'm so tight, so desperate.

A few taps on her clit have her squirming before I push into her. Sure, it's not the most comfortable position, but none of that matters as my two fingers slide into her flesh, the sucking sound leaving me smirking. Then I pull them out and press my fat thumb all the way in. She moans.

"How can it feel so amazing?" Her eyes are glazed over, and her hips are making small bucking motions.

My thoughts are wild as I contemplate how I'll fuck her like a damn beast.

"Sometimes just having an Alpha's touch, feeling them inside you, can tame your heat," I explain.

"I had no idea," she gasps, squirming, clearly wanting more. "So, you're just going to stay in there, then?"

"Yes, until I get you home, then we can take it from there. But I don't want you to be in pain before that. And I love being inside you. It's fucking everything."

She's staring at me like she might climb onto my lap, but instead, she rests and takes a few long breaths, closing her eyes.

The drive is sweet fucking torture. Every breath fills the car with her scent, and my Alpha instincts are going haywire, demanding I pull over and finish what we started. But for her, I'd sacrifice anything— including my sanity, apparently. My knuckles are white on the steering wheel, while the other hand between her thighs, which is definitely not helping me stay calm.

When I glance over, she's breathing deeper, head

tilted against the window. "You sleeping on me, gorgeous?"

No response. Damn, she's actually passed out, face completely relaxed, lips parted slightly. It's so fucking cute, I can barely handle it. We hit the town limits, and I know I should wake her up for her house key, but… I can't bring myself to disturb her. Instead, I turn north, a plan forming. Or maybe just an excuse to keep her close a little longer.

The gates open silently—perks of having more money than I know what to do with—revealing what my realtor called a *prestigious estate* but is really just a fancy prison most days. Three stories of showing off how well the Andersons did for themselves, all stone and glass and emptiness. Too big for one person, too quiet, too fucking lonely. My eyes drift to Ruby, curled up in my passenger seat, and something in my chest does a weird flip. *Time to change that*, says the guy who has his thumb inside her delicious pussy.

Once parked outside my front door, I force myself to withdraw from her without waking her and step out into the cold night air. Deep breaths. Trying to get my shit together. Adjusting my cock with a groan. This night has been nothing but building tension with zero relief. But that's not what this is about. Not yet. Even if my body strongly disagrees.

I move to open the front door to my home and leave it open, then collect her.

She doesn't even twitch. I gather her up, kicking

the car door shut as quietly as possible, and carry her inside. She fits against me perfectly, head tucked into my neck like she belongs there, as if she's always belonged there. Christ, I'm in over my head.

I navigate the house in darkness, muscle memory guiding me up to my bedroom. She's completely out as I lay her on my bed—reminds me of finding her in that storm, thanks to those assholes who left her out there. She's a heavy sleeper.

The memory makes my jaw clench, so I focus on removing her shoes and pulling the blanket over her instead.

"Sleep tight, pretty girl," I murmur, brushing hair from her face. "I've got you."

I force myself to leave before I do something stupid like crawl in beside her. The bathroom beckons—time for the coldest shower known to man. Maybe then I can stop thinking about how right she looks in my bed. Maybe I can pretend I'm not already imagining her there permanently.

The water hits like ice but does jack shit for the burning need under my skin or my rock-hard dick. My fierce little Omega, who keys cars, makes me laugh, and drives me absolutely fucking insane. God, I'm so far gone already, it's not even funny.

Tonight, she's safe in my bed, and that's enough. Even if I have to freeze my balls off in this shower to keep her that way.

Fuck, the things this woman does to me without even trying. But I wouldn't be anywhere else.

I wake up feeling like I'm floating on a cloud, which is weird because my mattress at home definitely has a spring digging into my lower back. As my eyes adjust to the soft morning light filtering through floor-to-ceiling windows, reality comes at me like a ton of bricks. This isn't my shoebox apartment above the bar—this is straight out of Architectural Digest or maybe Bruce Wayne's summer cabin.

I know instantly I'm in Knox's place. It smells like him; it screams him. The last thing I recall is being in his car with his finger inside of me—fuck, I tingle with the memory—then exhaustion came over me, and I assume I fell asleep. He must have brought me to his place.

The room is massive, all clean lines and minimalist luxury. A California king bed, which I'm currently sprawled in the middle of like some sort of starfish, is flanked by ornate dark wooden nightstands. The walls are a soft charcoal gray, decorated with black and white photographs of mountain peaks and snow-covered trails. There's an absolutely ridiculous chaise lounge by the window that looks like it's never been sat on.

The built-in bookshelves catch my attention—they're filled with adventure magazines, travel books, and what appears to be a complete collection of wilderness survival guides. Clearly, someone takes their mountain man persona seriously. But it's not just for show—some of the books are well worn, their spines cracked and pages dog-eared.

But it's the scent that really gets me—chocolate, crisp snow, and something wild that reminds me of thunderstorms. Knox. It's all over these obscenely soft sheets, and my head is spinning with it. I bury my face deeper into his pillow, inhaling deeply. God, who even is he? Batman in disguise? Some secret millionaire who gets his kicks leading hiking tours?

Last night plays on my mind—the kiss and mind-blowing orgasm in the gondola, him punching Marcus in the face, which I can never forget. The way Knox looked at me like I was something precious, something worth protecting. How much I'd wanted... still want him to fuck and knot me. The memory of his hands, fingers, and tongue on me makes my skin tingle, and I have to press my face into his pillow to muffle my groan.

I flop back, hugging his pillow close. His scent wraps around me. Part of me wants to curl up here forever, surrounded by his scent, preferably with him in the bed, too... And that thought right there? That's exactly why I need to order those suppressants. I'm losing my damn mind. Next thing you know, I'll be picking out curtains and naming our future children.

With a herculean effort, I force myself to untangle from his sheets. The bed is ridiculously high, and I slide down rather ungracefully, my red dress from last night falling around my ankles in a wrinkled mess. Right. No underwear. Fantastic. Nothing says *walk of shame* quite like going commando in last night's party dress.

I try what I think is the exit door and instead find myself in a bathroom that's bigger than my entire apartment. The mirror shows me exactly what I feared —raccoon eyes from smeared makeup and messy nest hair. I look like I've been thoroughly kissed, and... well, I have been.

Knox's shower has multiple heads, and I'm already making my way in that direction, turning on the hot water.

Once in, I can't resist using his shampoo, and yeah, maybe I spend a little too long enjoying how it makes me smell like him. The water feels amazing, and I may or may not pretend I'm in some sort of luxury spa retreat rather than hiding out in my... what is Knox, exactly? My potential boyfriend? My Alpha? One of my Alphas? God, I'm in so much trouble. Not only am I falling for Knox, but there's Garrett, too, and… My stomach does a little flip just thinking about them both. Oh right, and my reaction around Dominic.

I'm so lost in thought, I nearly slip on the fancy stone tiles and have to catch myself on the wall.

After my shower, there's no way I'm putting that dress back on—it smells like sex. I find a white, fluffy robe that has to be Knox's, hanging on the back of the door. It's huge on me, wrapping around me almost twice, but once I cinch it tight, I feel somewhat decent. The sleeves hang past my fingers, and I have to roll them up several times.

Gathering up my dress and shoes, I venture out into the hallway. The house is just as impressive as the bedroom. A plush red runner carpet leads to a sweeping mahogany staircase, complete with a crystal chandelier. Everything's very bachelor pad chic—lots of clean lines and muted colors, minimal furniture, but what's there screams money. There are more photographs on these walls, but these have people in them. A younger Knox with what must be his parents, all of them geared up for hiking. Another of him teaching what looks like a kids' ski class, his smile bright and genuine.

I pause at one that shows him on top of a serious mountain peak, arms raised in triumph, the sunrise painting the snow pink behind him. He looks so alive, so free. Something in my chest aches looking at it.

Downstairs, I find myself face-to-face with a massive white Christmas tree, decorated with the kind of precision that speaks of professional help. My throat tightens at the sight. I haven't put up all the decorations in years, not since... The memory overwhelms me without warning—my father throwing my mom into our tree, ornaments shattering, blood mixing with broken glass. Her trying to smile through split lips, telling me it was just an accident, just like always. The way she'd still insisted on cleaning up all the broken ornaments herself, as if somehow that would make everything okay...

"Morning, beautiful."

I whirl around to find Knox leaning against the stair railing, one hand tucked into the pocket of his low-slung jeans. His white t-shirt clings to every muscle, and those biceps... He's barefoot, looking completely at home in this palace of his. The heat must be cranked because I'm suddenly very warm.

"So, this is where mountain guides live nowadays? I think I chose the wrong career."

He pushes off the railing and walks toward me with a devastatingly sexy grin curling on his lips. "I prefer *outdoor recreation specialist*."

"Fancy title for someone who basically gets paid to go hiking."

He stops inches from me, close enough that I have

to tip my head back to meet his eyes. "I do more than just hike. I'll have you know I'm an expert in making trail mix and telling top-notch jokes."

"Oh, no."

"Oh, yes. What did the mountain climber name his son?"

I groan. "Please don't..."

"Cliff."

"That's terrible."

"I've got more. What kind of photos do mountain climbers take?"

"Knox..."

"Cliffies."

I can't help but laugh, which makes his whole face light up. "Do you actually tell these to your clients?"

"Only the special ones."

"And why's that?"

His eyes flick upward, and I follow his gaze to a sprig of mistletoe dangling from the ceiling. I take an immediate step back, my chest tightening. "Nope. Not happening. Never beneath the mistletoe."

I try to push away the memories that surface - Dad's cruel laugh, Mom's face crumpling as he tore into her for being so pathetic, so desperate for a Christmas kiss. Just marketing for weak-minded fools, he'd snarled.

Knox's watching me carefully, his earlier playfulness dimming. "Something wrong with mistletoe?"

"Let's just say my father wasn't a fan when I was

growing up." I shrug, aiming for casual and probably missing by a mile. "Guess some things stick with you."

"Not sure how anyone can hate a symbol that encourages kissing."

"You hungry?" He changes the topic and I respect him even more for not prying.

Something sweet and cinnamony wafts through the air, making my stomach growl too loud. "Is that what I think it is?"

Instead of answering, he cups my face and kisses me on the mouth. It's not gentle—it's hungry and deep and makes my toes curl against the hardwood floor. He tastes like cinnamon and coffee, and my insides just melt. When he pulls back, I'm breathless and a little dizzy.

"Come on," he says, taking my hand. "I've got something to show you."

I join him, unable to stop smiling.

The kitchen is a chef's dream—all stainless steel and granite, with a huge island in the center. Lily and Hannah would go insane for this kitchen. Industrial-grade appliances gleam, and there's a coffee maker that looks like it could power a small city. But what catches my attention are the cookies cooling on a rack by the window. "Are those..."

"Snickerdoodles." He lifts me easily onto the counter, stepping between my legs like he belongs there. My heart does a little skip when his hands settle on my thighs. "My specialty."

"Liar. They're my favorite."

"Mine, too." Something shadows his expression. "My mom used to make them. Taught me before..." He clears his throat, and I resist the urge to smooth away the crease between his brows. "Said every man should know how to bake at least one thing properly. Want to be my taste tester?"

He holds up a cookie, and I take a bite, trying to be objective even as the sugar and cinnamon melt on my tongue. There's something different, something that makes me want more...

"Did you put ginger in these?"

"Family secret." His smirk is almost mischievous. "Addictive, right?"

I finish the cookie in two bites, not even trying to be ladylike about it.

"I should warn you... I'm a cookie addict. This could get dangerous. I once ate an entire batch of chocolate chip cookies during a single shift at the bar."

He laughs, the sound warming me more than any cookie. "I'll risk it. Been baking early in the hours when I couldn't sleep."

"A man after my own heart. I do my best baking at three a.m." I steal another cookie. "Coffee?"

"Already on it." He moves to the fancy machine, and I definitely don't watch the way his back muscles move under his shirt.

"But I need to grab my phone from the car first. Think I left it there."

"Already handled." He reaches across the counter and hands me my phone. "It was dying, so I plugged it in. Figured you might need it."

My stomach drops when I see all the notifications. Messages from Ash checking I'm okay, so I quickly send back that I'm fine. One from Lily asking about the Christmas party, and suddenly Dominic's face flashes in my mind, making guilt curl in my gut. But it's the message from Marcus that makes me feel sick.

> You think you were real clever last night. The gloves are off, cousin.

"Everything okay?"

I look up to find Knox watching me, concern etched on his face. His hands are wrapped around two coffee mugs—both, I notice, decorated with terrible mountain puns. One says *Life is peak-uliar*, and the other says *Don't take these views for granite*. This man is such a dork.

I force a smile and put the phone face-down. "Yeah, just work stuff. Speaking of which, I should probably get back soon. Ash is alone at the bar..."

"I've got some clothes that might fit you for the drive," he offers, but his eyes say he knows I'm lying. He sets the mugs down and moves back between my legs, hands settling on my hips. "Ruby..."

"A lift would be great," I cut him off, not ready to deal with any of it—not Marcus' threats, not my growing feelings for both Knox and Garrett, not the call I know I need to make between these Alphas. Instead, I steal another cookie and try not to think about how perfect this kitchen would be for stress baking at three a.m. or how easy it would be to imagine a life here with him.

His thumbs trace small circles on my hips through the robe, and I have to fight not to lean into him like a cat seeking attention.

"You know," he says carefully, "I'm a pretty good listener. And I make excellent stress cookies."

"I noticed." I try for a smile. "What's your stance on stress brownies?"

"Double chocolate, with extra chocolate chips." He tucks a damp strand of hair behind my ear, and the gentle touch nearly breaks me.

I want to tell him everything—about Marcus, about the bar, about my Aunt Eve—but once I start, I'm not sure I'll be able to stop. And right now, in this perfect kitchen with these perfect cookies and this perfect man, I just want to pretend for a little longer that my life isn't a complete mess.

So, I lean forward and kiss him instead. His hands tighten on my hips, and for a moment, I let myself believe that everything might actually be okay.

I'm in so much trouble.

18

DOMINIC

The satisfying thud of my fists hitting the heavy bag echoes through the gym. Left hook, right cross, repeat. My muscles burn, but I keep going, working out the restless energy that's been plaguing me since that night at Ruby's bar. Since I felt her small body pressed against mine as I pulled her to safety. Since I watched her clean the blood from my split lip and wished it was her mouth instead...

Movement catches my eye as the front door to the studio opens, and everything in me goes still.

Ruby.

She's standing in the doorway, afternoon sunlight catching her reddish-blonde hair like a halo. For a moment, I forget how to breathe. She's wearing a long black coat, but underneath, I can see the curve-hugging lines of workout gear. Already, several of the guys have noticed her, their heads turning, eyes following.

A growl builds in my throat.

Mine.

She hasn't seen me yet. She's talking to Cherry at reception, fidgeting with the strap of her backpack. When she shrugs off her coat, I have to grip the heavy bag to keep from stalking across the room and covering her up again. The black tank top and leggings she's wearing are all smooth lines, high-lighting curves that make my mouth water. That tiny waist, the round breasts, those legs I want wrapped around me...

I'm moving before I make the conscious decision, drawn to her like gravity. She turns at my approach, and that smile—fuck, that smile ruins me. It's all for me, accompanied by a pretty blush as her gaze drags over my tank top and arms. Her breath catches, just like it did at the bar, and satisfaction groans through me. Good to know I'm not the only one affected.

"Ruby." I reach for her elbow, needing to touch her, to ground myself. "So happy you turned up."

"Hey." She tucks a strand of hair behind her ear, trying for casual, but I can smell the nerves on her. Honey and cardamom, sweet enough to drown in. "Nice place you've got here. Very... intimidating."

I chuckle, using my hold on her elbow to guide her away from prying eyes. "Wait 'til you see the private training rooms."

"Oh?" Her thin eyebrow lifts. "Mr. Chase. Are you planning to take advantage of me?"

The teasing lilt in her voice makes me want to show her exactly what I'd do with her in private. Instead, I lead her down the hallway to one of the smaller rooms, closing the door behind us. The padded floor takes up half the space—perfect for any practice falls.

"So, what made you finally decide to come for some training?"

"Oh, you know." She drops her bag in the corner, stretching in a way that makes my mouth go dry. "Dealing with asshole cousins makes a girl consider her options."

"You have any issues, let me know, and I'll take care of him or anyone for you, angel." The promise slips out, and the way her pupils dilate tells me she knows I'm not joking.

She glances up at me through those long lashes, and my gaze locks onto the pouty lips I haven't stopped thinking about.

"I had no idea if you'd be at the studio, but I took a punt."

"If I'm not on a job, I tend to come here either super early in the morning or late afternoons." I move closer, drawn into her orbit. "How have you been?"

"Just dandy." But there's something off in her tone, a tension in her shoulders that makes my protective instincts flare.

"You want to talk about something?"

"Nope." She pops the *p* playfully. "What about you? How's your lip?"

"Right as rain. Trust me, I've been beaten up a lot. I'm a tough son of a bitch to take down."

Her eyes dance in my direction. "Oh, is that a challenge for me or game talk to scare me?"

The laugh bursts out of me. Fuck me, but I'm falling way too fast for this woman.

"Let's start with some stretches, angel. Then we'll see about taking me down."

I guide her through basic warm-ups, and it's torture of the sweetest kind. Every bend forward, even her arms in the air, brings her scent closer and makes me more aware of her.

"Relax your shoulders," I murmur. "First, we'll practice breaking a wrist grab," I explain, moving to stand in front of her. "When someone grabs your wrist, most people try to pull away. That's exactly what they expect." I demonstrate by gently taking her wrist. "Instead, you want to rotate your arm like this—" I guide her through the motion. "And step to the side while pulling down and away. The movement breaks their grip using leverage instead of strength."

"Like this?" She tries to copy my movement, but her form is off. She's rotating her arm but not stepping properly.

"Here." I press closer, my chest to her back, arms

wrapping around her to adjust her stance. "You want to use your attacker's momentum against them. Step with your left foot—" I tap her leg with mine, guiding her into the correct position. "Good. Now rotate and pull while stepping. The movement should be quick and fluid."

My lips brush her ear as I demonstrate, and her sharp intake of breath goes straight to my cock. She's trembling slightly. Her scent spikes with something sweeter, headier. Beneath the honey and cardamom, there's the subtle, intoxicating scent of approaching heat. Does she even realize what's coming?

"Let's try it again," I say, forcing myself to focus. "I'll grab your wrist, and you execute the move we just practiced."

I circle around to face her, reaching out to grasp her wrist firmly but not hard enough to hurt. Her skin is soft under my fingers, and I have to resist the urge to stroke my thumb across her pulse point.

"Ready?"

She nods, determination replacing the nervousness in her amber eyes. When I tug on her wrist, she moves exactly as I showed her—stepping to the side while rotating her arm and pulling down. The movement breaks my grip cleanly.

"Perfect." Pride mingles with desire as I watch her face light up. "Your timing was excellent. How did that feel?"

"Like I actually did something right." She laughs,

brushing escaped strands of hair from her face. "Can we try it again?"

"Of course. This time, I'll grab a little harder. In a real situation, they won't be gentle about it."

We practice the move several more times, her confidence growing with each successful attempt. Her smile gets broader, more genuine, and the way she looks at me after each success tightens my chest.

"You're a natural," I tell her, and her answering blush is worth any amount of restraint it takes to keep teaching instead of pressing her up against the nearest wall and licking her all over.

"One more time?" she asks, practically bouncing on her toes now.

I grab her wrist, and she executes the move flaw-lessly—but this time, she adds a little twist of her own, using the momentum to step inside my guard. Her free hand comes up to brace against my chest, and suddenly, we're toe to toe, her face tilted up to mine.

"How was that?" she asks, slightly breathless.

Dangerous woman. "Creative." My voice comes out rougher than intended. "But now you're in range for this—" I slide my free arm around her waist, pulling her flush against me. Her small gasp shoots straight through me. "An attacker could easily grab you like this."

She's so tiny against me, fitting perfectly under my chin. Every point of contact burns—her hands on my chest, her hips against mine, the sweet curve of her waist under my palm. I want to slide my hand lower, grab her ass and lift her up, pin her to the wall and—

Damn it.

"So, what's my move here?" she asks, looking up at me through those lashes. She has to know what that does to a man.

"First instinct might be to push away." I tighten my grip slightly. "But I'm stronger. Instead—" Fuck, her scent is intoxicating this close. "Instead, you want to drop your center of gravity. Bend your knees."

She follows my instruction, but the movement just makes her body drag against mine in all the right ways, mostly her rubbing against my groin. Wrong ways. Focus on the lesson.

"Now, remember how we used momentum before? Same principle, but you are twisting away from me." My voice has gone hoarse. "Your elbow—" I guide her arm into position. "It goes here, into their solar plexus. Quick jab, then spin out."

"Like this?" She demonstrates the movement in slow motion, her body rolling against mine. Has to be deliberate, the way she does it.

"Faster," I manage. "Element of surprise is crucial."

She tries again, this time with more speed. The elbow comes up—still pulling the punch, but better— and she spins away. But she's smiling over her shoulder at me as she does it, and that smile is pure trouble.

"How was that?"

"Better. But a real attacker won't let you go that easily." I reach for her again, this time catching both her arms from behind. "They might grab you like this."

She fits too perfectly against me, her back to my chest, her ass pressed against my cock. I have to grit my teeth against the urge to grind against her.

"Now what?" Her voice has gone breathy.

"Stomp down... not now, just demonstrating," I quickly add as she shifts. "Hard as you can on their instep. Then throw your head back into their face."

"Into their nose?" She demonstrates the movement in slow motion, her head barely brushing my chin. "Like you got hit?"

I chuckle darkly. "Exactly like that. Though I'd prefer you didn't demonstrate that one at full speed."

"Scared I'll break your nose, tough guy?"

"Scared I'll do something entirely inappropriate if you keep wiggling against me like that." The words I hadn't intended slip out.

She goes still in my arms, but her scent spikes—sweet and wanting. My hands flex on her arms.

"Like what?" she whispers.

I should step back. Should put space between us and continue the lesson. Should not drag my nose along the curve of her neck, breathing in her scent. Should definitely not press my lips to her thundering pulse.

"Like pin you to that wall." The words rumble out of me. "Like lift you up and wrap those gorgeous legs around my waist. Like kiss you until you forget every damn thing that worries you."

She shivers. "That's... not very professional of you, Mr. Chase."

"Neither is coming to my gym purposefully rubbing yourself against me like sin itself, Ms. Winters."

She turns in my arms, and suddenly, we're face to face again, her hands sliding up my chest. "I think,"—her fingers trace my collarbone—"we should probably get back to the lesson."

"Most likely," I agree, but my hands are already spanning her waist.

"Because I came here to learn self-defense." Her gazes drop to my lips.

"Absolutely." I walk her backward to the wall.

"And you're supposed to be teaching me." Her back hits the padding with a soft thud.

"I am teaching you." My hands slide down to her hips. "I'm teaching you exactly what happens when you tempt an Alpha."

At the last second, Ruby ducks under my arm and dances away, leaving me bracing against the wall, desire and frustration warring in my gut. Her laugh is pure temptation.

"Now, who's being unprofessional?" She backs toward the center of the mat, eyes sparkling with desire. "I thought you were going to teach me self-defense, not how to drive an Alpha crazy."

"Seems to me you've already mastered that latter part." I turn slowly, tracking her movement. She's practically bouncing on her toes, all fluid grace and curved smiles. Everything in me wants to chase her, catch her, and—

"You coming?" she taunts, and fuck if that doesn't drive me wild.

I move faster than she expects and swing around to stand behind her in seconds. My arm loops around her waist, pulling her back against my chest.

"Rule one," I growl in her ear. "Never turn your back on an opponent."

"I didn't." She tries the move I taught her—dropping her weight, going for the spin-out—but she loses her balance, starting to fall, and instinct takes over. I grab her, turning so I take the impact as we hit the mat. She lands on top of me, facing me, with a surprised *oof*, her hair falling around us like a curtain.

Her laugh vibrates through me. "Well, that didn't go as planned."

"I don't know." My hands find her hips, holding her in place. "Seems pretty perfect from where I'm lying."

She pushes up slightly, bracing her hands on my chest, but doesn't try to move away. "You did that on purpose."

"Protecting my student from injury? That's literally my job."

"Mm-hmm." She shifts, and the friction makes me

grit my teeth. "Your hands seem to be wandering from strictly professional territory."

They are. My thumbs have slipped under the hem of her tank top, stroking the soft skin of her waist.

"You complaining?"

"Not yet." Her eyes are darkening, pupils blown wide. "But I should probably mention that I have a thing about men in positions of authority."

I raise an eyebrow. "A good thing or a bad thing?"

"Depends." She leans down, her lips brushing my jaw. "How do you feel about difficult students?"

Christ. "Ruby…" It's meant to be a warning, but it comes out like a plea.

"Yes, Mr. Chase?" Her teeth graze my earlobe, and my control snaps.

I roll us, pinning her beneath me. Her gasp of surprise turns into a moan as I capture her mouth, kissing her hard and deep. Her hands slide into my hair, nails scraping my scalp, and I growl into the kiss. She tastes like desire, and I can't get enough.

"This is a terrible idea," she pants when I move to her neck.

"Probably." I suck at her pulse point, loving how her body arches into mine.

"I mean it." But her legs wrap around my waist, pulling me closer. "We shouldn't—oh God." My teeth find that spot where her neck meets her shoulder, and she shudders.

I raise my head to look at her, taking in her flushed cheeks and swollen lips. "Do you want me to stop?"

Instead of answering, she pulls me back down, kissing me as if she's drowning and I'm air. My hand slides up her ribs, thumb brushing the underside of her breast through her top. She makes a little whimpering sound that nearly undoes me.

"Dominic..." The way she says my name, all breathy and wanting, makes me want to wreck her completely.

"I know, angel." I press my hips into hers, grinding my huge cock against her pussy, letting her feel exactly what she does to me. "I know."

Her scent is overwhelming now—honey and cardamom and approaching heat, all mixed with arousal.

A knock at the door has us both freezing.

"Dom?" Cherry's voice. "Your three o'clock is here."

Fuck. I'd completely forgotten about the new client consultation. Ruby's looking up at me with those big amber eyes, lips parted, chest heaving.

"I'll cancel," I whisper to my angel, not moving.

Ruby's laugh is shaky. "No, I think this is perfect timing."

"That's cruel," I murmur. I drop my forehead to hers, breathing her in one last time before pushing myself up. "I need to see you again, and soon." I help her up, pulling her against me for one more quick, hard kiss. "We're going to finish this lesson properly."

"The self-defense lesson or the other kind?" Her smile is wicked.

"Both." I tuck a strand of hair behind her ear, letting my fingers trail down her neck. "How does tomorrow sound?"

"And if I don't?"

"Then I'll come find you." I back her against the wall one last time, caging her in with my arms. "And trust me, angel,"—I lean down, my lips brushing her ear—"you won't like what happens when I have to chase you."

The small sound she makes tells me she might like it very much indeed. "Maybe it's not a great idea. I-I don't think I'm a good person." Her voice breaks on the words, and I pull back enough to see her face.

"What do you mean, angel?"

She turns her face away, but I catch her chin, forcing her to look at me.

"I'm doing things... things that will make people hate me. That's not who I am, but lately..." She swallows hard. "Lately, it feels like that's exactly who I am."

Ice slides down my spine as understanding hits. She's talking about Knox and Garrett—has to be. They both told me about their encounters with her, how neither of them could resist her pull. Just like I can't. And now, she's drowning in guilt, thinking she's playing us all.

Fuck.

I should tell her everything. Tell her about our plan

—my plan—to let her see each of us as we really are. No fake dating bullshit, no pretense. Just three Alphas who all want the same Omega, who all agreed to let her choose naturally.

But looking at the pain in her eyes, the self-loathing... I know I've fucked up. We all have.

"Ruby." I brush my thumb across her lower lip, watching it tremble. "You're the best person I know. Whatever you think you're doing wrong... it's not as bad as you think."

She laughs. "If you knew the truth."

"I know enough."

But she's backing away like the spell she'd been under moments earlier has cleared from her mind. Her eyes hold mine, and I see the worry behind them. Then she grabs her bag.

"I gotta go," she calls as she flees the room, everything in me screaming to chase her down, to make her understand. But my legs don't move and suddenly, Cherry is at the door with my new client.

Fuck!

This is my fault. I made the rules of this game, thinking it would be better to let things develop naturally. But all I've done is hurt her—we all have.

Time to change the rules.

I pull out my phone, sending the same text to Knox and Garrett.

We need to talk. Pronto.

19

I'm wiping down the same spot on the bar counter, trying to ignore Ash's pointed looks. It's been two days since I trained with Dominic, and I haven't seen any of the guys since... on purpose. I've kept my distance, deciding I need to come clean. So, I've been hiding in my bar since.

"If you clean that spot any harder, you'll find the secret passage to Narnia," he quips, juggling three glasses on the way back to the bar.

"Shut up," I mutter, but my lips twitch into a grin.

"Make me." He snatches the rag from my hand. "I swear, between your brooding and your cleaning obsession, you're one leather jacket away from being a romance novel heroine."

"I don't brood."

"Oh, really?" He strikes a dramatic pose, hand to

his forehead. "'Oh, woe is me. I'm too pretty, and too many hot guys want me. Whatever shall I do?"

I throw a maraschino cherry at his head. He catches it in his mouth... because, of course, he does.

My phone buzzes, and I grab it like a lifeline, ignoring Ash's smirk.

It's Lily.

> Guess who just dropped an entire bowl of buttercream on her favorite shoes? This girl! But on the bright side, my feet smell delicious.

Despite everything, I laugh and respond.

> How do you even function?

> Pure talent and questionable life choices Also, coffee. So. Much. Coffee.

> Miss you. The bar feels empty without you popping in with your stories and baked goodies.

> Aww, honey, you getting soft on me? Must be serious if you're admitting feelings. You good?

I bite my lip, fingers hovering over the keyboard.

> Just... boy trouble.

SPILL •• This about those hotties from
the other day? Because if you're not
interested, I volunteer as tribute.
Especially for Mountain Man. Those
ARMS.

My stomach twists with guilt. If she only knew...

It's complicated.

Isn't it always? But OMG, speaking
of complicated, you will NOT believe
what happened to me the other night

Did you set another mixing bowl on
fire?

That was ONE TIME. No... I may have
accidentally messaged a stranger.

...accidentally, how?

Okay, so I was trying to text Hannah
about this massive wedding cake, and
I typed the number wrong, and my first
message to this complete stranger
was, "I need help hiding this body; it's
bigger than I thought, and I can't lift it
alone"

LILY NO

LILY YES 😜 I was talking about the CAKE BODY, but this poor guy thought I was a legit murderer for like 10 minutes! Then I sent a pic of me covered in fondant, looking like a flour-dusted serial killer, and somehow, we ended up talking for THREE HOURS

Only you could accidentally attract a man by pretending to be a murderer 💀

In my defense, he said my "murder cake" text was the most interesting wrong number he's ever gotten. Also, he's a pastry chef, so like... fate? 😇

Or your bizarre serial killer energy finally found its match

Hey, some girls attract guys with their looks. I attract them with accidental homicide texts. Don't judge my methods! 🔪

Are you telling me you're cyber-flirting with a stranger? 🫢

Says the woman currently juggling multiple admirers 😅 But also YES, and he's so funny and smart, and we've been trading pictures...

My eyes go wide.

LILY. Tell me he didn't send you a 🥖 pic.

GET YOUR MIND OUT OF THE GUTTER 😂😂😂 I meant, like, baking pictures! He sent me his sourdough starter (her name is Bertha, and she's beautiful). Though I wouldn't say no to other kinds of pictures... 👀

I can't believe you're thirsting after bread boy

Excuse you, his name is James, and his baguettes are magnificent

I snort so hard, Ash gives me a concerned look.

Are we still talking about bread? 😏

Yes, his baguette does look very impressive 🥖😳

I'm dying 💀

No dying allowed until you tell me what's really bothering you. And don't say nothing because you've been radio silent for days, and that only happens when you're overthinking something

I stare at the phone, chest tight.

What if... what if you really like more than one person?

Then I'd say you have excellent taste and should probably buy a lottery ticket because, clearly, luck is on your side

I'm serious

So am I. What's the actual problem here? Are they jerks? Because I will absolutely come home early, and we can egg their houses

No! God, no, they're... they're amazing. That's part of the problem.

Only you would think amazing guys being into you is a problem 🫤 Look, remember that romance novel series you got me hooked on? The one with the reverse harem?

This isn't a book

No, but maybe it could be better. Real life usually is. Just saying... 😏

"Earth to Ruby!" Ash's voice makes me jump. He's dangling a towel in front of my face. "As riveting as your text conversation clearly is, we've got customers."

I look up to find the after-work business crowd starting to trickle in. Great. Just what I need—an audience for my crisis.

Gotta goes, work calls

This conversation isn't over! And
Ruby? Just be honest with them. With
yourself, too. Also, send pics of
Mountain Man's arms for scientific
purposes 🔬

I put my phone away, trying to ignore how it feels like it's burning a hole in my pocket. Three unread messages from three different men sit in my inbox, each one making my heart race for different reasons.

"You know," Ash says as he passes me with a tray of glasses. "For someone who owns a bar, you're terrible at handling shots."

I blink at him. "What?"

"You know, taking your shot? Making your move? Going for it?" He grins. "Though I suppose you're doing okay in that department considering how many—"

I slap his arm with my bar towel. "Don't you have glasses to wash?"

"Don't you have a love life to sort out?"

I groan, dropping my head to the counter.

He pats my head. "Now come on, these hipsters aren't going to serve themselves. Though we could probably convince them that's the new trend—self-serve craft cocktails—it's very underground."

Despite everything, I laugh. Maybe Lily's right. Maybe I need to stop overthinking and just... be honest.

But first, I have to survive this shift without combusting from anxiety.

"Ruby!" Ash calls. "Table three needs their lavender-infused, locally sourced, artisanal gin and tonics!"

I got this.

Eventually, the after-work rush slows down, leaving only a few stragglers nursing their drinks in the corners of the bar. I'm wiping glasses while Ash regales me with his latest dating disaster—something about a guy who turned out to be a professional clown. Literally.

"So, there I am," he's saying. "Thinking I'm about to get lucky, and he pulls out this red nose—"

The front door chimes, and I glance over.

Knox and Garrett walk in. Together.

My heart stops beating, and I freeze.

They're talking like old friends, and something about that makes my stomach twist. Before I can process what I'm doing, I drop behind the bar counter, barely avoiding knocking over a rack of glasses.

"What are you—" Ash starts.

"Shhh!" I hiss, pressing myself against the lower cabinets. "Oh my God, oh my God, did you not see who just walked in?"

He stares out over the bar, then crouches down next to me with an amused expression.

"Ah yes, Mr. Hunk, one and two. They're chatting like they know each other." He stands, then frowns and looks down at me. "Oh, Mr. Three is here, too."

"What?" I risk a peek over the counter, and, yep, there's Dominic, all dark intensity in his fitted black t-shirt, striding in like he owns the place. The three of them together are like a perfect storm of everything I want and everything I can't have. "Oh, fuck, kill me now." My hands are shaking so bad, I have to grip the edge of the cabinet to steady myself.

"I need to get out of here. I need to run…" My chest feels too tight, each breath shorter than the last. "They know, they found out I've been with all three, and now they're going to tell me I'm the worst person in the world…"

Ash crouches back down next to me, his usually playful expression serious for once. "Listen, it's going to be okay, no matter what. I promise I have your back. And if they really like you, then they'll find a way to work this out with you."

"And if not?" My voice cracks. I don't know why, but the fact of losing them now feels like I'm being gutted. I wrap my arms around my middle, trying to hold myself together. Something has changed in me. I don't feel like the girl I was before, but someone who had fallen for three men stupidly, not thinking, and now, instead of trusting my instincts and going to speak with them, they've made that call for me.

Ash pats my hand. "Trust me, it will be okay."

He stands up suddenly, and my heart ricochets against my ribs.

"Boss, you may want to come up…"

"Nope, I'm staying here forever. They can't break my heart if they can't find me."

"No, seriously, you need to come up now."

There's something in his tone that makes my stomach drop. Slowly, I rise from my hiding spot—and immediately wish I hadn't. The guys are halfway to the bar, but their attention is focused on someone else.

Marcus.

"Oh, fuck," I murmur. "Because I need him here during this, too." I close my eyes briefly. "What did I do wrong to deserve this?"

When I open them again, I find myself caught in a crossfire of stares. Knox's blue eyes are full of something that makes my chest ache—concern? Pity? Garrett's usual playful expression is nowhere to be found, replaced by a seriousness that scares me. And Dominic... His dark gaze flicks between Marcus and me, his jaw clenched tight enough, I can see the muscle jumping.

I focus on Marcus instead. Monsters, at least, I understand. He's striding toward the bar with that smile I hate—the one that says he knows something that's going to hurt me. His glance between the three Alphas is calculated, smug. Of course, he recognizes Knox and Garrett since he saw them with me, but something about the way he looks at Dominic makes my skin crawl.

I need the earth to crack open and swallow me whole.

"Drinks, anyone?" Ash calls out, breaking the awful silence. God bless him.

Marcus slides onto a barstool, still wearing that demon's smile.

"What a fortuitous gathering. I came to speak with my dear cousin, and look who else shows up."

"What do you want?" I snarl, grateful for the anger. Anger is better than anxiety.

"Well, after your little stunt the other night, I started doing some investigation…"

I'm going to be sick. I've been here before. Three years ago, when I started dating a local restaurant owner, Marcus dug up every health code violation the guy had ever had. Two years before that, he'd gotten another guy fired by revealing his gambling problem to his boss. Every time I try to have something good, Marcus finds a way to poison it.

"I don't want to hear it." My voice shakes despite my effort to keep it steady. "I told you before, you're not to step foot in here again."

Marcus doesn't move. If anything, his smile grows wider.

"It's interesting what you discover when you pry a bit around, when you follow people." His gaze slides to the three Alphas. "Do you really think you know who these three are?"

"What the fuck are you talking about?" Knox's voice is sharp enough to cut.

Dominic steps forward, his expression murderous. "You had us surveilled, you fucker?"

Garrett closes in, too, but his stare is on me. What is he thinking? What an awful person I am?

"Oh, wait for it." Marcus' laugh makes my skin crawl. "Because that's not even the good part. It's what Ruby doesn't know." He pauses for effect, clearly savoring the moment. "How these three men she randomly met? Not so random after all. They've been working together, planning to meet you for weeks. Setting up those perfect little meet-ups, pretending they didn't know each other. But it's all fake!"

The words are like a punch to my gut. "Wait, what?" My chest is so tight I can barely breathe. "What are you talking about?"

"Ruby—" Garrett starts, taking a step forward, but I hold up my hand.

"Is it true?" The words taste like ash in my mouth.

Knox runs a hand through his hair, looking pained. "It's not what you think—"

"Is. It. True?"

"Angel." Dominic's voice is softer than I've ever heard it. "That's why we came here, to explain."

But I can't. I can't look at any of them, can't process the fact that every moment I thought was real was actually choreographed. The cable car ride with Knox. The dance with Garrett. The training session with Dominic. All of it planned, all of it fake? A sense of betrayal cuts through me.

"Did any of it even mean anything to you?" My voice cracks.

"Damn it, Ruby, of course, it did." Garrett runs his hands through his hair like he always does when he's stressed. "I haven't been able to get you out of my thoughts. All three of us were fucking captivated by you. Every laugh, every touch... that was real."

Dominic's dark eyes burn into mine. "Your friends asked us to take you out on a blind date, and once we saw you, we all knew we needed to meet you for real. But fuck, Ruby... you weren't just some random date. You broke down every wall I had, made me feel things I've spent years running from. Never meant to fall this hard."

"Wait, my friends?" Lily and Hannah come to mind, about their plan to set me up with three Alphas. And they are standing before me, aren't they?

Fuck, I'm such an idiot for not seeing this.

I blink back tears, trying to process everything. Each memory feels tainted now—those casual meet-ups, those moments I thought were spontaneous. Sure, I kept my own secret, never telling them how I felt about all three of them. We never put a label on what-ever this was—just coffee dates, training sessions, late-night talks that felt like they meant something more.

But this? This feels like they tricked me.

Heat creeps up my neck as a horrible thought hits me. Did they see me as some sad little Omega who couldn't land an Alpha on her own? My cheek burns, and I force myself to meet Knox's gaze.

"Ruby, please. We never meant to hurt you. You are the truest thing I've ever felt. You mean everything to me. We should have been honest upfront."

"Yes, you should have!" Tears burn behind my eyes, but I refuse to let them fall. "God, I'm such an idiot. Here I was, feeling guilty about being with all of you, when you were all in on it together. Was it a game to see who got me first?"

"It wasn't like that." Garrett takes another step forward. "We just wanted—"

"To what? To see which one of you could bed the Omega first? Was there a bet? A timeline?"

"That's not—" Dominic starts, but Marcus cuts him off.

"Oh, this is so good."

"Fuck you. You'll be lucky if you walk out of here in one piece for this stunt." Dominic growls in his direction.

The blood drains from my face, and it's too much. My head spins, my chest hurts, and I feel bile at the back of my throat.

"Get out." My voice doesn't even sound like my own. "All of you, get the fuck out of my bar."

"Ruby, please just let us explain." Knox looks desperate now. "What started as a blind date became real. What we feel for you—"

"I can't cope with this." Ice spreads through my

veins, numbing everything. "You lied to me and made me think I was special to each of you, but now I feel like you were maybe exchanging stories in the background. Then what? A lucky dip to see who got to keep the sorrowful Omega?" A laugh bubbles up, harsh and bitter. "You made me think I was the bad guy, feeling guilty about leading you all on, when this whole time you were doing the same but worse."

"Angel—" Dominic reaches for me, and something in me snaps.

"Don't!" I pull back. "Just get out. I need to process this…"

Marcus's laughter rings out. "Oh cousin, you really know how to pick them. Though, I have to admire their technique. Three Alphas working together to—"

"You, too." I turn on him, and something in my expression makes him step back. "Get the fuck out of my bar before I call the cops."

"You can't—"

"Try me." I bare my teeth in what might be a smile. "I've got nothing left to lose now, do I? You're going to take it all in just over a week's time. It's what you wanted, and you won. Fucking happy now?" Tears sting my eyes.

For a long moment, no one moves. Then Ash clears his throat.

"You heard the lady. Out. All of you."

Slowly, they file out. Knox looks back once, his expression devastated. Garrett opens his mouth like he wants to say something, then closes it again. Dominic's face is a mask of sorrow—at Marcus, at himself, at me, I don't know anymore.

The door closes behind them with a final sounding click.

"Ruby..." Ash starts.

"Don't." My voice cracks. "Just... don't."

I turn and walk into my office, closing the door behind me. Only then do I let myself slide to the floor, wrapping my arms around my knees as the tears finally come.

Outside, I can hear Ash telling the remaining customers we're closing early. Can hear the scrape of chairs, the murmur of voices, the sound of the door opening and closing multiple times.

My phone buzzes in my pocket. Three messages, all at once.

> Knox: I know you probably hate me right now, but please let me explain.

> Garrett: It wasn't supposed to be like this. What I feel for you is so real, it's going to kill me if I lose you.

> Dominic: Don't let him win, angel. Don't let Marcus take you from us.

I turn off my phone.

Through the door, I hear Ash's voice.

"Ruby? Everyone's gone. Do you want me to call Lily?"

I press my forehead to my knees and don't answer. What would I even say? *Hey, remember how you mentioned those blind dates? Turns out they were making plans behind my back on how to best take turns and lie to me. Surprise!*

The worst part isn't even the lies. It's that even now, my heart still trips over itself, remembering Knox's gentle hands, Garrett's playful smile, Dominic's intensity.

I'm such a fool.

A knock at my door makes me jump.

"Ruby?" Ash again. "I know you probably want to be alone, but... I made coffee. And I may have those chocolate chip cookies you like."

Despite everything, a wet laugh escapes me. "You've been hiding cookies from me?"

"You don't have to talk. But you don't have to be alone, either."

For a long moment, I don't move. Then, slowly, I reach up and turn the handle.

In moments, Ash is sitting on the floor outside my door, a plate of burned shortbread cookies he made. He lays it beside him and two mugs of coffee that probably have way too much whiskey in them.

"You're a disaster," I tell him, voice rough from crying.

"Yeah, well." He hands me a cookie. "Takes one to know one."

I take a bite. It's simultaneously overdone and underdone and possibly the best thing I've ever tasted.

"What am I going to do?"

"Right now?" He bumps his shoulder against mine. "You're going to eat these terrible cookies and drink this terrible coffee and let yourself feel terrible. Tomorrow..." He shrugs. "Tomorrow, we'll figure it out."

"Promise?"

"Promise." He hands me a coffee. "And hey, look on the bright side—at least none of them turned out to be professional clowns."

The laugh that bursts out of me is half-sob, but it's something.

It has to be enough for now.

20

RUBY

My hands are shaking so bad, I nearly drop the keys to my bar. I glance around Winterscape Bar, my baby, the one thing I've poured my heart into and my last real connection to Aunt Eve.

God, I miss Ash today. He's been my rock through this whole mess, telling me to woman up and hear them out. Easy for him to say—he's not the one who got played by three gorgeous Alphas. Even if they were just doing Lily and Hannah a favor...

Speaking of my well-meaning but completely insane best friends, at least I'll get proper answers from Lily tonight since she's back home from her work trip. Four days of crying into my pillow is probably enough, right? Four days of ignoring messages from the three men is ripping me apart. Their scents are still everywhere.

Nope. Not going there.

I pull my hood up against the snow, watching the festive lights flicker through the storm like multicolored fireflies. *All I Want for Christmas* is belting out from the street speakers, and I can't help but snort. Yeah, all I want for Christmas is not to lose my bar to my douchebag cousin Marcus in four days. Oh, and maybe for my heart to stop feeling like it's been put through a meat grinder.

The snow's coming down in thick flakes now, turning everything into a weird winter snow globe. A few cars crawl past, probably full of people headed home to their normal, drama-free lives. Must be nice.

"Okay, Ruby, get your ass in gear. Just cross the street. Even you can't mess that up."

I step out from under the awning and... holy shit!

Headlights blind me as a van swerves way too close, way too fast. I stumble back, heart in my throat, but before I can even process what's happening, the side door flies open with a screech that sets my teeth on edge.

Black emptiness. A figure in a mask. Hands grabbing me—rough, strong, wrong.

I scream and kick out like a wildcat, but it's like fighting a brick wall. The world spins as I'm yanked into the van, and something clamps over my nose and mouth. The smell hits me—sickly sweet, chemical—making my head swim.

"Get off me, you—" The words slur, my tongue

feeling too thick. The door slams shut, and darkness closes in, even as I try to fight it. My last coherent thought before everything goes black is that I guess the universe wasn't satisfied with just taking my bar and my love life—it had to go for the hat trick.

21

GARRETT

My fingers drum against the desk in my office, each tap echoing my growing frustration. Five fucking days of radio silence from Ruby, and it's eating me alive. The snow's been coming down hard outside, turning the brewery's courtyard into a winter wasteland that matches my mood.

Knox hasn't stopped pacing since he got here. His usual easy-going nature is nowhere to be found. He's all tense shoulders and grinding teeth as he stares out the window. Even his designer outdoor gear looks rumpled, as if he's been sleeping in it. Knowing him, he probably has.

"I can't take this anymore." Knox turns, raking his hands through his already messy hair. "Sure, we're giving her space and time, but she's fucking ignoring our messages and calls. I've done fuck all since she found out we planned our dates with her. And I've been such a mess."

I get it. My brewery crew's been giving me a wide berth lately. Apparently, I've been a bear to work with. The latest batch of stout needs testing, but I can't focus on shit. Every flavor reminds me of her.

Dominic's sprawled on my leather armchair, but there's nothing relaxed about him. His dark eyes are sharp as ever, and his fingers keep twitching toward his phone. Guy's probably fighting the urge to hack into every security camera in town just to get a glimpse of her.

"We're in the same damn boat," he says, his voice rough. "And I agree. I want to go see her again. We've given her time, and I need to explain our part." He sits forward, jaw tight. "Fuck, I want to apologize, to make her know we fucked up. And you know I'm not a man who apologizes lightly."

The leather of my chair creaks as I lean back against my window. Cold seeps through my flannel shirt, but I barely notice it. My brewing notebook's been sitting untouched in my back pocket for days—can't think about new recipes when all I can taste is guilt.

"I'm ready," I say, surprising myself with how raw my voice sounds. "This waiting game is fucking strangling me." The words barely leave my mouth when a knock comes from the room. "Come in," I call out, expecting one of my brewers with a crisis.

Instead, Cindy, my assistant, pokes her head in. Behind her stands Ash, Ruby's bartender, looking like he hasn't slept all night. My stomach drops. Whatever brings him here can't be good.

"He insisted on talking to you," Cindy says, worry creasing her forehead as she pushes her mousey blonde hair out of her face.

The moment Ash steps into my office, I stiffen, on high alert. Knox stops pacing, and Dominic straightens in his chair.

"Ruby's missing," he says.

Two words. Just two fucking words and my world tilts sideways.

The words turn my veins to ice, and I'm across the room before I realize I've moved.

"What do you mean, missing?"

"She didn't show up to work yesterday." Ash runs his hands over his face. He looks like hell, with dark circles under his eyes and hair a mess. "Thought maybe she was sick, you know? But she's not at home, not answering her phone. Lily, her best friend, hasn't heard from her, either, and trust me, that girl would know."

"When's the last time you saw her?" Dominic's voice is deadly calm, but I know that tone. It's the one that makes smart people start running.

"The day before last, at closing. She was..." Ash

shakes his head, swallowing hard. "Man, she was devastated. Like, I've known Ruby for years, seen her through some shit, but this was different."

Knox makes a sound like he's been punched. I know exactly how he feels. My chest hasn't stopped aching for days.

"She gave each of you a piece of herself," Ash continues, looking at each of us in turn. "Her heart. And finding out about the setup? That broke something in her. She's spent years building walls, protecting herself, and you guys? You got through them. All three of you."

"We didn't mean to hurt her," I say, my voice rougher than intended. "We wanted to have her experience something real, not a fucking blind date. Something real in the way she met us."

Knox quietly nods, still staring out the window.

Dominic stands abruptly, phone already in hand. "I'm calling my team. We'll access every camera in town, track her movements. Something will show up." His fingers fly over the screen. "I'll head to the office now."

"Knox and I are paying Marcus a visit," I announce, already grabbing my jacket.

"I'm coming with you," Ash starts, but Knox cuts him off with a flick of his hand.

"No. We need you at the bar in case she shows up or tries to contact you." I pull out one of my business cards, scrawling my personal number on the back.

"Call me immediately if you hear anything. Anything at all."

Minutes later, we're in Knox's massive SUV, chains on the tires crunching through fresh snow. The streets are still busy with evening traffic, brake lights glowing red through the swirling white. Knox is driving more carefully than I'd like, but even I have to admit, the roads are treacherous.

"We should have gone to her sooner," Knox mutters, knuckles white on the steering wheel. "Should have camped outside her door until she talked to us."

"If that bastard Marcus touched her..." I let the threat hang in the air. We all know what that piece of shit is capable of. Dominic's background check had turned up enough red flags to cover a firing range.

"We'll bury him," Knox says simply, and coming from him, it carries extra weight.

The investment firm's building looms ahead of us, all glass and steel. Normally, I'd appreciate the architecture, maybe note how it would look on a beer label. Right now, all I can think is that Marcus better be in there somewhere.

I'm through the revolving doors and halfway across the marble lobby before Knox can even park. The receptionist startles as I approach, probably because I look like I'm about to commit murder. Which, depending on what I learn here, isn't entirely off the table.

"Marcus Winter. Where is he?"

She blinks up at me, manicured fingers hovering over her keyboard. "I'm sorry, sir, but I can't—"

"Now." The word comes out as a growl. Behind me, I hear footsteps, and I turn to see Knox approaching.

"Is there a problem here?" A deep voice cuts through the tension. I twist back around to find an older man approaching us at reception, white hair perfectly styled, wearing a pinned suit. Two security guards flank him, but they're hanging back, watching.

"Douglas Sterling," he says, extending his hand. "I own Sterling Capital Partners. And you are on my premises…"

"Garrett Reynolds." I accept his handshake. "I need to speak with Marcus. Now."

His eyes narrow slightly, taking in my flannel shirt and jacket, my worn jeans, and the brewery logo on my jacket. There's something calculating in his gaze.

"Perhaps we should discuss this privately." He gestures toward a hallway.

Knox steps forward. "We're not leaving without answers."

Sterling's expression doesn't change, but something in his posture shifts. "Follow me."

His office is exactly what you'd expect—all mahogany and leather, with a view of the mountains that most likely makes him feel like the king of the world. I remain standing even when he motions to the chairs.

"Ruby Winters is missing," I say without preamble. "And your stepson has been threatening her for months."

That gets his attention as one of his thick eyebrows arches. "Missing? Explain."

"Nobody's seen her for close to two days. And Marcus has been trying to run her out of business at the Winterscape Bar for months. Coincidence?" I lean forward, palms flat on his desk. "I want to find him before I get the police involved and start crawling all over your company. Because I promise you, Marcus will be suspect number one."

Sterling steeples his fingers, studying me. "You said Winterscape Bar? Eve Winters' place?"

"Ruby's place now. Her aunt left it to her."

"Ah." He leans back. "And you're aware of the condition in Eve's will? About marriage by Christmas Eve?"

The words hit me hard. "What?"

"If Ruby isn't married by Christmas Eve, the bar passes to Marcus." Sterling's eyes narrow. "You didn't know."

"I thought..." My mind is racing. "I thought he was just trying to run her out of business to buy the place for investment purposes."

Sterling sighs heavily, rubbing his temples. "That fucking idiot had plans to develop the property, but I told him not to get his hopes up on inheriting the property from Eve. I've kept him out of my business dealings because of his temper, but I promised his mother on her deathbed that I'd look after him." He looks up at me sharply. "He has... issues. Rage issues."

"Where is he?" The words come out barely controlled.

Instead of answering, Sterling pulls out his phone, dialing. After several rings, he frowns. "No answer." He tears a page from a notepad, writing quickly. "His address and number. I need to know immediately if he's involved. He's had too many warnings already, after his last few charges—"

"Sexual assault and battery," Knox cuts in, and I watch the man's face go pale. Dominic's background check had been thorough. Too thorough, now that I think about what Marcus might be capable of.

I snatch the paper. "If he so much as touched her—"

"He frequents O'Malley's Bar on 5th, The Red Room downtown, and there's a cabin retreat up at the other end of town," Sterling rattles off. "Give me your number. I'll make some calls, see if anyone's seen him."

I recite my number, already heading for the door, when his voice stops me.

"Mr. Reynolds." There's something heavy in his tone. "I want him alive."

I turn, meeting his gaze.

"For his mother's sake, I can't bear to see him go that way," Sterling continues, his voice hard. "But I promise you... if he's done what we fear, I'll make his life such hell, he'll wish he was dead."

The drive to Marcus' mansion feels endless, each mile stretching like an eternity through the swirling snow. Knox barely says a word, the air in the car thick. I keep checking my phone, willing it to ring with news from Sterling or Ash. Instead, Dominic's name flashes on the screen. I put it on speaker.

"She was fucking kidnapped." Dominic's words hit like bullets. "Yesterday, late afternoon." There's a sound like something shattering in the background, and knowing Dominic, it's probably an expensive piece of tech meeting his fist. "I've got the footage. A black van, no plates, pulled up outside the bar. Two men in masks." His voice breaks slightly. "They grabbed her. Ruby fought like hell, but they used something, probably chloroform. Those fucking cowards."

The heaviness in my chest threatens to suffocate me. Knox's hands tighten on the wheel, and I watch his jaw working as he grinds his teeth. She's been gone, and we had no idea. I've been sitting in my brewery, drowning in self-pity while she...

"There's more," Knox forces out, his voice rough as old gravel. "Sterling told us something about Eve's will. If Ruby's not mated and married by Christmas Eve, Marcus inherits the bar."

"That cock-sucking piece of shit!" Dominic's voice explodes through the speaker. Something else crashes in the background. "He's behind this. Has to be. The timing's too fucking perfect."

"Of course, that motherfucking bastard is," Knox snarls, slamming his palm against the steering wheel. His usual easy-going nature is gone, replaced by something feral. "That's his game? Keep her locked up until Christmas Eve passes?"

"Three days." The words taste like ash in my mouth. "He only needs to hold her for three days, then she loses her bar."

My fingers dig into my thighs hard enough to bruise. "Why didn't she tell us about this? About any of it?"

"Because maybe she didn't exactly trust us? Didn't want to seem like she wanted our help?" Knox's voice is bitter.

The snow's coming down harder now, thick flakes dancing in the headlights. My brewing notebook digs into my back pocket. How many times had Ruby sat at my bar, helping me taste test new recipes while this deadline was hanging over her head? While that bastard was threatening everything she loved?

"We're headed to Marcus' mansion," I tell Dominic. "I'm messaging you the address. Meet us there."

"Already on my way."

The mansion looms ahead of us through the storm, a sprawling Victorian monstrosity set back from the road. Dark windows stare out like dead eyes, and despite the perfectly maintained grounds, there's something abandoned about the place. Dominic's black Aston Martin is already parked out front.

"Place is empty," he says once we approach, his dark eyes hard. Snow dusts his hair, and there's a raw scrape across his knuckles that wasn't there this morning. "I checked the back, broke in. No alarm system—amateur move—but no one's home."

He pulls out his phone, fingers flying across the screen as he approaches my driver's window. The security footage plays stark black and white, and my stomach lurches. Ruby steps out of the bar, tugging her hood up against the snow. The van appears like a ghost, and then... God. Her struggle. The way she kicks out, fighting with everything she has. Then, her body goes limp inside as the door slides shut.

Knox makes a sound like he's been gutted. I taste blood and realize I've bitten through my lip.

"The van heads north out of town," Dominic continues, his voice clinical, but his hand's shaking with rage as he flicks through camera feeds. "We lose it after the Morrison turnoff. No more cameras out there."

"Let's go out there," Knox states. "I know that area like the back of my hand. Done trekking up there. If they're holding her somewhere, we'll find it. There are only so many places accessible in this weather."

"Drop your car down the road," I tell Dominic. "We'll pick you up. No sense leaving evidence we were here if Marcus returns."

Soon, all three of us are in Knox's vehicle. I can't shake the image of Ruby going limp in those bastards' arms. The woman who kissed like sin. Who crashed into my world and left me chaotically obsessed with her.

The snow falls harder as we head north, but nothing can erase the fire burning in my chest. *Hold on, Ruby. We're coming for you. And God help anyone who stands in our way.*

Knox steers us through the worsening storm, the headlights barely cutting through the thick curtain of snow. Every minute feels like an hour. The surveillance footage Dominic pulled showed their vehicle heading north, but after thirty miles of careful driving, we hit a fork that splits three ways into the darkness.

"We lose camera footage farther back. So, which fucking way now?" Dominic states.

Knox's eyes narrow as he studies each road, the windshield wipers fighting a losing battle against the storm. He leans forward.

"Those two paths on the left? Just highways. Nothing but empty road for hours. But up there?" He gestures to the right fork. "There's a bunch of old buildings. Some abandoned ranches. Marcus isn't trying to skip town. He just needs to keep Ruby hidden until Christmas Eve."

"Three days," I growl, the words tasting like ash in my mouth.

"Exactly." Knox shifts into drive. "He'll want to stay

close to town himself. The main roads are too obvious. Has to be this way, and we're going to hit every single one until we find her."

Dominic murmurs his agreement as Knox takes the turn, our headlights illuminating the snow-covered path ahead.

Hold on, sweetheart.

We're coming...

Marcus looms over me, a self-satisfied smirk twisting his face into something ugly. The dim light filtering through the grimy window catches the silver threading through his hair. Everything about him makes my skin crawl.

"You really should thank me for this, Ruby."

"Thank you?" I spit the words like poison. "For what, exactly? Showing your true colors as a pathetic excuse for an Alpha who has to chain up women to feel powerful?"

My wrists throb where the chains bite into them, but I force myself to sit straighter on the bed I'm tied to, refusing to cower. He had taken my bag and my phone and left me useless.

"Don't feel bad. You were running that bar into the ground. Omegas like you can't run businesses; you have better things to do serving your Alphas. So, I'm doing you a favor, even if you don't see it right now."

"Running it into the ground?" A harsh laugh escapes me. "I guess that must really burn you up inside, watching an Omega succeed where you failed. How many businesses are you running right now? None! Or do you just hate Omegas because you can't find any to love the monster you are?"

"Shut the fuck up," he snaps. "You don't know anything." His smirk falters for just a second, and I press harder.

"What would your stepfather say if he could see you now? Kidnapping women because you can't handle—"

The back of his hand connects with my face, snapping my head to the side. A metallic taste of blood fills my mouth, and I whimper as it feels like my head's cracking. Fuck, that hurt so bad.

"The police will come for you when they find out." My thoughts fly to the three Alphas who have broken me, yet they never leave my thoughts. I want to believe they might come for me. Except, who am I kidding?

He chuckles like a lunatic. "You think anyone will believe you? Besides, you have no Alphas at your side, and this is just a little insurance to ensure those fucking pricks don't stick their nose around you until after Christmas Eve. Then, Ruby, I recommend you go to them, spread your legs, and become their Omega so you don't end up homeless."

I grind my back teeth, never realizing I can hate someone as much as I do him.

"You're even more fucking pathetic than I thought."

"Such language..." He straightens his shoulders. "Here I am caring, even giving you advice because I don't want to see you with nothing. You just need to learn your place, is all. Your Aunt Eve wasn't that much smarter, you know, but saying nice things to people like her can make them think the world of you and add you to their will."

His words stab through me. He played my aunt? She told me he was a decent man who was just lost and needed guidance in this world, but he lied to her the whole time.

My blood runs cold. "Don't you dare talk about her. You're not fit to speak her name, you piece of—"

"Enjoy your time, Ruby," he cuts me off, heading for the door. "Maybe some quiet time will help adjust that attitude of yours."

Then he's gone, and I'm alone in this rundown room with light only from the window across the room.

Outside the door, voices murmur—Marcus and at least one other person.

I yank at the chains again, hissing as they cut deeper into my already raw wrists. Bet Marcus bought these at a garage sale. The room grows darker, and panic claws at my throat. I force it down.

No. No, you don't get to fall apart now, Ruby. Think.

The old bed frame creaks as I flop down onto the mattress, scanning the room for anything useful. The decorative finial on the corner post catches my eye—it's been loose since I got here, wobbling slightly every time I move.

I stretch an arm toward it until my shoulder screams in protest. My fingers brush the cold metal, but it's not quite enough. "Seriously?"

I pull my knees under me, trying for better leverage. The mattress groans, and I freeze, not wanting to make too much noise and get Marcus' attention.

This time I manage to grip the metal finial, my fingers curling around it. The thing's cold and rough with rust, but it moves when I twist it.

Nothing happens.

Come on, you son of a bitch. I work it back and forth, ignoring the burning in my muscles.

A sound from outside the room makes me stop breathing. Footsteps? No, just the wind. The house groans around me like it's in pain.

My arms are shaking now, but I keep working on the finial. I think about the bar and how Marcus is probably doing inventory right now on how he will tear it down and destroy all my memories with Aunt Eve.

I put everything into that bar this past year to

make it succeed, and I don't want to lose it. I feel at home there, like Eve is still around.

Pausing, I rest my wobbling arm, then try again. I won't give up.

The finial comes free so suddenly, I almost smack myself in the face with it. I barely catch it before it can clatter to the floor, my heart pounding in the process.

Quickly, I study the lock on the chains. Then I start working the pointed, thin screw attached to the underside of it into the lock. Lily taught me how to break locks after I locked myself out of my bar.

It's all about feeling for the pins, she'd said, demonstrating with a bobby pin. *You need to push them up one at a time until they catch. Like solving a puzzle with your fingers.*

I angle the metal just right, the way she showed me, pressing upward with careful pressure. My fingers work blindly, searching for that telltale resistance that means I've found one. The metal scrapes against metal as I probe deeper. A tiny click sounds, and I smile. One pin down. Now for the others.

Minutes crawl by as I probe the lock, refusing to give up.

Another tiny click and another, the sound almost lost in the howling wind outside. The shackle suddenly springs open.

Yes! Fuck you, Marcus.

Free of the chains, I slide off the bed. The floorboards creak under my feet, and I wince. *Shut up, shut up, shut up.*

A burst of laughter from somewhere in the house makes me jump. Marcus's voice carries through the old walls, something about making a phone call. My stomach churns at his casual tone, as though he's at a business meeting instead of holding someone captive. Bastard's probably calling his investment buddies, planning how to carve up my bar.

I decide to avoid the door and go right for the window. The wind blows louder outside, rattling the windowpanes. Snow swirls beyond the dirty glass, thick enough to obscure anything more than a few feet away.

My fingers trace the window frame, finding a lock similar to the one from my shackles, but one crusted over with years of paint and rust. Throwing something through the glass is out of the question. Might as well ring a dinner bell for everyone downstairs.

So, I lift my finial lockpick and start work. Minutes later, nothing. The lock is worse than I thought; each subtle movement feels like I'm trying to shift concrete rather than metal.

Come on, you rusty piece of—

The lock finally gives out with a grinding sound that seems loud enough to wake the dead. I freeze, holding my breath, but the voices in the house continue their muffled conversation.

My hands shake as I ease the window up, praying

the ancient frame won't squeal. Cold air rushes in, bringing with it stinging pellets of snow. The sloped roof below is covered in at least six inches of white powder, but it looks solid enough. I'm up on the second floor.

I hesitate at first, not wanting to break a leg, but if I do nothing, I lose everything. I swing one leg over the sill, then the other, grateful I'm still wearing my boots.

Easing onto the lower roof that juts out from the room I am in, I find a steady footing, the snow crunching under my feet. The pitch isn't too steep, but one wrong move on this slick surface and I'll make enough noise to bring Marcus running. Or just fall and break my neck, which would probably make his day.

Footsteps outside the room.

My heart stops.

"No, no, no..." I press myself flat against the outside wall near the window, snow coating me, coldness seeping through me. The footsteps pass the door to my room and continue down the hall, but I know my time is running out. They'll check on me soon.

In better weather, it would be an easy climb. In this storm, with numb fingers and shaking legs...

I need to move.

Heart thundering, I grip the window frame with numb fingers as I perch on the narrow ledge near the window. Eight feet below, the lower section of the roof disappears into swirling snow. I lower myself to a sitting position, the rough shingles scraping against my clothes as I scoot toward the edge. My muscles tremble from both cold and fear. A sharp point—a loose nail or broken drainpipe—catches my coat, and I have to pause, barely breathing as I work to free myself without making noise.

I reach back to pull myself free.

The snag in my jacket suddenly releases, and the world tilts as I pitch forward, tumbling onto the snow-covered shingles. My stomach turns as I hit the snowy ground, the air rushing from my lungs, and I taste copper where I've bitten my lip to stay quiet. I lie still, heart pounding so hard, I worry they'll hear it inside, listening for any sign I've been discovered.

Nothing.

Through the swirling snow, I spot the black van at the side of the property. My chest tightens as memories surface of me stuck in a storm up in the mountains—stormy night, my fingers turning blue, the dangerous confusion of hypothermia setting in. The woods in this weather would be certain death. The van might have keys, might be unlocked… I have to try.

I push to my feet, hunching against the bitter wind. Hastily, I round the corner of the house. The snow muffles my footsteps but also hides patches of ice. I'm halfway to the van—

White-hot pain explodes across my scalp as someone grabs my hair, yanking me backward. A cry tears from my throat as I crash to the ground. The cold seeps through my clothes instantly while fury burns in my chest like a living thing. Before I can scramble up, rough hands seize my throat from behind me.

Dominic's training cuts through the panic. I drive my elbow back with everything I have, feeling the satisfying crunch of impact and a pained grunt. My heel comes down hard on a foot, and I wrench away… only to have Marcus appear like a nightmare. The asshole behind me kicks my legs, and I crash face-first into the snow. A scream rips from me.

Fuck. Fuck!

I push up on trembling arms, but Marcus shoves me down again.

"Stay down, bitch," he barks.

I sprawl, rolling onto my back to see both him and his masked thug looming over me like dark giants against the snowy sky.

"Drag her back inside," Marcus spits out. "You're watching her this time. Make sure she stays put."

The man in the balaclava grunts, meaty hand reaching for my throat—

He vanishes backward in a flash. Three familiar shapes materialize from the storm like angels. Dominic and Garrett slam into the huge thug, driving him to the ground. The crack of Knox's fist connecting with Marcus's jaw is loud, and I find Marcus on his knees, getting the beating he fucking deserves.

"You came for me," I whisper, the words catching in my throat as tears freeze on my cheeks.

The massive henchman shoves to get to his feet,

but Dominic's already behind him, locking an arm around his throat.

"You touched her," he growls, voice promising retribution. "Big mistake."

The massive thug thrashes against Dominic's hold, his beefy arms swinging wildly as he tries to break free. His feet kick out, scattering snow, but Garrett is there, slamming fists into him while Dominic's grip tightens around his throat. The thug's face pales, and his movements become sluggish. I don't want to see this, but I can't look away.

The hands that were clawing at Dominic's arms begin to fall away, his legs buckling beneath him. A wet, choking sound escapes from behind the balaclava, and his eyes roll back. Finally, his massive body sags, dead weight in Dominic's arms as consciousness leaves him. He drops him in the snow.

Garrett breaks away the moment the henchman falls, crossing to me in three long strides. His hands are impossibly gentle as they frame my face, brushing away snow and tears I hadn't realized were falling. Those deep eyes scan my face.

"Are you hurt, sweetheart?" His voice breaks. "Fuck, I would die if anything happened to you. Please, Ruby, tell me he didn't hurt you. Tell me we weren't too late."

I shake my head, emotion overwhelming me. The familiar scent of him has my chest aching with how much I've missed them. Even through the memory of betrayal, the fact that they came for me breaks something open inside.

"I'm okay," I manage. "Just cold. So cold."

Dominic drags the unconscious thug inside by the foot while Knox keeps Marcus pinned to the ground, one heavy boot on his chest. Blood runs from Marcus's nose as he whimpers pathetic apologies.

"Shut the fuck up," Knox snarls, pressing down harder. His ice-blue eyes find mine, softening instantly. "I almost died not seeing you these past days, pretty girl."

I'm melting on the inside.

"We're going to make this right." He swallows hard. "You have to let us try. Please."

Dominic returns with rope from inside the house and begins binding Marcus's legs at the ankles, then his wrists, as Knox hauls him up. I stay pressed against Garrett, craving his warmth and protection despite everything. The pain in Dominic's dark eyes is raw as he catches my gaze.

"I'm so sorry, angel," he says softly, moving to my side. "We've been searching everywhere since you disappeared. Going out of our minds." His hand hovers near my cheek but doesn't quite touch it. "We're going to make it right, you'll see. Whatever it takes."

Words fail me as tears sting my eyes. The cold has set my teeth chattering, and Garrett holds me tighter, his chin resting on my head. Knox speaks quietly to Dominic, something about taking care of the backup he called, while Marcus continues to whine.

I still can't believe they found me, that they saved me, that they made that asshole pay.

"We need to leave," Garrett murmurs against my hair. "Get you somewhere warm." He hesitates. "Home, if you'll let us."

I nod. "I'd like that."

They load a bound and sobbing Marcus into the back of the SUV, and Knox returns to me, pulling me into his arms. His scent of chocolate and thunderstorms wraps around me like a blanket.

"You're mine. Ours." He kisses my brow, his lips warm against my cold skin.

"Ours?" I question, glancing at the three of them as the other two approach, their boots crunching in the snow. We're beneath the overhang at the back of the house, sheltered from the worst of the storm, but their breath still comes out in white puffs in the freezing air.

To my shock, all three Alphas sink to their knees in front of me, snow soaking through their jeans. Knox's ice-blue eyes shine with unshed tears while Garrett's hands tremble as he reaches for mine. Dominic's usual stern expression has crumbled into something raw and vulnerable.

"We had every intention of sharing you from the beginning," Garrett starts, his voice rough. "If you'd have all three of us. But we wanted to meet you first, to make sure we connected naturally, without pressure."

"Then we experienced the scent match," Dominic continues, running a hand through his black hair. "That irresistible connection that none of us could walk away from if we tried. You have to understand, Ruby... the moment I caught your scent, my whole world shifted."

Knox squeezes my hand. "We planned to meet you separately because we wanted you to see us in our everyday lives. No fake first-date behavior, no pressure. Just real connections forming naturally at the bar, the brewery, during ski lessons. But we fucked up." His voice cracks. "We took away your right to make that choice for yourself."

"Without you, I'm losing my mind," Garrett confesses, snow melting in his dark hair. "Every time someone orders a drink at the brewery, I turn, expecting to see you. I'll burn down the whole damn world to make this right."

Tears sting my eyes as I look at them—three powerful Alphas on their knees in the snow, their faces etched with regret and longing. Deep inside, past the hurt, I know they're telling the truth. But...

"I'm still pissed at you," I say, my voice wobbling. "Do you know how many people in my life have tried to tell me what an Omega can or can't do? What choices I'm allowed to make?"

"We fucked up," Dominic acknowledges, his dark eyes intense. "What can we do to show you we're sorry?"

I wrap my arms around myself, fighting the urge to fall into their embrace.

"Time," I whisper. "If you're serious about this, about us, you'll be patient. Maybe we can try normal dates again, start over..."

"Yes," they say in unison, hope blooming on their faces.

"Whatever you want," Dominic adds, then exchanges loaded glances with the others. "We'll take all the time you need, except for one thing..."

My heart stutters as they look at each other, then back to me.

"We don't have anything to give you right now," Knox says softly.

"But..." Garrett continues.

"Will you marry us?" they ask together.

I stare at them, wild snowflakes catching in my eyelashes, my heart threatening to burst from my chest. Three pairs of eyes—ice blue, forest green, and dark brown—watch me with such naked hope and love, it steals my breath away.

"Why are you saying this?" I choke out, my throat thickening as tears blur my vision. "I wanted you to suffer a bit longer, and then you say that?" I shake my head, but something in their intense gazes makes my heart stutter. Deep down, I suspect I know why.

Garrett rises to his feet, snow falling from his knees. The others do the same.

"We know the truth about your aunt's will, and

fuck if we're going to let Marcus take your bar. We'll marry you, gorgeous, and if you don't want us, we'll step aside and take nothing from you. We have everything we could want... money, success, except for one thing... an Omega to love."

"You're everything to us," Knox adds, his voice raw. "These past days without you, not knowing if you were safe, were torture."

Dominic steps closer, his presence achingly tender. "We'll spend our lives protecting you, cherishing you, if you'll let us."

I cover my face with my hands as tears spill freely, my chest tightening. This is crazy; this whole situation is insane. It's like a wild dream where everything I've wanted comes true in the most chaotic way possible. Part of me worries it's too fast, too soon, but another part knows with bone-deep certainty that this is it. And after what Marcus just tried... I can't let him win. Not when I have three days left...

They surround me, strong arms enveloping me in warmth and familiar scents. Suddenly, I'm off my feet, cradled against Dominic's chest.

"Okay, let's get you somewhere warm," he murmurs in my ear.

In the SUV, Marcus whimpers from where they've shoved him between the door and back seats, begging to be released. Dominic glances back.

"Oh, we're dropping you with your father. He wants to see you... knows everything you've been up to." His smile is all teeth. "And just so you know, you come anywhere near any of us, especially Ruby, and I will break a bone in your body every fucking time, starting with your neck. Thank your stars we didn't bury you out in the woods today. But there's always another day if you cross our paths again."

The silence is beautiful.

I'm nestled between Dominic and Garrett while Knox drives, his ice-blue eyes finding mine in the rearview mirror with soft smiles that have my heart flipping. It feels surreal—the warmth of their bodies, the gentle way they touch me as if I might disappear if they let go. After everything that's happened, I should be more scared, more uncertain. Instead, I feel... home.

They pause in front of a massive business building, Knox and Dominic dragging Marcus inside.

"What's going to happen to him?" I ask Garrett.

"Something bad, hopefully."

"Really horrible," I add, and we both laugh. He pulls me close, nuzzling my neck. "Just so you know, we're never letting you out of our sight. Every day, we'll be at your bar until you're ready to have us... to live with us."

I blink at the speed of it all, even though it feels right. "Three homes, three Alphas... what is this, some kind of rotation schedule?" I tease.

Garrett chuckles, cupping my face.

"Our biggest regret is ever hurting you. We're going

to spend the rest of our lives making it up to you. You know that, right?"

Tears well up again—will they ever stop? "I'll hold you to it."

After a solid fifteen minutes, the others return, and Knox is laughing as we pull away.

Knox

Marcus stumbles between Dominic and I as we drag him into the building. The lobby security guard barely glances up – one look at us hauling in Marcus probably tells him all he needs to know.

"I called Sterling earlier that we're coming to see him," I explain, and the guard nods, passing us through security.

"Come on, guys," Marcus tries, his voice taking on an oily tone. "We can work something out. Name your price. Everyone has one."

Dominic shoves him into the elevator, slamming him against the back wall. "Stop talking, dickhead."

"I've got friends in high places," Marcus continues, apparently too stupid to shut up. "You have no idea who you're dealing with—"

"No," I cut in. "You have no idea who you're dealing with." I lean in close. "The only reason you're still breathing is because we thought your stepfather, Sterling, might want a word first."

He swallows hard, glaring at me.

The elevator doors open to the executive floor, and Marcus suddenly straightens up, plastering on a smile for the receptionist. "Call security!" he shouts. "These men are—"

Sterling emerges from his office as we drag him out of the elevator, and Marcus's face goes pale. "Dad! They attacked me! They're going to—"

"Shut the fuck up," Sterling snaps, his voice like ice. "Bring him to my office."

We do just that and practically throw him into one of the chairs facing Sterling's desk. Sterling radiates authority from behind his massive desk.

"What happened?" His eyes are cold as he looks between us.

Dominic steps forward. "Your stepson here kidnapped our Omega, Ruby Winters. Threatened her and us to try to ensure he took her bar in her aunt's will. The fucker's lucky we didn't throw him off a bridge."

Sterling's hands curl into fists on his desk. A vein pulses in his temple, and his jaw clenches. "Marcus," he snarls. "I've had enough of your childish bullshit. Your greed. Your entitlement. This is the last fucking straw."

"What do you mean?" Marcus's voice cracks. "Do you believe their lies?"

"You're done. Disinherited. I'm cutting you off completely. If you want money, you can apply for a job like everyone else. Maybe we'll have an opening in the mailroom."

Marcus leaps to his feet. "You can't do that! This is my family too! I've worked hard! You promised Mom—"

"Sit. Down." Sterling's tone could freeze hell. "Your mother would be ashamed of what you've become."

I can't help but smirk as Marcus collapses back into the chair. Beside me, Dominic's practically vibrating with what I can only imagine is his own discipline.

"Please," Marcus whimpers. "I can explain everything. It's all just a misunderstanding—"

"The only misunderstanding," Sterling cuts in. "Was me thinking you could ever be trusted with any real responsibility."

Sterling gives us a look and his chin points to the door. Our time to exit. We leave Marcus blubbering in Sterling's office.

In the elevator, Dominic rolls his shoulders. "Would've felt better to knock him out a few more times."

"True." I laugh. "But watching Sterling destroy him was pretty satisfying."

The elevator descends in silence for a moment. "You know, I still can't believe we got so lucky with Ruby," he says.

"I know what you mean." I lean against the wall,

thinking of her. "I adore everything damn thing about her. I never thought I'd feel so deeply for someone."

A rare smile crosses his face. "Never meet an Omega I wanted to simultaneously protect and push up against a wall. She has me twisted up so fucking tight, my chest tight, that I can't imagine her not in my life."

"She makes everything feel... more," I say, struggling to put it into words. "More intense. More real. More worth fighting for."

"She's ours," Dominic growls, and I hear the possession in his voice that matches what I'm feeling. "And anyone who tries to hurt her again..."

"Won't live to regret it," I finish, and we share a look of perfect understanding.

Ruby

I'm fidgeting in the back seat of Knox's SUV when I finally spot them emerging from the building. My heart does this stupid little flip — even after everything that's happened, just the sight of them makes me feel safer. Stronger.

Knox opens my door first, and before I can ask what happened, he's cupping my face in his hands. His kiss is gentle but possessive, and I melt into it, breathing in that addictive scent of chocolate and snow.

"Everything's taken care of, sweetheart," he murmurs against my lips.

Dominic appears next, nudging his way to replace Knox, his dark eyes intense as he lifts my face toward him. His kiss is harder, more demanding, and I moan against him. "No one's going to threaten what's ours ever again," he growls softly.

"That prick Marcus was just disowned by his step-father. Everything taken from him, leaving him penni-less..." Knox explains.

My jaw drops. "After all those times he told me I'd end up with nothing, homeless..." I let out a whoop that makes them all laugh. "You have no idea how happy it makes me to hear he's going to suffer. And I have you three to thank."

"Just the beginning of everything we'll do to ensure you always smile," Knox promises, climbing into the driver's seat, his eyes meeting mine in the mirror with such tenderness it makes my chest ache.

And somehow, despite everything, I believe him. Believe in them. In us.

23

The SUV pulls up in front of the Marriage Registry Office, its imposing stone facade dusted with fresh snow. Warm light spills from a few windows despite the late hour, making the snowflakes dance like falling stars. My stomach does a nervous flip when I realize this isn't the route to my house.

"What are we doing here?"

Knox's blue eyes catch mine in the mirror, a hint of mischief in them.

Dominic takes my hand in his. "Called in a favor while we were dropping off Marcus." He winks, and my insides do that melty thing that I'm still mad about. "If you agree, we want to marry you this evening. Get the paperwork filed immediately since you only have three days. My lawyer's meeting us with the will documentation, too."

"We aren't taking any chances," Garrett says, his hand warm on my thigh.

That touch sends heat spiraling through me, and I shift in my seat, earning devious looks from all three Alphas. Damn them.

"But... how does this even work?" I gesture between the four of us, trying to ignore how good they smell, how right it feels to be surrounded by them. "I mean, legally?"

Knox turns in his seat, those ice-blue eyes dancing. "There are special provisions in Alpha-Omega law for multiple marriages. Specific circumstances where up to five Alphas can marry a single Omega."

"Like what?" I ask, genuinely curious despite myself.

"Scent compatibility is the big one," Garrett explains, his thumb making distracting circles on my thigh. "When multiple Alphas experience an irreversible scent match with the same Omega, it's considered a biological imperative."

"Plus, business entanglements," Dominic adds. "When multiple Alphas' businesses are interconnected with an Omega's establishment. The law recognizes the practical need for legal protection of all parties."

"Our lawyer helped establish our case," Knox continues. "None of us could bear the thought of only one getting to call you wife." His voice drops lower, making me shiver with excitement. "We all want our mark on you, our name with yours."

I'm blushing furiously, but remind them, "You three still have a lot of making up to do."

They're all watching me with such intensity, my skin tingles.

"You're gorgeous when you smile," Garrett murmurs, tucking a strand of hair behind my ear.

"Yeah, well, I'm still angry at you three," I say, trying to sound stern.

"And you should be," Knox admits, looking appropriately contrite.

"But maybe for today only, give us leniency if we're going to marry," Dominic suggests.

I burst out laughing, the sound filling the car with warmth. They join me, knowing it's crazy, yet I love the idea.

My heart's racing as I look at these three incredible men who've turned my world upside down. I'm still mad, still hurt, but watching the snow fall around us, feeling their love and protection wrap around me like a blanket, I can't help but think that sometimes the craziest decisions are the right ones.

"Well?" Garrett prompts softly. "Ready to become Mrs. Reynolds-Anderson-Chase?"

"That's quite a mouthful," I tease, but my voice catches as three pairs of eyes fix on me with such heated intensity, I forget how to breathe.

"Just the beginning of what we'll give you," Knox purrs, and suddenly, the car feels very, very warm.

Right. Wedding first. Then, I can figure out how to

stay mad at them while also knowing my heat is bubbling just below the surface. Being an Omega is complicated.

My heart thunders as I stand just outside the doors of the Bridal Ceremony hall, barely able to believe this is happening. An hour ago, Lily and Hannah had swept in like whirlwinds with Ash in tow, armed with a dress, makeup, and determined expressions.

The dress they brought is perfect—a pearlescent white silk that flows like water, hugging my curves before falling in a gentle sweep to my knees. Delicate beading catches the light across the straight neckline and cap sleeves. My hair is swept up in a twist, courtesy of Lily's skilled hands, with soft tendrils framing my face. The overall effect is bridal without being overtly a wedding dress.

"Ready?" Lily squeezes my hand, her eyes bright with happy tears. "You look so beautiful."

I take a deep breath, my eyes already stinging. "I can't believe I'm getting married. Hours ago, I was escaping through a window."

Hannah laughs softly. "And now you're marrying three of the hottest Alphas in town. Life's funny that way."

My stomach is swarming with butterflies.

The doors open, and my breath catches. The room feels surreal in the evening light, snow falling softly outside tall windows. My Alphas... dear God. They're standing at the front in borrowed registry suits, and the sight of them steals what's left of my composure.

Knox's ice-blue eyes lock onto mine, his normally casual demeanor transformed into something powerful in the black suit. Garrett's gentle smile has an edge of possession that has me grinning at his wickedness. And Dominic... the dangerous grace I've always sensed in him is on full display, dark eyes burning as they track my every move.

My feet carry me forward. Here I was worried about telling them how I felt about each of them, and the whole time, they had intended to share me. I shouldn't be thinking about how this will work in the bedroom—I'm still mad at them. But with studying them watching me, it's hard to hold on to that anger. Especially when I know why we're rushing this ceremony.

It's to help me with the will.

The lawyer's addition to the marriage contract sealed it for me—if we split, I keep my bar completely and get half of their combined assets, while they can't touch what's mine. It wasn't about money for them. It was never about anything but me.

When I reach them, they arrange themselves around me—Garrett and Knox on either side of me, Dominic creating a protective semicircle by standing behind me. Their scents wrap around me like a shield, making me feel safer than I ever have.

"Dearly beloved," the officiant begins, but I barely hear the words. I'm too caught up in the intensity radiating from my Alphas, the way they keep touching me—Garrett's hand on my lower back, Knox's fingers brushing my shoulder, Dominic's breath warm against my neck.

A tear escapes, and Knox catches it with his thumb. They hold me closer, and I know with absolute certainty that I'll never forget this moment. As magical and rushed as it is, it's perfect in its own way.

The officiant's voice breaks through my haze.

"Do you, Ruby Winters, take these three Alphas as your lawfully wedded husbands?"

"I do," I manage, despite my cracking voice filled with emotion.

Their individual *I dos* purr through me.

We sign the papers—me first, then my Alphas, then our friends as witnesses. The lawyer adds his official seal, making everything legal and binding. And just like that, I'm married. To three men. Who are now kissing me one by one—Garrett soft and sweet, Knox passionate and claiming, Dominic deep and possessive. And I kept my bar...

My fingers drift to the snowflake pendant at my throat, and I send a silent thank you to Aunt Eve. I'd cursed that crazy marriage clause in her will, hating how it tried to control my life, but without it, I might never have found my three heroes. Maybe she knew something I didn't all along.

"Tomorrow, we're getting you proper rings," Dominic murmurs against my temple.

"We're doing everything backward," I laugh through my tears.

"Been backward since the start," Knox grins. "Why change now?"

Our friends surround us with hugs and congratulations. Lily and Hannah are both crying, too, squeezing me tight and declaring it was meant to be.

Ash pulls me into a bear hug. "About damn time. Though I gotta ask... taking time off for a honeymoon?"

I shake my head, still dazed. "This is so sudden... I just want to focus on now." I hug him back, so blessed by the friends I have around me.

Before long, the celebration moves to Lily and Hannah's bakery, transformed into an intimate reception space with short notice. Soft music plays while fairy lights twinkle overhead. They've somehow produced a gorgeous three-tiered cake decorated with fresh flowers and silver ribbons.

"I can't believe I have three husbands," I say for probably the hundredth time, making everyone laugh as we gather around the cake.

"So... sleeping arrangements?" Lily wiggles her eyebrows. "Because, honey, I've seen your bed. Not exactly built for four."

"Lily!" I feel my face flame, suddenly very aware that I haven't actually thought about the logistics.

"Don't worry, we have it covered," Dominic says with a smirk that leaves me simultaneously nervous and excited.

"We do?" I ask, earning chuckles from all three of them.

Garrett pulls me close, his lips brushing my ear. "Angel, you're not spending our wedding night alone. Especially not this close to your heat."

I try to hide my blush as everyone pretends they didn't hear that very personal observation, but it's impossible when my Alphas are looking at me like they want to devour me whole.

"Anyway," I say loudly, making everyone smirk. Garrett just hugs me tighter, dropping a kiss on my head.

The party is perfect, filled with laughter and so much love, I'm about to burst. By the time we're ready to leave, I'm floating on a cloud of happiness and cake. Then it hits me—a wave of heat so intense, my knees nearly buckle. I fall into Knox's arms, and he's got me in his arms instantly. Slick floods my panties, and my core clenches with sudden, desperate need.

Oh fuck. My heat's here, and it's hit like a freight train.

All three Alphas freeze, their nostrils flaring as they catch my scent. Their eyes darken with synchronized hunger that makes me whimper.

"My place," Dominic says, his voice a low growl. "I definitely have the biggest bed."

"Always bragging about size, aren't you? We'll see!" Knox smirks. But the heated looks all three Alphas give me suggest Knox isn't just teasing about the bed dimensions.

Knox leans in close, his breath hot against my ear. "Ready to be fucked by three Alphas, pretty girl?"

The possessive promise in his voice has me shuddering. This night is about to get very, very interesting.

"You can put me down... I have legs," I manage to say as Dominic carries me from the back seat of Knox's SUV, but even I can hear how breathless my voice sounds. Warmth floods through me, a tightening deep in my gut following close after, and my fingers clutch at Dominic's shirt. My whole body feels like it's humming, every nerve ending buzzing. "Oh God, what's happening to me? Is it meant to feel like this?"

Dominic's dark eyes lock onto mine, filled with an intensity that makes my breath catch. "Your body knows what it needs," he murmurs, and the growl in his voice sends shivers down my spine. "And we're going to give it to you. All of it."

"It's calling to your Alphas," Garrett adds softly, his hand finding mine. "We're right here for you, angel." His thumb traces circles on my palm, and even that small touch feels electric. "You're so perfect like this, all flushed and needy for us."

Knox appears beside us, brushing my hair back from my forehead. I reach for him, drawing him closer until our lips crash together. The contact sends sparks through my entire body, and I moan into his mouth. He tastes like winter nights and sex, and I crave more, more, more.

"Look at how responsive she is already," Knox breathes against my lips. "So beautiful. So ours."

"Okay, we need to get inside, or I doubt my neighbors are going to be happy with the scene about to play out," Dominic mutters. At the door, he transfers me to Knox's arms, and I immediately curl into his chest, seeking his familiar scent of chocolate and snow.

"Can't get enough of your smell," Knox murmurs into my hair, followed by a deep inhale. "It's driving me insane."

"Garrett," I call out, reaching for him. My head is spinning with their heady scents. The rational part of my brain is trying to process how fast this is all happening, but my body is ten steps ahead, craving their touch like oxygen. "I have no idea how we're going to do this, but I need all of you... please. The pain..."

"We've got you, sweetheart," Garrett soothes, catching my outstretched hand and pressing a kiss to my palm. "Going to take such good care of you, make you feel so good you forget everything but us."

Through the haze, I try to hold on to some rational thoughts. We just got married. This is happening so fast. But when I look at each of them—Dominic with his brooding stare, Knox with his wild stare, Garrett with his possessiveness—my heart threatens to burst. They're my world now, all three of them. A month ago, I was alone in my apartment above the bar, and now, I have three husbands who look at me as if I'm everything they've ever desired.

Somewhere in the back of my mind, I hear Mom's voice. *"You'll see…"*

I push that thought away. These men aren't anything like my father. They're protective, they care for me, and even… love me. I believe that deep in my soul. I see it in how carefully Knox holds me, how tenderly Dominic strokes my hair, how softly Garrett whispers endearments.

"Going to worship every inch of you," Dominic promises, his voice dark with need, then he moves to unlock the front door.

Garrett's in my ear, too, whispering, "We're going to mark you up so everyone knows you're ours."

His voice and his words leave me giddy.

The house blurs past as Knox carries me inside; all I catch are glimpses of soaring ceilings, leather furniture, and enormous windows. A massive Christmas tree sparkles in the corner, green branches laden with twinkling lights and ornaments. Everything screams bachelor pad meets luxury, but I barely process it as another wave of need crashes through me.

"Please," I whimper. Everything feels too hot, too sensitive. My skin is crying out for their touch, and every inch of me is dying to submit, to let them take care of me.

They bring me to a huge bedroom with the biggest bed I've ever seen, with dark sheets and puffy pillows. When Knox sets me on the mattress, I cry out at the loss of contact.

I sit up on the bed, reaching for them.

They're all there instantly, surrounding me, their scents mixing together—cedar and smoke, chocolate and snow, hops and leather. Hands stroke my body, my hair, my face, and I arch into their touch, a purr grazing my throat.

"Look how desperate she is for us," Knox groans. "Been waiting so long to have you like this, baby."

"Don't worry, angel," Garrett soothes, pressing a kiss to my lips. His fingers thread through my hair, tugging gently in a way that makes me gasp. "We're going to keep you safe. Take away the pain. Though you should know... this could last a week."

"A week?" I gasp, my eyes going wide. Nobody told me that part. A week of this burning need, this desperate hunger? "I don't think I can—"

"You can," Dominic cuts in. "And you will. Because we're going to be right here, fucking you, licking you, giving you everything you need." His hand cups my face, his thumb brushing across my bottom lip. "Going to make you scream for us, little Omega. Make you ours in every way possible."

My world narrows to the overwhelming sensations curling between my thighs, but no matter how much I squeeze them, it doesn't alleviate the desire.

"You're trembling for us, sweetheart," Garrett murmurs against my neck, kneeling on the bed to get closer to me, his breath hot against my skin.

I try to form words, but another wave of heat rolls through me, stronger than before. My fingers clutch at Knox's shirt, pulling him closer, while my other hand is on Dominic, tugging at his belt. "It's too much," I manage to gasp. "I've never... I can't..."

"Shhh," Dominic soothes, brushing my hair from my face. His touch is gentle, but I can feel the restraint in his movements. "We know it's overwhelming. First heats always are. But we've got you."

Knox's hand finds mine, squeezing gently. "You're doing so well, Ruby. So perfect for us."

My skin tingles wherever they touch, the heat under my skin building to an almost unbearable level.

Knox's hands cup my face, his eyes searching mine.

Dominic's fingers trace along my collarbone, leaving trails of fire in their wake.

The rational part of my brain is still trying to process it all—three Alphas, all mine, all wanting me at once. And I love it so much! My instincts are reveling in their attention, their touch, the way they stare at me like savages desperate to fuck me, to knot me.

"I need you," I whimper, past caring how desperate I sound. "Please…"

Turning my head, I seek Knox's kiss, and he obliges immediately. His lips are soft but demanding, and I melt into them. His grip finds my hips, fingers digging into me, showing me just how much he's barely holding on. The other two have their hands all over me, tugging at my clothes.

The zipper at my back slides down, and my dress slips from my shoulders. I shiver despite the warmth flooding through me. Three sets of eyes darken at once, and the possessive growls that fill the room leave me purring with satisfaction.

"Beautiful," Knox breathes against my neck. "Our beautiful Omega."

My fingers tremble as I reach for Knox's shirt buttons, pulling at them hard, needing it off. "I can't wait," I whisper.

They're my Alphas. My mates. My everything.

In moments, they tug the dress down my body and off me, leaving me in my white thong. Garrett is already taking off my heels.

"Gorgeous," I hear Dominic murmur, his gaze traveling down my body and back up, pausing on my breasts.

"Fuck me!" Knox licks his lips.

"Are you wet for us?" Garrett asks, his gaze

narrowing in on my thong. "Do we make your little cunt drenched?"

Those words leave me undone as I watch my Alphas turn into savages for me, hungry for sex. I'm breathing heavily, my chest heaving, nipples so tight, I might explode when one of them touches me.

"Only one way to find out," I tease and lean back on my elbows.

Dominic throws himself at me first, fingers curling into the elastic of my thong, and he drags it down over my hips. I lift them off the bed, and he tugs my panties all the way down. His gaze settles on the fire between my legs as though he's about to lose himself.

I keep my thighs clenched tight, and I feel my pussy swelling, growing uncontrollably wet.

As if they read my mind, the three of them strip, yanking their shirts off and tossing them aside. My gaze drops to their abs, their chests, and my body's heating up worse. Shoes off, they unbuckle their belts and unzip their pants. I lean forward, desperate to see everything they're packing.

Nibbling on my lower lip, I take it all in, knowing I must be the luckiest girl in the entire world to have these three hunks all to myself.

Three cocks and I'm gasping for air.

They're all huge, long, and their girth... I swallow hard, unsure how they're going to fit inside me.

Their tips are glistening with their precum, and I notice they each have the bulbous knot at the base of their shaft just above their balls like all Alphas do. The one that enlarges once they're inside an Omega, locking us together. I may not be experienced with an Alpha because my first time was with a Beta male, but I know how Alphas work.

And right now, I'm being spoiled for choice, and one thing they all have in common is their damn size. Naked, erections so stiff and standing upward... I'm struggling not to gawk, especially when they're all built like tanks, muscles everywhere.

"Ruby," Dominic growls. "Show us. Let us see your beautiful little pussy."

I'm shivering, breathing faster, but he's there, tender hands on my knees, and he pushes them open wider. I let them fall apart, a mewling sound in my throat to offer myself to them all.

All three men hover closer to the end of the bed, their gaze sliding down my thighs to where I feel my pussy fluttering with arousal.

"She needs to be licked and fucked," Knox murmurs, leaning a bent knee on the bed while Dominic and Garrett do the same. "Spread wider for us. Do it," he orders.

There's no hesitation as I spread for them, giving them what they crave—me.

I'm shaking, feeling partly vulnerable but so fucking sexy.

"Beautiful. I knew you'd made me addicted to you," Dominic rasps.

Garrett strokes his fingers up my leg, staring at me with sexy eyes.

Knox reaches over, his calloused fingers pushing between my swollen lips, tracing from my clit to my entrance.

I moan out loud, my chest sticking out, breasts bouncing, desperate for them. He's using two fingers to spread my lips wider while I'm writhing, clinging to his every touch.

"Look at that sweet hole," Knox says.

Dominic reaches over as well and pushes two fat fingers into me.

I scream out, the sensation of him inside me driving me insane. It's intense, more sensitive than previous times I've been fingered.

"She's so ready. Look how her sweet cunt sucks down on my fingers." He pushes a third one into me, and I gasp for air, my hips rocking. "How many fingers do you think I can get inside you, sweetheart?"

"Fuck, I love seeing her stretched," Garrett groans.

Knox is palming his cock. "She might beg us for two cocks in that little hole."

My breaths are coming so fast, but my eyes are widening. "Wait, two? No, that's too—"

I'm moaning again as Dominic pumps those three fingers into me faster, harder, my whole body rocking. I'm gushing, growing wetter, my body arching as I collapse back on the bed, my legs splayed wider.

"And that tight little puckered ass," Garrett

mutters, staring at me wickedly. "I want to fuck that tight, pretty hole."

"Are you going to just talk about it?"

Dominic pulls out, and I groan in protest, staring up at them.

"She's ready, but first, I need a taste," he says. He leans in with his whole body, then his mouth is on my pussy, and I cry out. He takes long strokes along my full length before flicking my clit, which tingles with uncontrollable sensitivity.

"Yes, I'm ready."

Knox and Garrett laugh as they move to either side of the bed, kneeling on the mattress. They each take a breast, sucking down hard on my nipple, flicking and nibbling it, then pulling it.

I thrash beneath them as all three devour me, and the pain from my heat begins to fade into ultimate pleasure. To have three mouths on my body is euphoric. I never imagined it could feel so good. Dominic's tongue keeps dragging over my clit, the friction building and tightening at my core.

He suddenly draws back, and the other two do the same. I'm lying on my back between them, wide and purring for more. My hands reach for them as Dominic shuffles closer, his hands sliding under my ass, dragging me closer to him. Next thing I know, I feel him pushing his massive cock into me, his girth inching in deeper, stretching me.

I fist the sheets, wriggling for more as Knox and Garrett watch me getting fucked.

"Take a deep breath," Dominic tells me, and the moment I do, he rams into me. The pain is sudden, but so is the glorious build-up. I yell out, tears in my eyes from both the savagery of his fucking, his hips punching into me, and from the euphoria of how incredible it feels to have him ram into me. He's rough, and part of me knew he would be.

The other two are gripping their cocks, watching me being ravaged, rocking on the bed, breasts jiggling with each deep plunge that feels like Dominic might split me down the middle.

My clit throbs, every inch of me clenching.

I reach out for my other two husbands' cocks, wrapping them in my hand and tugging on them. They are kneeling on either side of me, grunting, and there's something so perfect, so primal in being taken by Alphas. They're animals, taking what they want, but it tells me that Omegas are made to handle them. My body buzzing for more because I never want to stop experiencing this sensation.

We're in sync, and it doesn't take long for Dominic to have his fingers on my clit, pinching and squeezing. His touch sets me off, and I shudder with the orgasm that tears me apart. Every inch of me tightens, but Dominic never eases.

The two cocks in my hands throb, and in seconds, they're spurting out ribbons of white cum all over me

—my breasts, my stomach, my neck, and my face. And God, there's so much of it everywhere.

Crying out from each slap deep inside me, Dominic pauses and grips my hips, then he's pushing in deeper, and it's so large…

I squirm.

"Just lay still, beautiful," he tells me. "Getting my knot into you will take a bit, but you're so wet, so greedy for me, aren't you?"

"Fuck, she is," Knox answers, pumping his last drops into me.

Garrett finishes off as well, then heads out of the room, returning seconds later with towels… lots of them. He tosses one to Knox, then uses another to wipe me down, cleaning me, which I love. That smile of his melts me.

But I might be losing my grip on control as the stretching sensation between my thighs brings me unbelievable arousal, alongside the heavy pressure of Dominic pushing himself in there… He glances up, smirking, while I pant for breath.

"You've taken me so well, opened up… Oh, Ruby, you have no idea how fucking sexy you look taking all of me."

All three are looking between my thighs, Garrett and Knox stroking their still-hard cocks.

"Look at that sweet, stretched pussy," Knox murmurs, practically drooling.

Before I can find my voice, Dominic is sliding his

hands under my thighs, lifting me slightly off the bed and working in and out of me, not as much as before, but enough to go deeper. Fuck, I feel him all the way in there, so thick, filling me completely. He growls, his eyes rolling up.

"When I come, I'm going to knot so hard in your pussy. I'll fill you with my cum," he tells me, smiling like he's been waiting for this moment. He's practically howling, his grip hardening as he shoves into me harder, our bodies slapping together.

"That's so fucking sexy!" Garrett snarls.

My body welcomes Dominic, and the stretch brings arousal more than pain now.

Moments later, Knox is at my side, his cock bopping toward my mouth.

"Open up, gorgeous," he instructs as he practically pushes himself past my lips. I taste the saltiness of his cum, and I greedily suck down on him, my body jerking in movement.

Garrett rolls onto his back on the bed next to me, glancing at me with a devious smirk. Before I know what's going on, Knox's cock pops out of my mouth as he and Dominic lift me, quickly placing me to lie down on top of Garrett, my back against his chest, his huge cock cradled between my ass cheeks.

The tempo of their movement escalates, as if they've talked about how they're going to all fuck me at the same time.

Before I can ask, Knox has his cock in my face, and I turn my head, hungrily taking it into my mouth.

Garrett's breath is in my ears. "I'm going to be gentle at first, angel. Are you ready for me to fuck your ass?"

I hum my response, giving my approval.

His fingers slide over my rear while Dominic lifts my legs to make it easier for him. In seconds, the hard pressure of his cock is teasing into my rear. I gasp for air, unsure if I can do this.

"You're so fucking beautiful," Garrett whispers as I suck down hard on Knox, all while Dominic pinches my clit. Garrett pushes a finger into me first, which feels strange, but as he works in and out of me, there's an unexpected arousal that tingles through me. The fact I'm so drenched offers plenty of lubricant, so the pain is the pressure of being claimed. I rock against his finger, which in moments, he replaces with his cock. He slips in the tip, and I'm sweating by now, gasping for air.

These men are not going to release me, and I don't want them to, not when my insides are on fire, and only their touch, their erections, can calm the flames.

"You're doing so well," Garrett murmurs in my ear as he pushes deeper into me.

I groan, that sensation unexpectedly having me shaking from another climax rushing forward. I never expected to be so turned on, but I'm at their mercy.

He's deep in me, and I feel all three buried in me, owning me, claiming me as theirs.

"You're so stunning, filled with our cocks," Knox says breathlessly, reaching over and pinching my nipple. Garrett has his arms on my hips, guiding me.

"How does it feel to have my fat cock deep in your ass?" he asks.

"And my massive cock in your tight pussy?" Dominic adds.

"You suck down on my dick so well," Knox adds.

I writhe and moan my approval, my pleasure.

"I know we're still getting to know each other, and so much has happened quickly," Dominic begins. "But I love you so fucking much, it hurts."

"Since that first night at the festival," Garrett breathes against my skin. "Love everything about you, Ruby."

"Our perfect Omega," Knox growls softly, his hand on my jaw, guiding me to take his cock deeper. "Love you so damn much, angel."

I can only manage a deep moan in response, tears pricking my eyes at the depth of emotion in their voices. My heart is screaming what my mouth can't say... I love you, I love you, I love you.

Then they start to really fuck me, to show me what it means to be truly claimed by three Alphas and loved by them.

EPILOGUE 2
RUBY

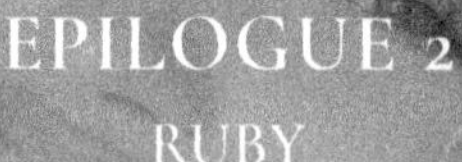

Three Weeks Later

I can't stop staring at Dominic's house from the front yard. No, *our* house—at least it is temporarily. The morning sun catches the enormous windows, making the modern mansion gleam like something out of an architectural magazine. Eight bedrooms, he'd said casually, like having a house bigger than some hotels was perfectly normal. The sweeping driveway curves past manicured gardens, leading to what has to be at least a four-car garage, and it's just as stunning as I remember it the first time I was here. The whole place screams *successful bachelor pad* with its clean lines and industrial-meets-luxury vibe.

"You're catching flies," Knox teases, coming up behind me, wrapping his arms around my waist and nuzzling my neck. His touch melts me.

"I still can't believe this is real," I admit, leaning back against his solid chest. "Any of it."

"Better start believing." His lips brush my ear. "Because you're stuck with us now."

The rumble of moving trucks interrupts my response. Two massive vehicles pull up, followed by Garrett's pickup with Dominic in the passenger's seat. My husbands emerge, and my heart flutters harder whenever I see them all together. It reminds me how lucky I am.

Garrett's already rolled up the sleeves of his flannel shirt, showing off that gorgeous brewing process tattoo that I love to trace with my fingers. His dark hair is messier than usual. He's talking animatedly with the movers, probably about carefully transporting his precious work desk he insisted on bringing.

Dominic prowls—there's really no other word for it—toward us, in dark jeans and a black t-shirt that does criminal things to his shoulders... and my insides. His black hair falls in his eyes in that way that has me itching to brush it back.

"Ready?" he asks, his devious gaze warming as they meet mine.

Before I can answer, Knox spins me around and steals a quick kiss that's anything but innocent. When he pulls back, looking entirely too pleased with himself, I hear Garrett's deep chuckle.

"Starting without us?" Garrett calls out, crossing the driveway. "That hardly seems fair."

I duck away before I can get thoroughly distracted by three very handsome, very determined Alphas. "Nope! We have work to do, gentlemen. Kisses later."

"Tease," Dominic mutters, but he's grinning.

The next hour is chaos as movers and my three Alphas begin unloading trucks. I'm directing traffic, trying to remember which boxes go where, when I spot something being carried into the house by a mover that has me pausing. "Is that... a guitar?"

Knox glances up from where he's carrying a box. "Oh yeah, that's mine. I play a little."

"A little?" Garrett snorts, passing by with what looks like part of a bed frame. "He's being modest. Wait till you hear him belt out a tune."

"You never mentioned you were musical," I say, following Knox inside. The foyer opens into that stunning great room with soaring ceilings and a wall of windows overlooking the backyard. A massive stone fireplace dominates one wall, while the open-concept layout flows into a kitchen that would make professional chefs weep.

Knox sets down his box and pulls me behind a massive support column, pressing me against the cool stone. "There's a lot you still don't know about me yet," he murmurs. "That's half the fun when I show you new things about me."

His kiss tastes like fresh rain, and I'm just softening into him when a throat clears nearby.

"If you two are quite finished..." Dominic's voice holds amusement.

I peek around Knox to find him watching us with that intense gaze that makes my knees buckle. "We were just... discussing furniture placement?"

"Is that what they're calling it now?" Garrett appears with another box, his green eyes dancing. "In that case, I need to discuss some placement with you too."

"Later," I promise, ducking away from Knox's grabbing hands. "We'll never get anything done at this rate!"

"That's a sacrifice I'm willing to make," Knox declares solemnly, making me laugh as I escape.

The kitchen isn't just gorgeous—it's a chef's dream with double ovens, a six-burner gas range, and the double door refrigerator that I'm sure costs more than my car. The main living area flows into a formal dining room I can't imagine ever using, and there's an honest-to-god library with built-in shelves waiting to be filled.

"Your office is upstairs," Dominic tells me, catching my hand as I explore. "Next to mine. Knox and Garrett's are on the other side of the house."

"I get an office?" I'm still not used to this—to being so thoroughly cared for, to having husbands who think about these things. It's always just been me on my own since I lost Eve, so this has me close to crying with happiness, my throat tightening in the process.

His expression softens in a way that's only for me. "You get everything." Dominic tugs me closer, one hand sliding into my hair. "Everything I have is yours now."

The kiss is slower than Knox's playful one, deeper, making my toes curl in my boots. Dominic kisses like he does everything else—with an intensity that makes me forget my own name.

"Hey!" Garrett's voice breaks through my daze. "No fair starting without us!"

I pull back, laughing at Dominic's growl of frustration. "Later," I promise again, pressing one more quick kiss to his lips. "Show me this office?"

The stairs curve up to a landing that branches into two wings. Dominic leads me down one hallway, pointing out rooms. "Master suite," he indicates double doors on the right. "Big enough for all of us."

My breath catches at the implications. A shared bedroom is a dream come true. For the past three weeks, I've stayed at their homes, or they came and crashed at mine, though space is super limited there. So to have such a huge bed for us is everything.

"Your office," he continues, opening another door. The room is gorgeous, with more windows overlooking the backyard and built-in desk space. But what catches my eye is the little corner nook with a comfortable reading chair and small table.

"For when you need space," Dominic explains quietly. "We all do sometimes."

The thoughtfulness of it, the way they understand my need for occasional solitude even as we build this life together, makes my throat tighten some more. I turn and wrap my arms around his waist, breathing in that intoxicating scent of his.

"Thank you," I whisper against his chest.

His arms tighten around me. "You are the world to me, Ruby."

I lift my chin, smiling, unable to believe this is happening. How can this be real life? "I love it here. But we should probably head downstairs as the other two will be up here in seconds and then we'll never finish unpacking," I tease, reluctantly pulling away.

"Most definitely they'll find us."

Downstairs, I'm surrounded by boxes, trying to make sense of this massive space. Seriously, who needs this many cabinets?

I've moved all my belongings from my old place, and now my bartender, Ash, has moved in. He insisted he needed to save money to buy his own home some-day, so I offered to let him stay here to help him out. He's always supported me in the bar, been there for me after Aunt Eve passed, so of course I will give him anything he needs if it helps him get ahead. So free rent between friends is the least I can do for him.

And now as I debate where everything should go, Garrett's warm hands settle on my waist.

"You look overwhelmed," he observes, stroking me gently. I lean back against him with a groan as his talented fingers work their way up to my shoulders to a knot.

"Just trying to decide if we really need four different coffee makers," I say, gesturing at the counter where I've lined them up. "I mean, I know we all have different coffee preferences, but this seems excessive."

"Mm, the black one's Dominic's. Touch it and he might actually growl." Garrett's laugh rumbles through his chest against my back. "The silver one's Knox's for his fancy pour-overs. The red one's mine because I like my coffee like I like my beer—strong enough to stand up on its own."

"And this cute little mint green one?" I ask.

"That's yours, sweetheart." He presses a kiss to my temple. "For your hazelnut cream concoctions that Knox insists aren't real coffee. I picked it up for you last week."

My heart soars to hear his thoughtfulness. I am still getting used to the generosity and love from my Alphas.

"Hey, I heard that!" Knox appears in the doorway, carrying another box. His shaggy blonde hair is damp with sweat, making it curl at the ends in a way that's unfairly attractive. "And I stand by it. Coffee should taste like coffee, not dessert."

"Says the man who puts maple syrup in everything," I tease, remembering the breakfast he made us last week.

"Maple syrup is a gift from the gods and I will not apologize for appreciating it," Knox declares, setting down his box and coming over to steal a kiss. He tastes salty from exertion, and I can't help but run my hands over his shoulders, feeling the lean muscle there.

"If you three are done canoodling in my kitchen..." Dominic's deep voice makes us all jump slightly.

"*Our* kitchen," I correct automatically, then freeze when I see his expression. Oh. Oh no. That's his predatory look, the one that usually ends with me breathless and begging. "Dom..."

"Our kitchen," he agrees, stalking closer. Knox and Garrett part slightly, making space for him but not letting me go. I'm surrounded by Alphas, three distinct scents mixing together in a way that makes my head fog up. "And what exactly are you planning to do in *our* kitchen?"

The way his dark eyes narrow tells me I'm not fooling anyone. Then his mouth is on mine, hot and demanding. I whimper as Garrett's lips find my neck, while Knox's hands slide under the hem of my t-shirt, callused fingers tracing up to my bra.

A loud throat-clearing from the doorway makes us all freeze.

"So, uh, where do you want the dining room

boxes?" One of the movers asks, looking anywhere but at us.

My cheeks are on fire as my husbands don't move from my side.

I'll show you," I manage, smoothing down my shirt and attempting to look professional. As I pass Dominic, he catches my hand.

"To be continued," he murmurs, and the promise in his voice makes me shiver with excitement.

An hour later, I'm actually making progress with the kitchen organization when music floats down from upstairs. The gentle strum of acoustic guitar pulls me away from my task, following the sound until I find Knox in what will be our shared living room, perched on a stack of boxes with his guitar in his lap.

He glances up as I enter, those ice-blue eyes melting me. "Taking a break?"

"Couldn't resist investigating the music," I admit, settling cross-legged on the floor near him. "You're really good."

His fingers dance over the strings, picking out a melody I almost recognize. "Used to play in college. Still do sometimes, when I need to think."

"What are you thinking about now?"

His smile turns softer, more intimate. "How lucky I am. How incredible it is that we all found each other. I've lived alone ever since losing my parents, and hated the emptiness of the house. I can't tell you how ready I am to not wake up to a silent home, to finally have a family again." The melody shifts into something sweeter, almost a lullaby, and my heart's aching at his loss, at his agony. I want to wrap him up and make sure he never feels alone again. "I'm also thinking how beautiful you look right now, with sunlight in your hair and that smudge of dust on your nose."

I reach up to rub my nose, feeling myself blush. Knox sets aside his guitar and slides down to join me on the floor, pulling me into his lap.

"You're ridiculous," I tell him, even as I curl into his warmth.

"Maybe." He nuzzles my neck, making me giggle. "But you love it."

"I love you," I correct without thinking, then freeze. We haven't said that yet—any of us—still finding our way through this relationship.

Knox goes very still for a moment, then his arms tighten around me. "Say it again," he whispers against my skin and when I do, he steals a delicious kiss.

Movement in the doorway catches my attention. Garrett and Dominic stand there, watching us. My heart hammers in my chest, but I meet each of their gazes as I say clearly, "I love you. All of you."

Suddenly I'm being passed between them, receiving three very different but equally passionate kisses. Knox's playful and sweet, Garrett's deep and thorough, Dominic's fierce and possessive.

"We love you too," Knox murmurs when they finally let me breathe.

"So much love," Garrett adds.

Dominic doesn't speak, but his kiss to my forehead says everything.

We might have stayed there forever, tangled together in our half-unpacked living room, if someone's stomach hadn't growled loudly. We all look at Knox, who grins sheepishly.

"What? Moving is hungry work!"

"I think there are some snacks in one of the kitchen boxes," I say, extracting myself from their embrace. "And we should probably actually finish unpacking if we want to have that housewarming barbecue tonight."

"Spoilsport," Garrett pouts, but he gets up and offers me a hand.

"The sooner we finish," Dominic points out. "The sooner we can properly break in our new bedroom."

Well. That's certainly motivation to get back to work.

The afternoon sun streams through those massive windows, creating pools of warm light across the hardwood floors as I tackle more boxes. I've just discovered my collection of vintage bar coasters—carefully wrapped by Garrett, if the precise newspaper bundling is any indication—when I hear a low whistle from the hallway.

"Dominic, you've been holding out on us," Knox calls out, excitement clear in his voice. "Ruby! Garrett! You have to see this!"

I follow his voice down a hallway I haven't explored yet, finding him bouncing on his toes outside a set of double doors. Garrett appears from the opposite direction, looking curious.

"What's got you so worked up?" he asks, but Knox just grins and pushes open the doors with a flourish.

Then I see it.

"Holy shit," I breathe.

It's a home theater. Not just a media room with a big TV, but an honest-to-god theater with tiered seating, reclining leather chairs, and a screen that takes up almost a whole wall.

"I take it you approve?" Dominic's amused voice comes from behind us, and I spin to face him.

"You have a movie theater in your house," I say, still trying to process this. "An actual theater."

"Our house," he corrects, echoing my earlier words. "And yes. Though it hasn't gotten much use lately."

"Oh, it's going to get used," Knox declares, already sprawling in one of the recliners. "Movie nights are officially mandatory now."

"After we finish unpacking," Garrett reminds him, yet he's examining the sound system.

I'm still standing in the doorway, shaking my head, when Garrett's arms slide around my waist from behind. "What are you thinking?" he murmurs in my ear.

"That this is insane," I admit. "All of this—the house, the four of us, everything. Sometimes I feel like

I'm going to wake up and it will all have been a dream."

He turns me in his arms, tilting my chin up until I meet his dark gaze. "Not a dream," he says. "Real. We're real." His thumb brushes over my bottom lip. "Should I prove it to you?"

Heat floods my cheeks as Knox whistles. "Get a room, you two!"

"We have several," Dominic points out dryly, but Garrett settles for a kiss that manages to leave me breathless. I wrap myself around him, unable to get close enough. He has a way of making me forget the rest of the world.

It isn't long before we're back to work because we keep seeming to stop to kiss, which shows how obsessed I am with them.

But it's getting darker outside, most of the boxes are unpacked, at least the kitchen ones. And we're holding a housewarming barbecue for only our closest friends today.

"I'll start marinating the steaks," Garrett offers. He's appointed himself head chef for the evening.

"I'll grab the string lights from my truck," Knox says. "This backyard needs some ambiance."

Garrett's heading upstairs, and I follow him to the great room which is starting to look more lived-in now, with photos appearing on walls and personal touches emerging from boxes. I pause at a framed picture of Aunt Eve that someone must have unpacked, touching it gently.

"She'd be happy," Garrett says softly. "Seeing you —seeing us—like this."

"She orchestrated the whole thing with the will and me getting married before Christmas Eve," I reply, thinking of that ridiculous will stipulation that started everything. "Somehow she knew it would turn out perfectly."

"Eve always knew," he agrees, pressing a kiss to my temple.

I watch him go, admiring the way his shoulders fill out his flannel shirt, then catch Dominic smirking at me. "What?"

Knox is suddenly calling us from downstairs to help with the lights. So we're rushing to his aid.

The next hour passes in a blur of activity. Knox and I wrestle with string lights while Garrett and Dominic work their magic in the kitchen. Dominic disappears briefly and returns with patio heaters I didn't even know he owned, positioning them strategically around the massive curved outdoor sectional.

"This backyard is huge," I comment, standing on the deck and surveying the space. It's bigger than my entire apartment, with carefully landscaped beds and what looks like the beginnings of a fire pit area.

"Too much?" Dominic asks quietly, coming to stand beside me.

I lean into him, breathing in that addictive scent of cedar and smoke. "No. Just... different and amazing. I'm used to my tiny balcony with a wobbly chair."

"We'll find our perfect space," he promises. "Something that's ours from the start."

"This is pretty perfect already," I admit.

He makes a noncommittal sound, but I feel him relax.

"Incoming!" Knox calls from above, and I glance up just in time to see him perched precariously on a ladder, attempting to string lights through the pergola.

"Be careful!" I yelp, but he just grins that adrenaline-junkie grin.

"Always am."

"Liar," Garrett calls from the kitchen doorway. "Need I remind you about the skiing incident?"

"That was one time!"

"What skiing incident?" I ask, curious.

"No!" Knox points accusingly at Garrett. "You promised never to tell that story!"

Garrett's green eyes sparkle with mischief. "I promised not to tell it to your clients. Ruby's not a client."

I stare between them, curious to know more. Sometimes I forget they knew each other before me, that they have a history I'm still learning about.

"Tell me?" I ask sweetly, batting my eyelashes at Garrett.

Knox groans. "Oh no, not the eyes. Help!"

But Dominic just smirks. "I'd like to hear this story too, actually."

"Traitors, all of you," Knox grumbles, but he's fighting a smile as he climbs down the ladder.

"Fine. Tell her. But remember, I was clearly stupid back then." Knox gives a dramatic sigh, which has me giggling at him.

"Was?" Dominic mutters.

Garrett leans against the deck railing. "So, this was about five years ago. Knox had just started his company, and he was trying to impress this group of wealthy clients with his skiing expertise."

"I am an expert skier," Knox interjects, his hands absently playing with my hair.

"Shush, you lost story privileges," I tell him, snuggling deeper into his warmth. "Go on, Garrett."

"So there's this really advanced trail—Devil's Drop. It's technically off-limits unless you have special permits and extensive experience. Knox decides he's going to take his clients there, even though there had been reports of unstable conditions."

"In my defense," Knox starts, but we all shush him.

Garrett continues, grinning. "I was doing a delivery to the resort's restaurant that day. I get there just in time to see Knox leading this group, all decked out in their designer ski gear. He's showing off, doing these fancy turns, really playing up the experienced guide angle."

"Oh no," I whisper, already knowing this is going somewhere amazing.

"Oh yes," Garrett's grin widens. "So he's demonstrating this complex maneuver, really getting into it, when suddenly—"

"The snow was loose!" Knox protests.

"—when suddenly his ski catches wrong and he goes flying. But not just any wipeout. He manages to lose both skis, tumble through the air, and land face-first in the only pink-dyed snow on the entire mountain."

"Pink snow?" I ask, twisting to look at Knox's increasingly red face.

"The resort had done this Valentine's Day thing," he mumbles. "With colored snow in certain areas."

"He came up looking like a very angry, very pink snow cone," Garrett wheezes. "And the best part? His clients thought it was part of the show. They started trying to copy him, diving into the pink snow. By the time ski patrol showed up to investigate the unauthorized trail use, there were six people rolling around in pink snow, and Knox looking like a frozen flamingo."

I'm laughing so hard I can barely breathe, and even Dominic is chuckling.

"I still made the sale," Knox points out, but he's laughing too. "They booked a whole week of lessons."

"Because they thought throwing yourself into pink snow was part of the advanced technique!" Garrett wipes tears from his eyes. "The resort had to put up signs specifically stating *No Intentional Snow Diving* after that."

"Though I think I wore pink better than Garrett wore that beer when his first brewing experiment exploded."

"Oh no," Garrett straightens. "That's not the story we're telling today."

"I don't know," Dominic drawls. "I think Ruby would be very interested in hearing about the Great Honey Ale Disaster."

"You know about that?" Garrett looks betrayed.

"I know everything," Dominic says simply, making me shiver in a way that has nothing to do with the evening air.

The doorbell chimes before we can start another story, and Hannah's laugh floats through the house. But as we all move to greet our guests, I file away this moment—this perfect snippet of shared history and teasing affection—in my heart. These are the stories I want to learn, the memories I want to be part of, the life I want to build with them.

"I'll get it," I say, but Knox tugs me back against him.

"Dominic's security system probably already let them in," he mumbles against my hair. He's right—moments later, Lily bursts through the French doors onto the deck, arms laden with what looks like enough baked desserts to feed an army.

"This place is insane!" she declares, setting down her burden. "Ruby, honey, you've officially won at life."

Behind her, Hannah appears with even more food. "The kitchen alone!" she gushes. "I'm moving in. You can't stop me."

"Get in line," Ash drawls, following them out. He's carrying several bottles of expensive whiskey. "Boss, this is a serious upgrade from your apartment."

My cheeks are on fire, and I'm up on my feet, rushing to hug them all. "It's just temporary," I start to say, but Dominic's arm tightens around my shoulders.

"For now," he agrees, but something in his tone makes my heart skip. "Until we find something even bigger and better."

"Better than this?" Lily looks skeptical, gesturing at the sprawling backyard with its professional land-scaping and the way the house seems to glow from within. "I'm having trouble imagining better."

"Everything okay in there?" Garrett calls from the grill, and I realize I've been quiet too long, lost in thoughts of permanent homes and futures.

"Perfect," I call back, and mean it. Standing up, I go to help him with the steaks, admiring the way the fading sunlight catches the silver in his hair. "Need any help?"

"Just your company," he says softly, pulling me close for a quick kiss that tastes like the beer he's been sipping. Behind us, I hear Knox launching into some elaborate story that has Hannah and Lily giggling while Ash adds sarcastic commentary. Then I hear the doorbell and in no time, more people are joining us. I don't recognize many of them, but my husbands wanted their closest friends and those from their work to join us.

"I can't believe how things turned out after everything," I admit, leaning against Garrett's solid body.

He hums thoughtfully, flipping a steak. "Good unbelievable or overwhelming unbelievable?"

"Both? Neither?" I watch as Dominic actually cracks a smile at something Ash says, while Knox demonstrates what looks like a particularly disastrous skiing move. "I keep waiting for the other shoe to drop."

"No shoes dropping on my watch," Garrett promises. "Now, go meet some new people while I finish these up. And tell Knox if he wants his medium-rare he better stop trying to convince Lily to let him teach her rock climbing."

I laugh and head back to the group, settling onto the space between Hannah and Lily. The evening air is perfect—just cool enough to justify cuddling closer to the nearest warm body, but not cold enough to drive us inside. Not with the outside heaters keeping the winter coldness away.

"I just don't understand how you got so lucky," Hannah is saying, watching Knox and Garrett argue playfully over grill temperatures while Dominic is chatting to someone else. "Here I am stuck with dating app disasters, and you somehow ended up with three perfect specimens of Alpha-hood."

"Specimens?" Lily snorts. "What are they, lab experiments?"

"You know what I mean!" Hannah waves her hand expressively. "Look at them. Just look! Knox with those stunning face and jawline and that whole rugged mountain man thing. Garrett being all cool and collected with his brewing genius. And don't even get me started on Dominic—"

"Please don't." I laugh, settling onto the spacious sectional between them. "His ego is big enough already."

"I heard that," Dominic calls over, not even turning around.

"You were meant to!" I call back, making Knox and Garrett chuckle.

"But seriously, Ruby" Lily says, her eyes twinkling as she turns to me. "Three gorgeous Alphas, a mansion, and what looks like the world's most expensive grill. Should I, your best friend, be worried about finding my own body in the river when you don't have time for me?"

"Lily!" Hannah smacks her sister's arm while I choke on my drink.

"What? I'm just saying, if this turns out to be the

start of a true crime documentary, I want credit for calling it first."

I'm laughing because Lily loves true crime docs and will thread it into conversations where she can.

"If it helps," Knox calls from where he's now attempting to juggle beer bottles. "I'm pretty sure Ruby could take all three of us in a fight."

"Damn straight," I agree, thinking of my self defense classes with Dominic.

"Besides," Dominic adds dryly. "If we were serial killers, we wouldn't be so obvious about it."

There's a moment of startled silence before everyone bursts out laughing. Seeing Dominic crack jokes and being super laid back still catches me off guard in the best way.

"Food's ready!" Garrett announces, and there's a general scramble for plates and seats.

I end up with my plate balanced on my lap and Dominic's thigh pressed against mine. Knox sprawls at my feet, using my legs as a backrest while he devours his steak. Garrett joins us after serving everyone, settling on my other side.

"This is amazing," Lily moans around a bite of steak. "Garrett, will you marry me?"

"Sorry, I'm taken," he replies easily, and my heart does that flutter thing again.

"Worth a shot," she sighs dramatically. "Ruby, you're a lucky woman."

"Don't I know it," I murmur, and feel three distinct hands squeeze different parts of me in response.

I'm just starting to think this evening couldn't get more perfect when the first fat raindrop hits my nose. Thankfully, it's as most of us finish our meals.

"Everyone inside!" Garrett shouts as the sky suddenly opens up. We're all scrambling, grabbing plates and glasses, trying not to slip on the increasingly wet deck. Dominic, naturally, is the only one who manages to look graceful about it.

"Quick, through here!" I call, holding open the French doors as a fast wind comes out of nowhere. Everyone piles in, laughing and slightly damp. Hannah's hair is plastered to her face, and Lily's carefully styled updo is starting to droop.

"Well," Ash drawls, looking at his soaked shirt. "That was refreshing."

"Sorry about that," Garrett starts, but I cut him off with a kiss that tastes like rain and barbecue sauce.

"Are you kidding? This is perfect." At his raised eyebrow, I grin. "Now we have an excuse to show them the theater room."

"The what now?" Lily perks up instantly.

Dominic appears with a stack of fluffy towels—of course he has extras ready—and starts passing them around. "Follow me," he says, that tiny smile playing at the corners of his mouth.

I hang back for a moment, watching all our friends trail after him like excited puppies. Garrett catches me around the waist, pulling me against his rain-damp chest.

"Penny for your thoughts?"

"Just... happy," I admit, turning to face him. Droplets of rain cling to his eyelashes. "Really, really happy."

I love falling into his embrace and just being held by him, when Knox's voice floats back to us.

"If you two are done making out in the hallway, you're missing Lily's impression of finding out about the theater room."

"We're not making out," I call back, then yelp as Garrett's hands wander over my ass. "Okay, maybe we're making out a little."

When we finally join the others, nearly every seat taken by my friends and my husbands', I have to laugh at Lily sprawled dramatically across one of the recliners. "I'm never leaving," she announces. "This is my home now. I live here."

"You'll have to fight Ruby for it," Hannah points out, already curled up in another chair with her feet tucked under her.

"Please, Ruby has three whole Alphas. She can share one room."

"I don't know," Ash comments, examining the state-of-the-art sound system. "Given how vocal our boss can be, you might not want to be too close to any of their rooms."

"Ash!" I sputter, feeling my face flame as my mates

all growl possessively. He just grins that gap-toothed smile at me, unrepentant.

"What? I work late at the bar, remember? Those office walls aren't as soundproof as you think."

If possible, my face gets even hotter. Knox is shaking with suppressed laughter behind me, while Garrett looks entirely too pleased with himself. Even Dominic's eyes are glinting.

"Right!" I say loudly. "Who wants to watch a movie?"

"Ooh, yes!" Lily bounces in her seat. "Something romantic!"

"Action," Hannah counters.

"Horror," Dominic and Ash say simultaneously, then eye each other and do a fist pump.

"Whatever we pick," Garrett says, pulling me down onto one of the larger recliners with him. "Can we agree no Christmas movies?"

I elbow him in the ribs as everyone laughs. Most of them know about my complicated relationship with Christmas, thanks to Aunt Eve's will stipulation about getting married during the holiday season.

"Actually," Knox says, settling into the chair on our right while Dominic takes the one on our left. "I have an idea."

He pulls up something on the insane tablet control system, and suddenly the opening credits of The Princess Bride fill the massive screen.

"Perfect," I sigh, snuggling back against Garrett's chest as Hannah and Lily cheer.

"As you wish," he murmurs, and I reach over to tangle my fingers with his.

The movie plays, but I find myself watching my friends and husbands more than the screen. Hannah and Lily quote along with their favorite parts, while Ash and Dominic debate the practicality of various sword-fighting techniques. Garrett's hands never stop stroking me, playing with my hair, lacing and unlacing our fingers. Knox keeps shooting me these soft looks that make my heart flip, and even Dominic seems more relaxed than I've ever seen him, his usual intensity softened in the dim light.

"You know," Knox murmurs in my ear during a quiet moment. "For someone who hates Christmas, you got quite a gift from it."

I think about Aunt Eve's will, about how angry I was at first. About how it brought me these three incredible men, about how they've filled spaces in my life I didn't even know were empty. About how my friends have embraced our unusual relationship without question.

"Yeah," I whisper back, feeling three pairs of eyes turn to me instantly, attuned to even my quietest sounds. "I really did."

As the movie credits roll, I'm fighting to keep my eyes open. The long day of moving, the emotional highs, and Garrett's warmth beside me are all conspiring to make me drowsy.

"I think that's our cue," Hannah says, untangling herself from her recliner. "Some of us have pastries to bake in the morning"

"But it's so comfy," Lily whines, though she's already standing. "Ruby, I meant it about moving in."

"Get your own Alphas," I mumble sleepily, making them laugh.

Others are up as well, yawning and starting to say their farewells. We're all up on our feet now.

"Speaking of," Ash drawls in my direction. "I'm assuming you won't be in early tomorrow to open the bar?"

"Maybe I can sleep in tomorrow?" I say sheepishly, feeling guilty.

"I got it covered," he adds smoothly. "Take the day, Boss. You've earned it."

"Ash, you're the best."

"I know." He grins. "Just remember that when review time comes around."

Once everyone leaves and we say our farewell, the house feels suddenly huge and quiet. I'm still curled up in the theater room with Knox, while Garrett and Dominic see our friends out.

"Ready for bed?" he murmurs against my ear.

My heart skips. "I should help clean up..."

"Already handled," Garrett says, returning with

Dominic. "The cleaning service will deal with every-thing tomorrow."

Of course Dominic has a cleaning service.

"So..." I bite my lip, looking between them. "Bed?"

The atmosphere shifts instantly, charging with electricity, and I'm here for it.

"If you're not ready..." Garrett starts, always the gentleman.

"I'm ready," I say quickly. Maybe too quickly, given Knox's chuckle.

"Let us take care of you," Dominic rumbles, holding out his hand.

I take it, letting him pull me up from Knox's lap. We make our way upstairs, and I'm hyper-aware of all three of them around me—Dominic leading the way, Knox and Garrett following close behind. The master bedroom door opens to reveal that space that's pure luxury, with a bed that has to be custom-made to fit four people comfortably.

With my clothes, I can't help but crawl onto the inviting bed, and collapse on the most comfortable mattress in the world. Immediately, I'm surrounded by warm skin and familiar scents. It takes some adjusting—a tangle of limbs, some gentle repositioning—but we finally settle with me curled against Garrett's chest, Knox spooned behind me, and Dominic's hand resting on my hip from where he lies on Garrett's other side.

"I think we missed the part where we have to get undressed," Knox says softly, causing me to burst out laughing. As if that's their cue, they are already pawing at my clothes, undressing me, then themselves. I'm giggling, trying to playfully push them away, which of course I'm failing at. Their kisses and hands are all over me, and I let myself fall for them because I can only resist them for so long.

And because this is everything I never knew I wanted. Everything wishes are made of.

This is home.

ABOUT HARLEY KNIGHT

Hi, I'm Harley Knight! I'm a romance author who's absolutely obsessed with books, writing, and happily-ever-afters. I love creating stories filled with emotion, passion, and unforgettable characters that stick with you long after the last page. When I'm not writing, you'll find me lost in a good book or dreaming up my next big adventure. For me, there's nothing better than crafting love stories that remind us all why love is worth fighting for.

www.ingramcontent.com/pod-product-compliance
Lightning Source LLC
Chambersburg PA
CBHW070825190726
48292CB00006B/2114